Praise for Deryn Lake's other
John Rawlings Mysteries

One of the best mystery series to hand at present is the John Rawlings historical crime line . . . ten out of ten'
DR JONATHAN GASH

'John Rawlings and the Blind Beak are developing into my favourite historical mystery heroes – tenacious in their search for villains, daring as they outwit them, yet always ready to pause for a moment of delightful domestic life. I'm eager for the next!'
LINDSEY DAVIES

'evocative Georgian mystery . . . if you love a good whodunnit you won't be disappointed'
Evening Argus, Brighton

'an absorbing murder tale set in Georgian London . . . splendidly evokes the atmosphere of the capital with all its elegance and intrigue. Wonderfully descriptive, it deserves to be a success'
The Kent and Sussex Courier

'A wealth of marvellous characters parade across the pages, their dialogue is lively and John Rawlings is proving to be a real charmer.'
Eastbourne Herald

'An effervescent tale. . . the author organises her large cast and colourful background with skill and gusto through a racily readable drama.'
FELICIA LAMB in the *Mail on Sunday's Night & Day Magazine*

Also by Deryn Lake

Death in the Dark Walk
Death at The Beggar's Opera
Death at the Devil's Tavern
Death on the Romney Marsh
Death at Apothecaries' Hall
Death in the West Wind
Death at St. James's Palace
Death in the Valley of Shadows
Death in the Setting Sun
Death and the Cornish Fiddler

About the author

Deryn Lake is the pseudonym of a well-known historical novelist who joined the popular ranks of historical detective writers with her gripping John Rawlings Mysteries.

Deryn Lake lives near the famous battleground of 1066.

Death in the Peerless Pool

Deryn Lake

Back-In-Print Books Ltd

Published by Back-In-Print Books Ltd 2002
ISBN 1 903552 38 9
Previously published in Great Britain by
Hodder and Stoughton 1999 under ISBN 0 340 71859 5

A CIP catalogue record is available from the British Library.

Cover illustration by Tim Barber based on an old print.

Printed and bound on demand in Great Britain by
Lightning Source

Back-In-Print Books Ltd
PO Box 47057
London SW18 1YW
020 8637 0975

For JONATHAN GASH
in appreciation

This is a Back-In-Print Book.

- This title was out of print for some time but Back-In-Print Books has brought it back in to print because of demand from Deryn Lake fans.
- This re-print was produced on demand using up-to-date digital printing technology.
- Paper and print quality are higher than most conventionally printed paperback novels.
- Digital printing may cost somewhat more but ensures that book titles need not go out of print as long as there are readers who want them.

What other titles are available from BiP?

Check out our web site at www.backinprint.co.uk for other titles released by Back-In-Print Books Ltd and news about forthcoming titles.

Do you want any other titles?

If you know of a title which is out of print and you think there might be a reasonable demand please contact us.

Back-In-Print Books Ltd
PO Box 47057
London
SW18 1YW
020 8637 0975

e-mail: info@backinprint.co.uk

Chapter One

'Last one in is an oaf,' called Samuel cheerfully, and breaking into a sprint dived into the Peerless Pool, sending up a vast spout of water which cascaded back on to the tranquil surface with the bright abandon of a royal firework.

Thoroughly soaked by this exhibition, John Rawlings, who stood on the paved surround, stripped to the waist and wearing a pair of flannel bathing drawers, shouted back, 'Watch what you're doing! I thought it was high tide.'

Samuel's head appeared. 'Come on, man. It's warm.'

'Oh, very well,' John answered, just a trifle tersely, and plunged into the Pool with a neat descent that hardly rippled the water.

His friend was already halfway down the swimming bath's length, flailing his arms and splashing considerably, much to he consternation of several old gentlemen, proceeding slowly through the Pool like a school of elderly porpoises.

'Have a care, Sir,' shouted one. But Samuel, deafened by his own wash, had reached the far end of the pleasure bath and was now heading back, hell for leather.

'I sometimes wonder,' said John Rawlings aloud, 'why I allow myself to be seen about town with you.'

Yet he didn't mean a word of it, for Samuel Swann, Goldsmith of London, had been his companion since childhood, when the boys had lived next door to one another, and it would take a deep division indeed to sever a friendship as enduring as theirs.

On this particular day, their meeting had been of a lighthearted nature. It being a cruelly hot summer that year of 1758, those beautiful birds of paradise known as the beau monde, who rose at noon then perambulated the streets in search of diversion, had taken to places of deep shade for their leisure. Thus, the city had been deserted, and there had been hardly a hint of custom for those who made a living as shopkeepers. In fact John had been on the point of closing his apothecary's shop, situated in Shug Lane, just off Piccadilly, when Samuel had come bursting through the door, setting the bell jangling.

'Well, what a waste of a day this has been,' he had stated jovially. 'Not one single customer over my threshold. I've decided to shut early and go swimming. What say you?'

'Yes,' John had answered without hesitation, removing the long apron which he always wore when compounding his physicks and potions.

'Shall I close the shop for you, Sir?' his apprentice, Nicholas Dawkins, had asked.

'No, we'll all do it,' the Apothecary had replied. 'Then you can come too.'

A smile had broadened the somewhat pale features of the young man, nicknamed the Muscovite because of his strange ancestry, which could be directly traced back to the court of Tsar Peter the Great. Now nearly twenty-one years of age, he had been issued indentures by the Apothecary three years earlier. 'That would be a pleasure, Mr Rawlings.'

'Then let's to it,' his Master answered, and leapt round the premises like a hare, tidying everything away for the night, and throwing covers over those objects that could not be moved.

This done, the trio had walked to Piccadilly and hired a hackney coach which had taken them to Holbourn, then up Hatton Garden and through Clerkenwell Green to St John's Street, and finally to Old Street where, a mere stone's throw from the well of St Agnes le Clare, the pleasant resort known as the Peerless Pool was situated.

Now, in hired bathing drawers, all three were in the water, Nicholas swimming beneath the surface like a fish, despite the fact that on land he walked with a limp.

It seemed that most of the male population of London had made for Old Street that late summer afternoon. Bankers and merchants, tradesmen and dandies, soldiers and actors, all overcome by the heat, had retreated to that delightful oasis created by the pleasure bath and its surrounding attractions. John even espied a beau, shaven head pale beneath the sun from constant wearing of his wig, swimming along in fully enamelled maquillage, carmined lips spouting water like a whale.

'Hare and hounds!' exclaimed Samuel, surfacing suddenly. 'I could spend the rest of the day here.'

'There's nothing to stop us,' answered John. 'We can swim, fish, have supper, and leave when the Pool closes at dusk.'

The Goldsmith gazed round at the other bathers. 'Pity this isn't family day so we could have some ladies present.'

'Do you think of nothing else?' asked the Apothecary, neglecting to say that his mind had been running along very much the same lines.

'No,' answered his friend cheerfully, and dived deep.

For the sake of decency the rules of the Peerless Pool stated that certain days were designated for members of the male sex to swim, others for females, but on one day of the week men and women were allowed to bathe together, the custom having been set in Bath, where much amusement was derived from seeing the fair sex wading with gentlemen, all up to their necks in water.

Despite the size of the Peerless Pool, a generous 170 feet long by 100 feet wide, it was by now becoming more than a little crowded. So much so that

John began to grow weary of making way for those who swashed along heartily like Samuel, or swam with erect head and swan-like necks in order to avoid the merest droplet of water ruining their appearance. Therefore, after another rapid ten lengths, these executed for the sake of his health, the Apothecary hauled himself out and made his way into one of the arched cubicles that lined the Pool on either side. Stripping off his flannel drawers, he rubbed himself down with a towel, then wrapped it around his body as if it were a toga.

'Where are you going in that?' called Samuel from the water.

'I thought about taking a turn in the cold bath.'

'I'll come too,' said the Goldsmith, and climbed one of the series of steps leading out of the water.

Though strictly speaking the Peerless Pool was not a pleasure garden, it was regarded as such by those who regularly walked there from their counting houses and shops in the City, and also by other visitors who came from further afield. Fed by a clear, sweet spring rising in Hoxton, just one of the many to be found in the marshes of Finsbury and Moor Fields, it had originally been known as the Perilous Pond because of its reputation for dangerous swimming conditions. In fact several young men had drowned there and some years earlier the Pool had been closed down. However, in 1743, an eminent citizen and jeweller, William Kemp, had leased the land from its owners, St Bartholomew's Hospital, and set about transforming the entire terrain.

First of all, Mr Kemp, who greatly believed in the therapeutic quality of the spring's water, had built a large brick wall round the property, thus guaranteeing privacy to swimmers and pleasure seekers alike. Then he had ensured safety by raising the pool's depth to three feet in the shallow end and five in the deep, all being kept clean by the springs which bubbled up through the fine sandy bottom, a drainpipe taking away excess water to maintain a constant level. A cold bath, fed by an icy spring, had been installed in a building close by, this pool being 40 feet long and 20 feet broad, faced with marble and paved with stone, the dressing boxes having floors of purest Purbeck.

Mr Kemp's greatest triumph, however, had been the creation of a fishing lake of stunning proportions. Situated between the two swimming baths, the Fish Pond was 320 feet long, 90 feet broad and 11 feet deep, was stocked with carp, tench and several kinds of other fish, and advertised as being 'for the use of those subscribers who admire the amusement of angling'. The owner had also established a handsome paved terrace walk on either side of the lake, well planted with lime trees and agreeably covered with shrubs. With the addition of a bowling green, a fine library and a place to take refreshment, the Peerless Pool had been transformed into a most desirable resort. So much so that Mr Kemp decided to spend all his time there and built himself a fine manor house in traditional country-squire style, the back of which looked over the fishing lake, the front the Peerless Pool itself.

On this particular day, extremely hot as it was, the cold bath was reasonably full, some gentlemen swimming in the nude as there were no ladies present. John left his towel in a dressing box and joined them, while Samuel, after a moment's hesitation, removed his drawers and did likewise, bellowing a hearty laugh as the freezing water consumed his privy parts. The Apothecary gazed at him fondly, thinking, as he had so often before, that subtlety was hardly his old friend's strong suit.

The breathtaking experience over, the two went in search of Nicholas and found him still swimming, having met some fellow 'prentice lads, who were diving and tumbling and generally annoying the other bathers. Shouting to him that they were going fishing, John and Samuel made their way towards the lake.

Surrounded by trees, the Fish Pond was approached by means of a sloping path winding to the left of William Kemp's stately house. This led down to the terraced walkway circling the lake, where benches for the comfort of those wishing to fish had been thoughtfully situated. Jetties, too, stuck out into the water, a wooden railing at the end providing something on which to lean as fishing tackle was plied. But neither of these two accommodations for gentlemen of rod and line appealed to John and Samuel, particularly in the high-spirited mood in which the challenge of swimming naked in chilly waters had left them. With much boisterous laughter, they proceeded instead to the arch in the embankment behind Mr Kemp's house, and from it pulled out a rowing boat, two of which were always kept there for those subscribers who wished to fish over the side. Then, carrying it between them, the friends somehow managed to get the thing launched, an achievement that left both of them extremely wet, particularly Samuel, who pushed the boat out from the terrace then made a somewhat unsuccessful flying leap into the craft, a move which almost sank it.

'You row, I'll fish,' he instructed John as he removed his coat and hat and sat down, wobbling dangerously.

'Very well.'

Samuel produced the hired fishing rod. 'Now, just you watch this cast. I've been practising recently.' And with that the Goldsmith whipped the line over his shoulder and tossed it into the water, neatly picking up his own wig and throwing it into the lake as he did so.

John bellowed a laugh. 'Is that the latest form of bait?'

'No, it isn't,' Samuel answered crossly. 'That wig is both new and expensive, and somehow I've got to retrieve it. Can you reach it with your oar?'

'No,' said John, attempting to do so and almost tipping them over as he tried. 'Can't you hook it back in again?'

Samuel cast frantically, narrowly missing the Apothecary's eye. 'Oh, this is infuriating.'

'It is also extremely funny. I wish you could see your face.'

'One more remark like that and I shall be forced to punch you.'

'One more complaint and I shall throw you in.'

They stared at one another beadily like two fighting cocks, then realised the stupidity of the situation and grinned, watching the water-logged wig as it first attracted the attention of a large and belligerent carp, who attacked it, then, growing heavier by the moment, sank slowly beneath the surface.

'I suppose you want me to dive for it?' John asked.

Samuel shook his head. 'If anybody has to do it it will be me.' He sighed. 'Do fish bite?'

'No, of course not.'

'None the less.'

'Oh, for heaven's sake. Cast for it, man.'

'Then you're not going to...?'

'No, Samuel, I am not. I've done quite enough swimming for one day, thank you.'

The Goldsmith gave another deep sigh, hunched his shoulders, reeled in, then cast once more, promptly catching a tench which he threw back into the water in a dispirited manner.

'Here, let me try. Give me the rod.'

Somewhat reluctantly, Samuel handed it over. Taking it from his friend, John peered down into the pond's depths, shading his eyes from the early evening sun in order to see more clearly.

In common with the Peerless and Cold Pools, the Fish Pond was fed by a series of natural springs which kept the water fresh. Further, weeds were not encouraged to grow in profusion, so that in places a clear view to the sandy bottom, eleven feet below, was possible. Leaning over as far as he dared, John sought the missing wig.

A glimpse of something white had him shouting an instruction. 'Pull to the middle, Samuel. I think I can see it.'

The Goldsmith guided the boat to the centre of the pond. 'Here?'

'Yes.'

It was Samuel's turn to lean over the side, gripping the boat tightly in order to keep his balance, but not quite succeeding. With a splash equalling the one with which he had entered the bathing pool, the mighty young man toppled over and disappeared beneath the glassy surface.

A few moments later his head broke water, and he gasped for air, obviously frightened, John thought, for his friend's face had a deathly pallor to it. Seeing the boat, he struck out towards it in a frantic crawl, his manner very agitated, even for one who had just fallen into a lake unexpectedly.

'What's the matter?' John asked, reaching out a hand to help him back in.

'There's somebody down there,' Samuel gasped, clambering aboard and nearly capsizing them.

'What do you mean?'

'There's a body lying on the bottom.'

'Are you certain?'

'Yes. I saw it as I plunged near the lake bed. Take a look for yourself.'

With an uneasy sense of apprehension, John leant over the side.

The waters, though translucent, still had a lovely greenish tinge, like glass that had been in the sea. Gazing through them, seeing where the shafts of early evening sun lit the bottom quite clearly in places, the Apothecary had the impression that he was staring into a fairytale and so, when he glimpsed the woman lying on her back on the bed of the lake, looking up at him, just for a moment he felt that she was not out of place. Then his brain engaged, and he hurriedly stripped off his wig, coat and shoes and dived in.

She was down there, waiting for him. As John plummeted towards the bottom, he saw her, the Lady of the Lake, lying so still, her hair floating out round her head, her eyes open and gazing into his. She was dead, of course, no nymph from legend she. And yet with the water eddying over her, causing a slight movement of her clothes, and the damage that her submersion had done not yet clearly visible on her face, just for a moment she gave the strange impression of being alive. Longing to draw breath, the Apothecary surfaced no more than a foot away from the boat, and filled his lungs.

'Well?' called Samuel.

'Yes, you're right. There's a dead woman down there.'

'Then we'd best get assistance,' the Goldsmith replied frantically. 'I'll row for the bank.'

John climbed aboard, shaking himself like a dog. 'Did you notice anything when you looked at her?'

Samuel stared uncomprehendingly. 'No. What?'

The Apothecary's expression became grim. 'She had chains binding her wrists and ankles, weighting her down. We must send Nicholas to Bow Street, Sam. This is clearly no case of accidental drowning.'

'God's mercy!'

'Upon her soul.'

'I have a sense that all this has happened to us before,' Samuel commented bleakly.

'And so, indeed, have I,' answered John Rawlings, his features set and unsmiling.

Chapter Two

'A body?' Mr Kemp repeated incredulously. 'In the Fish Pond?'

'I fear so, Sir,' John answered grimly.

But how could it have got there?'

'I'm afraid somebody threw the woman in. And with evil intent at that. Her wrists and ankles were bound together with heavy chains.'

'In order that she might be held down and drown?' William Kemp went pale. 'Are you trying to tell me that she was put into the water whilst still alive?'

'It's certainly possible.'

'Dear me,' said the eminent citizen, and adjusted his jewelled cravat pin with a shaking hand.

John stood in the spacious salon of the delightful home that the proprietor of the Peerless Pool had created for himself, a country mansion surrounded by a walled garden and an orchard of pear and apple trees, built on the land lying between the swimming bath and the fishing lake.

In this clean and beeswaxed room, the Apothecary had never been more horribly aware of the fact that he stank. Weed from the Fish Pond, hard though he had tried to brush it off, clung to his clothes, which stuck to his body, still damp from his recent dive. Further, his white stockings and neckwear were by now an unpleasant shade of grey, while a dirty smudge smeared his face where he had rubbed his hand across it. In short, John Rawlings, who loved high fashion with fervour, felt a regular tatterdemalion, and wished that he had been in better sartorial condition to bring to the Peerless Pool's proprietor the news that there was a body in his fishing lake.

As though this thought struck him simultaneously, Mr Kemp gave the Apothecary a piercing look. 'Who did you say you were?' he asked.

'John Rawlings, Apothecary of Shug Lane and occasional assistant to Mr John Fielding of Bow Street.'

The magic name had been uttered. William Kemp's brow cleared and he said, 'Ah,' as if everything were now quite plain to him. 'Then you will wish me to call for the constable,' he added more politely.

John shook his head. 'No, Sir. I have taken the liberty of sending my apprentice to the Public Office by hackney coach. I have requested that Mr Fielding send us two of his Brave Fellows, those prepared at short notice to travel anywhere in the kingdom to investigate a crime. I thought it might be better if the Blind Beak were involved from the very beginning.'

Mr Kemp looked apprehensive. 'It won't mean that the Pool has to be closed, will it?'

The Apothecary spread his hands. 'That is beyond my control, alas. However, I think the anglers should be moved away from the Fish Pond as soon as possible. My friend Samuel Swann is standing guard but has no authority to give orders to anyone.'

The proprietor nodded emphatically. 'Of course, it shall be done immediately. The waiters will see to it. Now, what next?'

John looked sheepish. 'I would very much appreciate an opportunity to wash myself.'

'Quite so,' answered the proprietor, and gazed down the length of his nose.

He was not at all what the Apothecary had expected of a prominent citizen of London, being, in John's eyes, altogether younger and shorter than such a role demanded. Yet the fact that William Kemp had started life as a jeweller was clearly revealed by his hands, small and manicured and supple as birds, obviously belonging to a creator of fine and beautiful things. As to the rest, the proprietor stood slightly below average height and, having kept a trim figure, had something of the air of a dancing master about him. It would not have surprised John in the least if Mr Kemp had suddenly produced a fiddle and bow from somewhere and executed a series of nimble steps. However, at the moment his dark eyes had a mournful, solemn look as the proprietor contemplated possible disrepute falling on his beautiful oasis. Unconsciously, he sighed.

'A wash, Sir. Yes, by all means. If you will follow me.'

He led the way down the hall to an extremely modern indoor water closet, a vast mahogany projection with brass handles and cocks surrounding its unventilated hole. Nestling in the corner beside the monstrous contraption was a washstand containing a bowl and ewer. John, ever practical, made full use of both, tidied himself as best he could, then stepped out to face the world that undoubtedly would soon be arriving at the Fish Pond.

The waiters had done their job well. There were no anglers left on the seats and jetties, the entire area having been cleared, while the second boat had been brought out of the boat arch and was moored beside the other one, ready for use. The path to the left of William Kemp's house, running between the Peerless Pool and the Pond, was guarded at both ends by a pair of hefty fellows whose usual job, besides waiting table, was to rid the grounds of any rowdies who might attempt to spoil the enjoyment of other bathers. Knowing that something was badly amiss but not quite sure what it was, they bristled with anticipation and looked ready to manhandle anybody who approached. Meanwhile, two other waiters had been despatched to the entrance to meet Mr Fielding's Runners when they approached in their fast coach. Of Samuel, John noticed as he gazed around, there was no sign.

Unfortunately all this strange activity had not gone undetected, and a crowd of curious onlookers, some dressed, some still in their drawers, had gathered at the top of the path to see what was going on.

'I think they'll have to be asked to leave,' John murmured to Mr Kemp as they stepped forth on to the terrace at the back of his house.

'Indeed they will,' the proprietor agreed. 'Frederick,' he called, 'a word with you, if you please.'

A burly stepped forward. 'Yes, Sir?'

'Be so kind as to tell the patrons that I will address them. Then if you can make sure that they quit as soon as possible, I'd be obliged.'

He pronounced it 'obleejed', much to John's amusement.

'Very good, Sir.'

Frederick strode up the path and loomed his six-foot frame over the onlookers. 'Gentlemen, Mr Kemp desires a word with you all. Please remain where you are.'

Nobody stirred as the proprietor descended the steps leading from the terrace and proceeded towards the crowd, which had now been joined by others from the library and the bowling green, and by one or two patrons of the restaurant, some with glasses still in their hand. Coming up behind him, the Apothecary noticed that Mr Kemp walked with a slightly mincing gait, perfectly enhancing his dancing-master image. The proprietor cleared his throat.

'Gentlemen, I am sorry to have to ask you all to withdraw, but so I must and as quickly as possible. The term of your subscription will be extended by an extra day to compensate. Those of you who have brought guests will have their shillings refunded.'

There was a general murmur of disappointment, then someone called out, 'Why must we go, Sir? What is amiss?'

'Yes,' chorused other voices. 'Tell us.'

'We have a right to know,' quavered a frail old fellow near the front.

Mr Kemp turned to John and raised a brow. The Apothecary held his thumb and forefinger close together, meaning 'a little'.

'There has been a fatality in the Fish Pond.' the proprietor stated firmly. 'A most unfortunate incident and not one for public scrutiny. Therefore, while the necessary actions are performed, I must insist that you clear the pleasure garden.'

One or two mouths opened to argue, but Frederick, arms folded across massive chest, jutted his jaw at them and they closed again. Finally, after a few further moments of muttering, the patrons reluctantly began to shift, those dressed towards the gates, the gentlemen in drawers to the changing rooms.

Mr Kemp turned to his companion and smiled for the first time since he had heard the news of the woman in the lake. 'Was that explanation sufficient?'

'Yes. It was well done.' John's eyes swept over the Pond, its calm surface broken only by the occasional ripple of a fish. 'I wonder how they will bring her up,' he said, almost to himself

William Kemp shuddered, his neat frame shaking from hat to buckled shoes. 'Lift her on a rope, I suppose.'

The Apothecary nodded. 'Are any of your waiters exceptional divers? And with strong nerves?'

'One is. Tobias, known as Toby.'

'I think you'd better warn him that he may have an unpleasant task ahead.'

'He's standing just over there.' Mr Kemp made to call out but was interrupted by the sound of a scuffle on the path. Both men looked round to see Samuel, his arms whirling like the sails of a mill, attempting to fight off two waiters simultaneously.

'They're here,' he was shouting excitedly. 'The Runners have arrived.'

'Samuel Swann, the friend I mentioned to you,' John explained.

'Let the gentleman through,' ordered William Kemp, and calm was restored.

The Goldsmith straightened his coat and attempted nonchalance. 'I went to the entrance when they asked me to leave the Pond and I've just seen the fast coach pull up and Nicholas Dawkins get out. He's leading them here.'

'Have the patrons gone?' John asked.

'Nearly all of them. Just a few stragglers taking their time over getting dressed.'

Mr Kemp pursed his lips. 'Typical. Terrified of missing something, I dare swear.' He raised his voice. 'Lads, two Runners from Bow Street will be approaching at any moment. Let them through without demur. Toby, come over here, if you please.'

A short, powerful waiter, built like a veritable bull, approached. 'Sir?'

The proprietor gestured towards John. 'Perhaps you would care to explain, Mr Rawlings.'

'To come directly to the point, Mr Swann and I have discovered a body, weighted down and lying on the bottom of the Fish Pond. The Runners who are on their way are duty bound to bring the poor wretch to the surface and, as Mr Kemp tells me you are an excellent diver, they may well call upon you to assist them. Whether you do so or not, however, is entirely your own choice.'

Toby looked stern of feature. 'I fought in the war till a few months ago when I was wounded. I've seen worse sights than dead women, Sir.'

The proprietor announced shrilly, 'I only employ the best, Gentlemen. None but the stoutest hearts.'

'And here comes another who could be described thus,' John answered as his pale apprentice, russet eyes gleaming with excitement, came hurrying down the path, his limp accentuated by the speed at which he was travelling.

'They're right behind me,' he called, 'and they've brought things.'

The Apothecary turned to see approaching the two Beak Runners whom he had met during the previous summer, when he had been investigating a mysterious death on the Romney Marsh. 'Mr Rawlings,' one shouted cheerfully. 'Mr Fielding asks me to convey his compliments and to request that you will attend him as soon as is convenient to yourself.'

'I most certainly will,' John answered, going to meet them and saying in a lower tone, 'The body is lying in the middle of the lake and we have a volunteer to dive down and fix a rope round her.'

The Runner, whom John recalled as being named George, gulped with relief 'That's as well, Sir. For Nathaniel here don't swim, and I myself can only paddle like a dog. Diving deep would be a little beyond us.'

'All you need to do is tell that solid-looking waiter over there what you require and he will do the rest.'

'Very good, Mr Rawlings.' George exhibited the things, which turned out to be a portable winch and a strong piece of rope. 'If he can fix this round the corpse's waist we should get her up in no time. Your apprentice said the victim was female. That's right, isn't it, Sir?'

'Yes, but she's weighted down with heavy chains.'

'So it's definitely a killing?'

'Her hands are bound behind her back, practically impossible to do to oneself.'

George nodded and beckoned Toby over, and after a few moments of discussion the lifting party set out; John and the waiter in the first boat, the two Beak Runners following just behind. One end of the rope was securely attached to the winch, which was manned by George and Nathaniel; the other Toby wore tied round his middle, joining one craft to the other.

The sun was setting now, and it was no longer possible to see into the Pond's depths, murky and menacing without the light shining into them. The trees that lined the lake were casting their own shadows and John could only get his bearings by reckoning the distance between the boat and Mr Kemp's house.

'I think this is the spot,' he called finally, shipping his oars.

'Right, Toby?' asked Runner George.

'Right as I'll ever be.'

'Get the rope round her and tie it securely. We'll do the rest.'

'Very good.'

The waiter stood up, clad only in his drawers, and dived so neatly from the boat that it hardly bobbed. John stared over the side but could see nothing except a dark shape disappearing towards the bottom.

'I don't envy him that task,' he said.

'I think he's found her,' George put in. 'He's just tugged the rope.'

'Was that the signal?'

'Yes. When he tugs again we're to start hauling her in.'

They waited in edgy silence but there was no further tug. John pulled his watch from his waistcoat. Toby must have lungs like a bull, he thought, to stay down as long as he had. But just as he was beginning to grow seriously worried, the rope suddenly went taut and then there was a flurry of water as the waiter broke surface and gasped in air. At this, the Runners hauled wildly, and a few moments later the corpse appeared alongside their boat.

To have lifted her aboard would have been hazardous indeed, so small was the craft. So, in one of the most bizarre spectacles John Rawlings had ever witnessed, the drowned woman was towed ashore, her body kept straight by the stoical Toby, who swam alongside. Reaching the bank first, the Apothecary, tottering precariously, stepped ashore, then wheeled round to see the Beak Runners securing their craft before they cut the body loose. Nathaniel, for all the fact he couldn't swim, had jumped into the shallows to hold the dead woman steady, and it was he who carried her to the bank, holding her in his arms like a bride. He looked at John.

'Where shall I put her, Sir?'

The proprietor answered for him. 'I've ordered a sheet to be placed over there. Lay her on that.'

Nathaniel raised his brows and the Apothecary nodded. 'Be careful with her, though. I want to see her much as she was.'

Delicately, the Runner lowered his burden, and John, kneeling beside the body, began the grim business of examining the dead woman, gazing into the shuttered face as if it would give him the answer to all the questions posed by her sudden appearance on the bottom of the Fish Pond.

The hair, a strand of which he picked up and loosely held in his hand, was long and dark, strikingly streaked with grey. Judging by her general appearance, the Apothecary presumed the woman to be about forty-five years of age. However, her face, handsome enough in a strong, masculine way, had been totally marred by the wild array of bruises which marked it.

Shocked, John unbuttoned the top of the dress and found further evidence that the woman had sustained a severe beating. Hating to do what he must next, he delicately raised her skirts and saw that the legs in their torn and pathetic stockings were also covered in marks.

'Well?' asked Samuel, coming to join him and shuddering slightly.

'She was battered within an inch of her life before she was thrown in.'

'How do you know?'

'By the contusions. She would only bruise like that if she had been alive when they were sustained.'

'Was she dead when she went into the water?'

John shook his head. 'No. Look at the marks on her wrists and ankles. Those were made by the chains which weighted her down. If she had been already done for, they would have left no impression.'

Samuel dashed his hand across his eyes. 'Christ's mercy on us, what a terrible end. Beaten half to death then thrown in to drown.'

The Apothecary looked grim. 'A ghastly fate certainly.' He leant forward over the face once more, noticing that the open eyes, still a recognisable shade of deep brown, were just starting to go cloudy. He closed them rapidly before anyone else could see.

'What are those little pink marks?' asked his friend, pointing to where pin-prick spots showed amongst the bruises.

'Shrimps,' John answered shortly.

'Do you mean...?' The Goldsmith's eyes widened in horror.

'I'm afraid so. They made a bit of a meal of her during the night.'

'I shall never eat a shrimp again,' Samuel announced, turning pale.

The two Runners approached. 'Should we take her away, Mr Rawlings?'

'Let me just quickly sketch her. She'll start to swell in half an hour or so and then the details of her injuries will be more difficult to see.'

'I'll get a pad and pencil,' announced Mr Kemp. who had been gazing out over the stretch of water, studiously avoiding having to look at the body.

'Thank you.'

'No trouble, I assure you.'

The proprietor turned to go towards the house, and in so doing his gaze fell willy-nilly on the thing lying stretched out on the sheet, the Apothecary still kneeling beside it. Staggering very slightly, Mr Kemp let out a piercing cry.

John looked up. 'Are you all right, Sir?'

'The clothes she's wearing...those stripes...' the proprietor answered incoherently.

The Apothecary got to his feet. 'Are you saying that you recognise the victim?'

'Not her as such, no. But she's wearing the uniform of one of the warders at St Luke's Hospital.'

John stared at him. 'Do you mean the asylum for the insane?'

William Kemp stared back, eyes wide, 'Yes, I do. The place that opened some seven years ago to relieve the overcrowding at Bedlam. It's not far from here, at Upper Moor Fields in fact.'

Samuel interjected. 'I've heard tell there are some violent inmates there. John, you don't suppose...'

The Apothecary shook his head. 'I don't suppose anything at this stage.'

'But the savagery of the attack! Might that not point to an unbalanced mind?'

'Yes,' said Mr Kemp, eagerly warming to the theme. 'Surely this murder must be the work of a madman?'

'It could, and there again it could be the doing of someone perfectly sane. Someone with a grudge against the poor woman, so strong that it led them to beat her to a pulp before they killed her.'

'I wonder what conclusion Mr Fielding will draw,' Samuel replied somewhat peevishly.

John smiled. 'Well, we shan't have to wait long to find out, for here he comes.'

And all three of them turned to watch the rare sight of the blind Principal Magistrate coming down the path towards them, one arm firmly held by his clerk, Joe Jago, the other by his wife, Elizabeth.

'My dear Sir, how are you?' enquired Mr Kemp, sweeping a bow.

'Never better, never better,' answered the Beak, and made a salutation in return.

Chapter Three

Darkness had finally fallen on that long summer's day. The waters of the Peerless Pool and the Fish Pond lay still and tranquil, reflecting on their glassy surfaces the rise of a glittering crescent moon. Similarly, the beautifully kept grounds, the bowling green, the cold-water bath-house, stood in shadow, quiet and deserted, the only sign of life in the entire pleasure resort the blaze of candles coming from William Kemp's manor house. The light from these spilled out over the walled garden and orchard on the one side, and on the other the terrace and banks of the Fish Pond, so still and blameless in the moonshine, as if no one could recently have breathed their last in its emerald depths.

Within the house itself there was an almost jovial atmosphere, for Mr Kemp, in company with his wife, a small, elegant lady of uncertain years, was entertaining. Much to the Apothecary's surprise, it had emerged early in the conversation that the proprietor and the Blind Beak were friends of long standing, John Fielding going to the Peerless Pool both to swim and fish at times when it was closed to the general public.

'Mr Rawlings,' William Kemp had said to the Apothecary in a confidential aside, 'I have observed that man, when I have placed him beside the Fish Pond with rod and line, catch perch of a pound weight as fast as Joe Jago could bait his hook. As for swimming, he is like a fish itself, and that with only a servant to attend him.'

'It is sometimes hard to believe that he cannot see.'

'Impossible,' Samuel had added loudly, afraid that he was being left out of the conversation.

John had grinned, and at that moment Mr Fielding himself started to speak.

'How congenial it is to be here again, William. If only the circumstances were a little happier.'

Mr Kemp sighed gustily. 'I fear this macabre incident will do the reputation of the Peerless Pool no good at all.'

The Magistrate had permitted himself a hollow chuckle. 'On the contrary, you will probably find the place packed when you reopen. The voyeuristic capacity of the public at large is well known.'

Samuel commented, 'Dirty devils,' and the two ladies present, Elizabeth Fielding and Jemima Kemp, both laughed.

There were seven of them, all seated round a large circular table in the dining salon. The lady of the house, Mr Kemp's diminutive wife, had hastily organised an early supper, which everyone present was attacking heartily, with the exception of Nicholas Dawkins. He had been sent home to tell Sir Gabriel Kent, the Apothecary's father, that his son was once again about the business of Mr Fielding. In the meantime the corpse had been removed to the mortuary, while the employees of the Pleasure Garden had removed themselves to a nearby hostelry as the gates were locked for the night.

'I am most impressed, my dear Sir,' said Mr Kemp reflectively, 'by the manner in which your Brave Fellows acted. It seemed to take them no time to get here and deal with the situation.'

The Magistrate contrived to look modest. 'I must admit that that part of the Public Office's activity is going very well. My boast that my Flying Runners, as I jokingly call them, are ready to go to any part of the kingdom at short notice is no idle one. Why, during the past year, in fact since we last met, Mr Rawlings, they have been called to places as far afield as Windsor, Maidstone, Bristol, Barnet and Faversham. To say nothing of the famous incident two years ago when they pursued a man to Portsmouth and had a most exciting boat race before capturing their quarry.'

Joe Jago spoke up, his foxy colouring bright in the candlelight. 'In the spring of this year the Brave Fellows went in hot pursuit of John Evans, the corpse snatcher.'

'How courageous,' murmured Mrs Kemp. 'Did they catch him?'

Joe looked slightly uncomfortable. 'Alas, no. He was last heard of heading for France.'

'Now, to present matters,' said the Blind Beak, and everyone fell silent. 'You say that the dead woman was wearing the uniform of St Luke's, William?'

'She most certainly was,' the proprietor answered, and with relish launched into his theory of a homicidal madman having killed a wardress.

The Magistrate nodded. 'It is possible, of course. We must check at the hospital first thing in the morning to see if they can throw any light on the matter.'

'May I go, Sir?' John asked.

The black bandage that concealed Mr Fielding's blind eyes from the world swivelled in the Apothecary's direction. 'I would be absolutely delighted, my friend. But as ever I have the usual reservations about keeping you from your livelihood.'

'These days, with Nicholas coming along so well, ably assisted by Master Gerard when I am absent, there is absolutely no need.'

Samuel spoke up. 'If you have no objection, Sir, I would like to accompany John. I do believe that I have certain skills when it comes to ascertaining facts.'

The Apothecary smiled to himself, remembering all too clearly some of the gaffes that his friend had made in the past. Momentarily the Magistrate's mouth twitched, but he said, 'By all means, Mr Swann, providing that Mr Rawlings is agreeable.'

'What I want to know,' said William Kemp, 'is how the killer got into the grounds to dispose of the body. The gates both to the Old Street and Pest House Lane entrances are locked at night and everything kept secure.'

'And the entrance to your own premises?'

'My house is reached by a path leading directly from Old Street which continues on to Islington. The gate is similarly safe.'

The Apothecary asked a question. 'Are all your staff utterly trustworthy, Mr Kemp?'

'What are you suggesting?'

'That one of them might be in league with the murderer and have opened the gates for him.'

The proprietor appeared a little put out. 'As I told you earlier, I employ none but the best at the Peerless Pool.'

'None the less,' interjected the Magistrate, 'in a case of murder one can trust nobody.' He turned his sightless eyes in the direction of Mr Kemp. 'Tell me, William, when do you intend to reopen?'

'Well, I had thought tomorrow. I have no wish to raise alarm in the minds of my subscribers by being closed.'

'I agree with that. However, if you could delay by one day I should be grateful. I would like to send some of my most experienced men here in the morning to comb the grounds for signs of unlawful entry. Further, I myself, in company with Jago, would like to question every member of your staff about their whereabouts on the night the poor woman was thrown in to drown.'

Mr Fielding's words had a sombre ring to them, and there was an uneasy silence after he had spoken. Eventually, though, the proprietor answered, 'It shall be as you say, of course.'

'In that case there is little further we can do until daylight.'

Mrs Kemp interrupted. 'Then may we forget this sad and sorry affair for an hour? It would please me if you finished your supper with a modicum of enjoyment.'

At her words there was a general but unsuccessful attempt to rally. For haunting them all as they sat in that pleasant house, picking at a cold collation and sipping wine, was the thought of the suffering of the woman who had died a terrified death but a few yards away from where they all sat at leisure.

It was well after midnight when John finally alighted from a hackney coach outside his home in Nassau Street, and looked up fondly at the house in which he had lived since Sir Gabriel Kent had taken himself and his mother off the streets of London where they had been begging for an existence. Though not a large building, it had once accommodated in comfort the Apothecary's adopted father and his new family, together with their servants. But when Phyllida Kent, as John's mother had honourably become, died in childbirth, the establishment had reverted to an all-male household, and the boy had been brought up by Sir Gabriel as if he were his own son. In fact the Apothecary thought of himself as such, and sometimes had to remind himself that he was in reality a bastard child of the house of Rawlings of Twickenham.

Creeping indoors quietly so as not to disturb the grand old man, John was thoroughly startled to hear a further set of wheels draw up outside, followed by the neigh and stamp of mettlesome horses. As the footman on duty threw open the door, the Apothecary turned to see Sir Gabriel's equipage just being driven round to the mews in which it was housed.

'Ah, my son,' his father said, alighting and swirling off his white-lined black cloak with a flourish. 'I take it you have just returned from the Peerless Pool. Nicholas told me the details of what happened there and I must say that it sounds a highly unpleasant and sordid affair.'

John nodded, then smiled at Sir Gabriel's arresting appearance. Clad as always in stark black and white, or black and silver for special occasions, tonight his father sported a top coat and breeches in dark silk velvet. The waistcoat that complemented this ensemble was made of contrasting ivory satin, however, profusely embroidered with a floral border pattern of silver silks, as was the coat. The total effect was stunning; a sight to behold with awe.

'You look very fine,' said the Apothecary appreciatively. 'Where have you been?'

'Playing whist with Lord and Lady Dysart, who are connected with the Hampshires. They've recently had a new town house built and wanted me to see it.'

'I wasn't aware that you knew them.'

'To be frank with you, neither was I. But the other night at Marybone, whilst throwing dice, Anthony Dysart came up to me. It seems we were at school together and he recognised me, even after this passage of time.'

John patted his father affectionately on the arm. 'Nobody could ever forget you, that's for certain.'

Sir Gabriel's golden eyes crinkled at the corners and he said, 'Tush,' though the Apothecary could tell that truly he was pleased.

'Would you care for a glass of port before you retire?' the older man asked.

'I certainly would. Besides, I want to discuss this latest event with you.'

They settled down comfortably in the library and John put more coal on the fire in order to avoid disturbing the servants, nearly all of whom had bedded down for the night. Then he told his father everything that had occurred since he and Samuel had taken a boat out on the Fish Pond.

'So you believe that someone employed by Mr Kemp must have given assistance to the killer?'

'Yes, I do. The woman was not dead, though grievously beaten, and must have been transported to the Peerless Pool in some kind of conveyance, even be it a wheelbarrow. It seems that the proprietor locks up securely enough, so it's my theory that a gate was opened from within. Now think back to the various remarks that were made to me and see if you notice the same thing that I did.'

Sir Gabriel imbibed his port, staring thoughtfully into the flames. Eventually he asked a question to which John nodded.

'Yes, that's it. I did not notice at the time but later on that evening it suddenly occurred to me.'

'Did you tell Mr Fielding?'

'No, I couldn't. There were too many people present. However, I shall send Nicholas round with a note early tomorrow morning.'

'A good plan. Forewarned is forearmed.'

Sir Gabriel's longcase clock chimed its tuneful melody, 'The British Granadears'* then struck one. 'I must go to bed,' said John, standing up. 'I have arranged to meet Samuel early so that we can get to St Luke's at breakfast time. I hope to be the first to break the news of the woman's death.'

'And thus have the element of surprise on your side?'

'Precisely.'

But as John mounted the stairs he wondered whether this would be the case, or whether someone more closely connected with the Peerless Pool had already taken the news of the wardress's death to the asylum for the insane.

* *Eighteenth-century spelling.*

Chapter Four

It was not until he approached St Luke's Hospital for Poor Lunatics on foot, walking up the length of Windmill Hill from Upper Moor Fields, that John Rawlings realised just how close to the Fish Pond the building actually was. It had once been used by John Wesley as a Meeting House, but the lease had been obtained by a consortium of six worthy citizens of London intent upon establishing a new dwelling to assist and supplement the ancient and overcrowded asylum known as Bethlehem Hospital, commonly referred to by all strata of society as Bedlam.

No provision being made by the state for the proper care and treatment of mentally ill persons belonging to the impoverished classes, Bedlam, the one refuge offered to them, was packed to suffocation point, and desperate patients were constantly turned away. Accordingly, much to the relief of the staff of Bethlehem Hospital, in the summer of 1751 the doors of St Luke's were opened, the asylum to be administered by Dr Thomas Crow, one of the six original founders. And it was to see this man that John, accompanied by an extremely eager Samuel, was presently making his way.

Turning through the gates, the Apothecary took stock of the lie of the land. Though the building had been extended beyond the boundaries of the original Meeting House, St Luke's was for all that small, an austere, joyless place, admirably suited to housing those whose madness brought about frenzies. But despite its harsh appearance, the hospital's surroundings were pleasant; fields to one aide, trees to the other. Apart from a few straggling cottages, the only other building in sight was the distantly glimpsed Lord Mayor's Dog House, owned by the City Hunt.

Just beyond St Luke's, the path known as Windmill Hill forked right, leading to the well of St Agnes le Clare, situated at the junction with Old Street. If one bore left at the well, the site of the Peerless Pool lay just a matter of yards away. In the other direction from the hospital gates was Tindal's Burying Ground, where the great Daniel Defoe was buried. Any number of back alleys led from there directly to the Fish Pond.

'Well?' said Samuel.

'I was just thinking that it wouldn't have been difficult to transport the victim from here to the Peerless Pool. That is if the beating took place near the hospital.'

'Would the woman have been conscious, do you think?'

'Barely. However, there is always the possibility that she walked to the Pond unharmed and was viciously attacked once she got there.'

Samuel looked portentous. 'It was the work of a lunatic, John. I feel certain of it.'

His friend regarded him gravely. 'Everyone is a lunatic when they kill. Even if you did so in self-defence, the heart would pound, the blood rush, and extra strength would come in a rush. Just for a split second, as you pitted your life against your assailant's, you would be mad, Samuel.'

The Goldsmith pursed his lips. 'I'm afraid I cannot agree. In such a situation I would remain in full possession of my faculties.'

'Like a drunk who considers himself sober?'

'No, not like that at all,' Samuel answered irritably.

They had traversed the path leading to St Luke's and were now standing outside a high and substantial brick wall, beyond which lay the hospital. Looking up, John saw that every window in the place was barred by iron grilles and that the door in the wall, complete with wicket, was equally well fortified.

'Appears to be more of a prison than a place of treatment,' he remarked.

Samuel shivered dramatically. 'I can just imagine what goes on behind those windows. Scenes from a nightmare, I dare swear.'

The Apothecary rolled his eyes. 'Well, be of stout heart, my friend. You are about to find out. Now remember, look neither to the right nor left of you, or you may never come out again.'

Samuel appeared fractionally startled, then gave a hearty guffaw and clapped John on the shoulder. 'Ho, ho, what a wit!' And with that he leaned across his friend and tugged the bellrope, which distantly echoed with a hollow and somehow sinister sound.

'I told you,' said John, smiling unevenly, a characteristic of his.

They waited in silence, listening as chains and bolts were undone; this sound followed by footsteps crossing the few yards that lay between the hospital and the wall. Then a small window opened in the wicket and a pair of nervous, pale grey eyes shifted uneasily from side to side, regarding them.

'Who is calling?' asked a muffled voice.

'John Rawlings and Samuel Swann, visiting on behalf of Mr Fielding of the Public Office, Bow Street. We would like to see Dr Crow, if that is possible.'

'This is not one of Dr Crow's days,' the voice replied. 'Mr Burridge is in charge.'

'Then may we see him?'

'I will enquire. If you would like to step into the waiting room.' There was a further dragging of bolts, and then the wicket opened to reveal the figure of a small tremulous being, badly afflicted by what appeared to be some form of palsy, for he shook uncontrollably as he ushered the visitors inside. John took him to be a former inmate, sufficiently recovered to carry out simple tasks.

Beyond the gate, the Apothecary saw that the wall widened out in a semi-circle to encompass a pleasant garden, in which several people were already sitting, taking the morning sun. Overlooking them were two warders, one male, one female, the last wearing a striped dress similar to that found on the victim. The man had on a dark blue jerkin and breeches, very plain and serviceable. As John passed close by, going into the main building, several of the inmates looked up, one particularly catching his attention, for she was utterly beautiful, lacking only the divine spark of sanity to make her incomparable. Fair hair, fine as flax, blew untidily round a magnificently boned face, its contours so perfect that it looked to have been carved by a master sculptor. Full and passionate lips curled above a small chin. But the girl's eyes, a shade of dazzling blue, had no expression in them whatsoever. A dead soul was peeping out and regarding the Apothecary, and it made him shiver as he walked into the shadowy confines of St Luke's Hospital for Poor Lunatics.

Though efforts had been made to brighten the place, no doubt by the wives of those Christian souls who had founded the asylum, nothing could combat the terrible feeling of despair which pervaded the entire atmosphere. Sitting uncomfortably in the small room into which they had been shown, John and Samuel regarded one another dismally. From a distance, like the murmur of the sea, came the muted sound of moaning, punctuated by the occasional loud cry or scream and the noise of running feet. It was totally unnerving, and the Apothecary found himself wishing that he had never volunteered for such a wretched task.

'Hope we don't have to wait much longer,' said Samuel glumly.

'It's not exactly jolly,' John agreed.

'In fact it's downright...'

But the Goldsmith got no further. There was a tap on the door and a warder appeared. 'Mr Burridge will see you now, he said. 'If you would follow me, gentlemen.'

They climbed a staircase, slippery with polish, and then proceeded down a corridor. All the while, the sound of muted cries continued, though the two friends could see no one.

John cleared his throat. 'Where are the patients?' he asked boldly.

The warder shot him a quizzical glance. 'There's some in the garden, some in the saloon, the others are locked in their rooms.'

'Are those the dangerous ones?' Samuel enquired earnestly.

'They're all dangerous,' the warder answered shortly. 'There's not one I'd turn my back on if they held a pair of scissors. Any of 'em is liable to fly into a frenzy soon as look at you.'

'So in your view any of them would be capable of killing someone?' asked Samuel, using the casual voice he always adopted on these occasions.

The warder gave a hollow laugh. 'Capable of it? Why, most of the creatures in here already have! Believe me, there is no patient of St Luke's who hasn't homicidal tendencies.'

'Even the beautiful girl, the one with the fair hair and blue eyes? Surely she wouldn't harm a fly,' said John, shocked.

'You mean Petronelle? Oh, she's all right as long as she doesn't see any children. Then she goes wild and has to be restrained. By more than one strong man as well.'

'Why is that?'

'Nobody has any idea, for nothing is known of her. She was picked up off the streets of London, quite crazed, rescued from a life of prostitution.'

'How old was she then?'

'Thirteen or fourteen.'

Both John and Samuel shook their heads in sorrow, though neither was surprised, such a thing being commonplace rather than unusual.

Reaching the end of the passageway, they drew to a halt outside an imposing door on which the warder knocked deferentially.

'Yes?' came the answer, and the man, cautioning the two friends to wait, went inside, closing the door behind him. There was the murmur of conversation and then the warder reappeared and ushered them into the room with a slight bow.

John led the way, then drew back, realising he was just a second or two too early. For the man in charge of St Luke's was in the very act of slapping a serviceable wig on to his head and adjusting his cravat into a more fashionable knot. Hearing them come in, he turned and smiled somewhat sheepishly, revealing a large pair of loosely fitting false teeth which he raised to gum level with a sucking sound.

'Good morning, gentlemen,' he said heartily. 'And what may I do for you?' It seemed clear from his manner that he either knew nothing about the missing member of staff or had not connected John with the matter. So it would appear that the news had not yet been broken.

Coming straight to the point, the Apothecary said formally, 'I am here on behalf of Mr John Fielding of Bow Street, Sir. This is his letter of authorisation.' And he handed Mr Burridge the document that the Blind Beak had given him before they parted company on the previous night.

The older man pushed his spectacles up his nose, thus magnifying his eyes which suddenly loomed, blue and bulbous. As he scanned the contents, his toothy smile vanished and his features became decidedly grumpy. 'What is all this?' he asked sharply. 'Mr Fielding requests my cooperation? Regarding what, pray?'

'Regarding a case of murder,' Samuel answered, stung to speak thus by the man's sudden irritable manner.

'I beg your pardon?' Mr Burridge retorted nastily.

'Murder,' replied John coldly. 'Last night, Sir, the body of a woman was found in the Fish Pond on the Peerless Pool estate. The state of deterioration of the corpse, or rather the lack of it, suggests that she had been thrown in quite recently, probably the night before. The victim was wearing the uniform of one of your wardresses. So I must ask you, has any of your employees not appeared for duty today?'

Mr Burridge's expression changed from surly to shaken. 'Why yes,' he answered uncomfortably, 'now you come to mention it, Hannah Rankin has not been seen this morning.'

The Apothecary continued ruthlessly, aware that he had the advantage. 'And would this Hannah Rankin be in her late forties, possessing dark hair streaked with grey, and brown eyes?'

Mr Burridge removed his spectacles and cleaned them with a serviceable handkerchief 'Yes, that's her. But I'm afraid I don't understand. You have the advantage of me, gentlemen.'

'That is a description of the body raised from the bottom of the Fish Pond last evening. The victim had been severely beaten, then weighted down and thrown in to die. The Public Office is looking into the manner of her death, Sir, and I am assisting Mr Fielding in this. Now, what can you tell me about the woman, presuming for the moment that it is one and the same person?'

Mr Burridge sat down behind his desk, rather swiftly John thought, and reaching into a drawer, poured himself a small tot of brandy from a bottle kept within. Forcing a smile, he said, 'For shock,' then gulped the draught in one. Mopping his brow, he sucked his false teeth into position.

'She hasn't worked here long...Hannah Rankin, that is,' he said rapidly, looking anxiously at the Apothecary.

'What do you mean? Six months or less?' John asked, taking a seat opposite while Samuel settled himself into a chair near by, his look intent.

'No, a little more than that. About a year or so.'

'And where did she come from? Do you know?'

'Originally from Bath I believe. As far as I can recall her references bore an address somewhere within that town.'

'I see.'

Samuel spoke up. 'Do you still have those references, Sir? They could be of vital importance in tracing the woman's background.'

Mr Burridge looked relieved, probably because he could answer positively for a change. 'Oh yes, yes indeed. All facts of that kind are kept on record.' He half rose. 'Would you like me to trace the papers now?'

John shook his head. 'No, Sir, pray sit down. That information is very helpful in its way but what I am looking for is something more recent. For example, was Hannah Rankin married, and where did she live? Did she have enemies here on the staff? Or is it possible that she could have fallen foul of one of the patients?'

Mr Burridge took another surreptitious tot of brandy, then leant his elbows on the desk. 'You do realise that it is Dr. Crow himself who employs the warders?'

'No, I didn't know that. But what...?'

'Simply put, he knows their background better than I. I do not hobnob with the staff, you understand.' Realising that he was implying that the worthy doctor did just that, Mr Burridge attempted to cover his error. 'Of course, Dr Crow is quite right in being on friendly terms with one and all. Ha, ha!'

Samuel cut to the heart of the matter. 'So when is the doctor coming back to St Luke's?'

'Not till next week, I fear. We alternate. I am an administrator, he a man of medicine.'

'So you cannot help us further in the matter of Hannah Rankin?'

Mr Burridge endeavoured to look genial but his eyes were unsmiling. 'I think, gentlemen, you might be better off talking to Forbes, the man who showed you in. As Chief Warder he is fully cognisant with all that goes on. I shall send for him.' And without further argument he picked up a small handbell and rang it.

With an alacrity that convinced John the man had been listening at the door, Forbes appeared. 'You summoned me, Sir.'

'Yes, my good fellow, I did. As you already know, these two gentlemen are here representing Mr Fielding of the Public Office, Bow Street. It seems that a woman resembling Hannah Rankin and wearing the uniform of this hospital met with an unfortunate accident in the Fish Pond near the Peerless Pool. They would like to ask you some questions about her.'

'Very good, Sir.'

'It was something more than an accident,' said John forthrightly. 'It was in fact deliberate murder.'

He stared into Forbes's face, looking for signs of surprise. There were none, but that, of course, could be accounted for by the fact that he had overheard the entire conversation rather than by any prior knowledge.

The Apothecary turned to Mr Burridge. 'May I claim your indulgence, Sir. May I speak to Mr Forbes in private?'

The administrator looked predictably put out. 'Well, really, I...'

'The reason is that a man does not feel as free to speak in the presence of his employer; that is a known fact and one in which Mr Fielding would bear me out.'

'Oh, very well,' Mr Burridge replied testily, and strode from the room, fuming.

Instantly John took his place behind the administrator's desk and produced paper and pencil from his pocket. 'Now, Mr Forbes, if you would be so kind as to tell me everything you known about Hannah Rankin, I'll take a few notes.'

'I suppose,' said Samuel practically, 'that she hasn't reappeared? I mean to say, we are talking about the right woman and not heading up a blind alley, aren't we?'

'Hannah has not reported for work, if that is what you are asking, Sir.'

'When did you last see her?' asked John.

'Not yesterday, which was her day off, but the day before. In the evening. She was going home at about eight o'clock. I called out goodnight to her but she didn't answer, just went hurrying away.'

'How do you organise your work here?' the Apothecary enquired, genuinely curious. 'Are there warders present throughout the night, or do you all go off duty?'

'Most goes home, Sir. The apothecary comes round after the lunatics have been fed and doses 'em up good and strong. Then the violent ones are tied to their beds and locked in. The others are just made secure in their rooms. There are no dormitories, it being too difficult to control a group of 'em if trouble should break out.'

'How many staff remain here?'

'We have found three warders to be enough. Two men and Mother Richard. She always does night-times. She likes it, you see.'

'And who is Mother Richard?'

'The midwife. She needs the extra money for gin, being very partial to the stuff.'

'She sounds highly unsuitable to be nursing the sick.'

'Well, the lunatics ain't exactly that, now, are they, Sir? A firm hand and a few chains are what they need.'

'I thought this place was meant to be more caring than Bedlam,' John answered, sighing.

'It is. We don't allow sightseers, for a start.'

The Apothecary shook his head, not knowing how to answer. For the fact was that for an entry fee of two pence, visitors were allowed into the Bethlehem Hospital to stare at the disturbed and suffering inmates, a circumstance violently deplored by the artist William Hogarth, who had painted a terrible scene depicting conditions within the asylum.

Thinking it better not to argue, the Apothecary said, 'Tell me about Hannah. Was she a married woman?'

'No, Sir. She lived alone in Ratcliff Row.'

'Where's that?'

'Not far from Pest House Row, near to the French Hospital.'

'My God,' said the Goldsmith, jumping to his feet. 'Do you realise where that is, John?'

'No.'

'Pest House Row runs directly behind the Fish Pond.'

'That's right,' put in Forbes, 'it does.' His eyes glistened. 'You say that Hannah met her end in that very place?'

'Indeed she did.'

'Then she wouldn't have far to go, would she?'

The Apothecary considered for a moment, then changed the conversation's direction. 'Did Hannah have any particular friends that you know of? Either on the staff or outside the hospital?'

Forbes looked thoughtful. 'No, she didn't. The fact was that she kept herself very much to herself. Spoke to few; did her duty; befriended no one but fell out with none. She had a way with her, if you understand me, that seemed to discourage comradeship. She was alone and happy like that.'

'Obviously an austere woman,' John stated with just a hint of a smile.

'Very. There was some that were quite nervous of her.'

'Why?'

'Only because of that. Because of her forbidding manner.'

'Might one of the inmates be sufficiently afraid of her to be driven to commit murder?'

Forbes screwed up his face to hide the fact that he was grinning. 'They hate all us warders, but her they hated most of all.'

John stood up, indicating that the interview was at an end. 'Mr Forbes, I must thank you. You have been most helpful. However, I'm afraid there is one other thing.'

'Yes?'

'If no kith or kin can be found, then someone who knew Hannah Rankin well will be asked to identify the body. Would you be willing to do so?'

Forbes gulped. 'If nobody else is available, I suppose I must.'

'I will inform Mr Fielding.'

They walked back down the corridor together, listening to the wail of the wretched patients, glimpsing through one open door a half-naked man, his hands on his genitals.

'Stop that!' bellowed Forbes, but the poor creature continued, totally oblivious of the world beyond his own pathetic needs. Very sobered, the two friends stepped through the heavily fortified front door and into the fresh air of the garden beyond, where both drew a deep breath.

'God grant that I never end in such a place,' Samuel said morosely.

'Amen to that,' John answered with feeling. He looked around him and saw that the beautiful girl, Petronelle, had started a meaningless solitary walk, wandering in circles, going nowhere, without purpose. Looking up, she caught his eye and began to head in his direction.

'Only a shilling,' she said sadly.

'Not now, my dear,' the Apothecary answered.

Petronelle burst into tears. 'But I need the money to buy food.'

John shook his head. 'No, they feed you here.'

She looked at him, very puzzled. 'Do they? What place am I in?'

'You're in hospital,' Samuel replied kindly. 'Where they look after you.'

Very briefly, a look of cunning came into Petronelle's eye. 'Some do, some don't,' she answered.

Thinking of the warders' attitude as personified by Forbes, John inwardly shuddered at the thought of cruelty being meted out to such a delicate creature.

'Who is unkind to you?' he asked, determined to take the matter up with Dr Crow himself, should it prove necessary.

Petronelle took his arm, her lovely face staring up into his. 'She's gone now,' she whispered.

'Who? Who's gone?'

'Her. The wicked one.'

'Tell me which she is.'

'The one who came for me. Oh, Sir, the one who came for me.' Petronelle's beautiful lips quivered and tears glistened in her eyes. 'Oh, Mama, Mama,' she sobbed.

John slipped an arm round the girl's heaving shoulders and was rewarded with a frantic clawing of his coat. 'You won't let her take me, will you?' Petronelle implored.

'Nobody's going to harm you. You're safe here,' the Apothecary answered, wishing he believed it to be true.

'She thinks I don't remember,' the girl continued in a whisper, close to his ear. 'She thinks that because I'm grown I've forgotten all about it. But I haven't. I'll always remember her and the way she came for me.'

So saying, Petronelle's mood seemed to swing and she wandered off again, her eyes vacant, her beautiful face as devoid of expression as a mask.

'I wonder what she meant by all that,' said Samuel, staring after her.

'I don't know,' John replied thoughtfully. 'But I have every intention of finding out.

Chapter Five

Pest House Row, as John and Samuel saw when they turned into the lane that ran between Old Street and Islington, stood, an untidy jumble of straggling houses, the sole reminder of the place in which the City Pest House had once been situated. Built in the last few years of the sixteenth century by money raised from companies interested in Sir Walter Raleigh's adventure at sea, namely his piratical exploits plundering Spanish galleons, the House had been erected 'as a lazaretto for the reception of distressed and miserable objects infected by the dreadful plague'. Having taken in many patients at the time of epidemic, principally those poor wretches who were homeless, moneyless and friendless and who regarded the Pest House with hatred and horror, the building had finally fallen into disrepair in the early part of the eighteenth century and, in 1736, had been sold to the French Hospital, the governing body of which knocked down what was left and erected new buildings on the site.

'Do you reckon there's a burial pit anywhere round here?' said Samuel, staring at the rise and fall of the land behind the cottages.

John shook his head. 'No, the poor bastards were all thrown in at Mount Mill, weren't they?'

Samuel looked vague. 'I'm not certain. Where is Mount Mill?'

'Just off Goswell Street, near Peartree Street. Supposedly there are hundreds of plague victims buried there.'

'Hurled into the ground with scant ceremony, just a few hastily mumbled prayers. Frightening thought.'

The Apothecary gave a cynical smile. 'One could say the same for Hannah Rankin.'

Samuel shivered. 'Don't! A goose walked over my grave when you spoke those words. Are you going to knock on doors in Ratcliff Row to find where she lived?'

'In a moment or two. First of all I want to get the lie of the land.'

They had been walking as they talked and now found themselves standing outside the French Hospital, a gracious and beautiful building erected round three sides of a quadrangle. Funds for the project had been provided by a French Huguenot, James de Gastigny, Master of the Buckhounds to King William III. Though it had originally been intended that the Hospital should be a place of refuge for 'Poor French Protestants and Their Descendants

Residing in Great Britain', the asylum also had its share of aged and infirm people, providing them with a permanent home. But for the rest of the Huguenots it was a place of sanctuary, a shelter where they could find friendly advice in determining their future plans. The Hospital also acted as an agency for locating other French immigrants who had already settled elsewhere in London. As he walked past the entrance, John thought what an excellent place it would be to cloak the activities of a French spy ring.

Directly opposite the Hospital, on the other side of the lane, stood the rear of the complex that housed the Peerless Pool and the Fish Pond, together with the other buildings belonging to the Pleasure Garden, including Mr Kemp's grand dwelling place. There was the back way in, the Apothecary noticed; a gated entrance leading off Pest House Row. Would it have been possible, he wondered, for someone to have come through that gate and stealthily make their way to the Fish Pond, hidden by the cover of the trees? Certain that at night it would have been all too easy, he put his hand out to give the gate a push, only to find that today it was locked.

'Interesting,' he said to Samuel.

'What?'

'If the gate is as secure as this at night, as Mr Kemp assures us it is, it means if the body were taken to the Fish Pond this way, the murderer either had a key or...'

'Was let in by an accomplice on the inside, as you suggested.'

'Exactly. Now listen to this.' And the Apothecary repeated to his friend the thought that had struck him after they had last parted company.

''Zounds!' Samuel's jolly eyes lit up. 'Have you told Mr Fielding?'

'Nicholas went round with a note containing the information early this morning. It should have reached the Beak before he set off for the Peerless Pool.'

The Goldsmith looked eager. 'Shall we present our compliments to him before he leaves?'

'By all means. But first let us find the lodging house of the late Hannah Rankin and see what information, if any, that yields up.'

On closer examination it was easy to see that the cottages of Ratcliff Row, which was situated a quarter of a mile further up the lane, directly opposite the fields and a path leading to Mr Kemp's house and the Pleasure Garden, had been rebuilt at the same time as the Cripplegate or God's Gift Almshouses. These had been founded by Edward Alleyn, the well-known actor and joint owner of the Fortune Theatre in Playhouse Yard. Originally put up in 1620, the almshouses had been modernised exactly one hundred years later. Each was one-storeyed, with a red-tiled roof, shuttered windows and a green front door that opened directly on to the street. The houses where Hannah had lived were similarly designed, except that their front doors were a bold, if somewhat weathered, blue. Jauntily approaching the first one, John raised the knocker.

Even before it descended, a woman appeared. 'Yes?' she said beadily.

John assumed his urbane expression. 'I am seeking the whereabouts of a Hannah Rankin. Would you be able to help me at all? Do you know where she lives?'

'I might,' the woman answered, narrowing eyes that had not been large to start with.

'So what must I do to obtain your assistance?' the Apothecary replied charmingly.

'State your business,' she retorted. 'That's what, young Sir.'

John conjectured possibilities, smiling the meanwhile. If he announced that he was conducting affairs on behalf of John Fielding, then he would have authority but little cooperation. If, on the other hand, he fabricated a feasible story, he might get a great deal further. His smile broadened and he bowed.

'Mistress Rankin and I are distant cousins. I was hoping that I might pay my respects to her now that I am in town.'

The mean eyes glinted. 'You don't look like no cousin to me. She's a rough thing, is Hannah.'

'So you do know her?'

'There's not many come and go in this row that I don't.'

Samuel entered the discussion with his usual disastrous approach. 'I'll wager there's not much goes on here that you miss, Ma'am.'

He laughed heartily and looked affable but the woman curled her lip. 'Are you saying that I am a busybody?'

Samuel began to bluster. 'Gracious me, no. Merely a lady with sharp eyes who notices what her neighbours do.'

The woman made to slam the door shut but John stepped in to retrieve the situation. 'Madam, as you correctly observed, I am not Hannah Rankin's cousin. However, I do represent the hospital of St Luke's, and the fact of the matter is that Hannah did not appear for work today, nor has she been seen there since the day before yesterday. I wondered, therefore, if you could tell me at which cottage she resides so that I might ask her landlord for information.'

'Two doors down from me she lives, with one Mother Hamp, who takes in lodgers being as she is a widow woman.' She drew in breath. 'So Hannah's disappeared, has she? I thought she'd been keeping strange company of late.'

The Apothecary raised a lively brow. 'Really? Who, for example?'

'A Frenchie from the Hospital, for a start. A right sly old fox he looks with his powder and patches. Then there was the coachman, a hulking big fellow. I wondered what she could be doing with such a pair of suitors.

'You think they were that?'

'Well, what else could they be, calling on a woman alone?'

'Business connections?' said John, doubtfully.

Samuel snorted. 'Hardly, I should have thought.'

Hannah's neighbour nodded. 'Who could be doing business with a warder from the lunatic asylum? Unless it was something shady, of course.'

'Perhaps that's the answer.' The Apothecary looked thoughtful. 'Perhaps Hannah was involved in some rum doings.'

The neighbour's ear for gossip was certainly acute; for she put her head on one side and said, 'Was?'

Furious with himself for making such a crass mistake, John answered, 'A figure of speech, that is all.'

But the woman did not seem altogether convinced for she watched the two friends closely as they went to the cottage where Hannah had lived, having politely thanked her for her help.

'Do you think she believed me?' John muttered.

'No,' Samuel whispered in reply.

'The rumour of her possible death will soon be down the entire row.'

'It's already started.'

And John saw out of the corner of his eye that the neighbour had gone to the house next door where she had been joined by another, very similar to herself, and that the pair of them were looking their way. Partly because of this, the Apothecary decided he must persuade Mother Hamp to let them in immediately and not stand talking on the doorstep, even if this meant revealing the true nature of his enquiry. Accordingly, when a greasy, grey-haired harridan of a great many years and exceedingly few teeth answered his summons, John, speaking in a low voice, said, 'Madam, I urgently require you to let my companion and me into your house. We are here on the official business of Mr John Fielding of Bow Street.'

His plan was instantly thwarted by the crone cupping her ear and saying, 'What? Speak up, young fellow. Can't hear a word.'

Horribly aware of the grin spreading over Samuel's jocund features, John leant close, his nose wrinkling at the terrible stink emanating from the hag's apparel and person, and repeated the message.

'Bow Street?' she bawled in reply. 'What have I got to do with Bow Street?'

'Nothing,' he thundered. 'Go inside.' And seizing her skinny elbow, the Apothecary hurried Mother Hamp within doors. He turned to his companion. 'If those two besoms come knocking the door, send them away with a nit in their ear.'

'To add to the others already there,' Samuel answered, and chortled.

Away from the street and in her own grim surroundings, Mother Hamp became somewhat more amenable and produced a bottle of gin from the depths of her rags, wiping the neck with her sleeve and offering it around. John gingerly took a swig to show there was no ill feeling. Samuel turned pale but did likewise.

'Now what's all this about, boys?' she asked, having taken a deep draught herself.

Briskly, and with a certain amount of authority, John explained, omitting the fact that Hannah Rankin's body had been found.

'So she's disappeared, has she?' Mother Hamp asked, echoing the neighbour's words. 'Can't say I'm surprised.'

'Why is that?'

The harridan downed a half-pint of gin. ''Cos she had no past, that's why.'

'What do you mean?'

'She never spoke of family, friends, places where she used to live, nuffink. She seemed to come from nowhere and know no one.'

'What about the two men who called on her; the Frenchman and the coachman? She must have known them.'

Mother Hamp flashed her gums in a silent guffaw. 'I wouldn't have called them friends exactly. She was afraid of them, I reckon. That Frenchie, with his white face and black beauty spots, he had some hold on her. She used to see him in her room and talk to him all meek and mild, not like the way she screams at them lunatics.'

'How do you know that's the way she treats the patients at St Luke's?'

''Cos I sometimes do shifts there, when Mother Richard is away delivering a child.'

John shuddered at the very thought. 'Go on.'

'As for the coachman, she lived in mortal dread of him. He only came here twice but each time she trembled and wept. And one day when she'd had a bottle of spirit, Hannah told me that she might have to run for her life if he came again.'

'Hare and hounds!' exclaimed Samuel from the corner. 'There's a clue, John!'

'Indeed. Tell me, how did you know this man was a coachman? Was it merely from the way he was dressed?'

Mother Hamp let out another soundless, toothless laugh. 'No. It was on account of his conveyance standing outside my front door.'

The Apothecary gazed at her. 'He drove a coach here! Was it a hackney?'

'No, bless you, it was a gentleman's carriage. It even had a coat of arms on the door.'

'And this man was up on the box, not inside?'

'He was on the box with the reins in his hands.'

'He was definitely a coachman,' said Samuel, sniggering at John.

The Apothecary shot him a black look. 'Would it be possible, Madam, to look at Hannah Rankin's room? There might be something there which could tell us more about why she disappeared.'

'It's up the stairs on the left,' Mother Hamp answered, and fell to consuming the gin in earnest.

It was quite extraordinary. Exactly as if Hannah had actually left home for good on the night she was murdered. No clothes hung in the ancient clothes press and there were no shawls or stockings in the drawers. Nor was there any sign of baggage. It looked just as if Hannah had packed up, taken her belongings with her, and in this state gone to her death.

'She must have planned to go away with her killer,' said Samuel, staring around him at the deserted chamber.

'Not necessarily. If the Frenchman or the coachman, or both, were menacing her, perhaps she ran away.'

'But not far enough.'

'Precisely.'

'I wonder what she had done in the past to have two such sinister characters on her trail.'

'And to merit such a terrible beating. For someone exacted a terrible revenge when they thrashed Hannah within an inch of her life, then threw her into the water alive to drown.'

For no reason an image of the beautiful Petronelle came into John's mind, together with the final words she had said to him. Under his breath he muttered them. 'I'll always remember her and the way she came for me.'

Samuel overheard him. 'There's darkness in this case, isn't there, John?' he asked fearfully.

'Darkness — and a great evil,' the Apothecary answered slowly.

There had been much activity at the Peerless Pool that morning. As arranged, the Principal Magistrate, John Fielding, accompanied by Joe Jago, had arrived by coach shortly after eight o'clock, having risen and breakfasted early. Once on the premises, he had gone to the Fish Pond and allowed Jago to describe the scene for him as it appeared in full sunlight, then report on what the team of Runners searching the grounds had so far unearthed. After that, the Blind Beak had set up a room in Mr Kemp's house and started to question those who had been present not only on the day when the body had been found but also at the Pleasure Garden during the previous day and evening.

An account of the Peerless Pool's routine had emerged from those examined. The Garden shut every evening at sunset, a bell being rung half an hour beforehand in order to warn bathers and those taking refreshment or in the bowling alley that closing time was drawing near. Then, when all the patrons had finally gone, the waiters would go around locking the gates for the night.

'I believe there are two ways into the Peerless Pool,' Mr Fielding had said, sitting back in his chair, apparently negligent, the bandage that covered his eyes this day giving the impression that he was resting.

'Yes, Sir,' the waiter being questioned had answered. 'One leading off Old Street, through which subscribers are admitted. The other a small gate going off Pest House Row, almost opposite the French Hospital. It leads to the west corner of the Fish Pond.'

'And what is the purpose of that?'

'It allows the dedicated anglers, those with a season ticket, to go straight to the Pond without having to walk through the rest of the Garden.'

Mr Fielding had nodded. 'I presume there is someone on daily duty there?'

'Oh yes, Sir.'

There had been silence, and then Joe Jago had asked a question, his ragged features harsh in the early morning light.

'But surely there is a third way in. Did I not spy a gate leading from the back of this property to a path going across the fields in the direction of Islington?'

'Yes, Sir. You did, Sir.'

'And is this, too, locked at night?'

'So I would imagine, though that is the duty of Mr Kemp's household servants, not the waiters.'

The Magistrate had fingered the curls of his long, flowing wig, a magnificent creation in its way, though nothing like as fine as that worn by Sir Gabriel Kent.

'So it seems there are three entrances by which the body could have come in, Joe.'

'It looks like it, Sir.'

'Though only of use to someone with a key or a friend on the inside of the Garden.'

'So it would appear.'

'Did you see the letter that Mr Rawlings sent me this morning? Nick Dawkins read it to me but I left it on my desk for you to peruse.'

'The one in which he...'

But Joe got no further. There was a polite tap on the door and the very person under discussion came walking in. John and Samuel had finished their morning's investigations and had arrived to compare notes with the finest brain in London.

As comprehensively as he could, the Apothecary described all that had taken place, especially dwelling on the extraordinarily empty state of Hannah Rankin's room. Mr Fielding nodded occasionally but deliberately asked no questions until John had finished speaking. Then he said, 'Tell me, was Mother Hamp sober enough to be questioned before you left?'

'Just about.'

'Did you ask her if Hannah had given notice of quitting?'

'I did, but she replied no. I then enquired when she had last seen the victim and she said early on the evening of the night before last.'

'Did she state in what circumstances?'

'Yes. Apparently Hannah went out with a bundle in her hand. Mother Hamp asked her what it was and she said it was some old clothes that she was taking up to the Hospital for Poor Lunatics and that she was on her way there immediately. However, the old besom did not believe her.'

'Why?'

'Because she swore that she glimpsed the Frenchman waiting for Hannah, loitering further down the lane, and that the pair of them set off in the direction of the French Hospital.'

Mr Fielding gave a quiet and rather shocking chuckle. 'Do you know, my friends, I have the feeling that this is going to be one of the most intriguing investigations any of us has ever undertaken. For what do we have so far? A victim who appears to have been up to no good, a frightened mad beauty, a waiter who knows more than he should, a gate leading from the scene of the crime into the fields and directly to where the dead woman lived, not to mention a powdered Frenchman and a menacing coachman. It is truly the stuff of novels. How my brother would have relished it.'

John smiled, one side of his mouth tilting upwards. 'Is it not said that fact is stranger than fiction?'

'Indeed it is. Now, did Hannah's landlady reveal anything further?'

'Only that the dead woman kept herself very much to herself. Something confirmed by the gossiping neighbour. But what of Toby, Sir?'

Joe Jago answered for the Magistrate. 'We have yet to see him. In fact we kept him to the last, Mr Rawlings, in the hope that you might arrive.'

Samuel looked excited. 'Then shall we call him in?'

'By all means.'

The man who had brought Hannah Rankin's body to the surface of the Pond was clearly the old soldier that he claimed to be. Scars of battle marked his face, one cut running down so close to his eye that he was lucky not to have lost the sight of it. With his sleeves rolled back, exposing his burly forearms, other healed wounds could be seen. There was a generally stoical air about the fellow, as if he had borne all manner of terrible conditions and still come out uncomplaining. John almost regretted the blow that would shortly fall upon him.

Mr Fielding leant back in his chair, his face impassive, his voice measured. 'Be so good as to stand in front of me. As you know, I am completely blind and it helps me to converse if I know whither I should address my voice.'

Toby did as he had been requested, then stood straight, military style, waiting to be questioned.

The Magistrate continued urbanely. 'I will, if I may, recount your part in the tragic events of yesterday, so that you can tell me if they are correct or otherwise. Then, perhaps, we might discuss any points that arise. Is that agreeable to you?'

'It is, Sir.'

'From what I have heard you were summoned by Mr Kemp to assist Mr Rawlings. He told you that a body had been found in the Fish Pond and asked whether you would be willing to dive in and retrieve it. To this you made the somewhat curious reply that you had fought in the war and seen worse sights than dead women.' Mr Fielding paused, then said silkily, 'How did you know that it was a female who lay at the bottom of the lake?'

Toby's eyes bulged in his head and his jaw sagged, then he recovered himself. 'Because he said so,' he answered, pointing at John.

'But that's just the point,' the Apothecary retorted, 'I did no such thing. I was very careful not to mention the gender of the victim.'

There was a moment's silence, then Toby fell back on the soldier's creed that attack is the best method of defence. 'Far be it from me to argue with a gentleman, but I must contradict you there, Sir,' he announced boldly. 'You definitely said she was female. How else would I have known?'

'How indeed?' repeated John Fielding reflectively. The black bandage turned in John's direction. 'I feel we must let the matter rest there, at least for the time being.'

And the Apothecary knew that he had been given an instruction not to argue until there had been a chance for further discussion. However, he could not resist shooting a quizzical glance in Toby's direction and slowly raising a dark svelte brow, just to show the waiter that he had not been deceived by the downright lie than had just been told about his own recollection of events.

Chapter Six

It had been a morning crammed with events and information and nobody felt more relieved than John when Mr Fielding finally announced his intention of returning to Bow Street, believing that, for the moment, all had been achieved that could be at the Peerless Pool. For so far several interesting facts had emerged. Not only had Toby told a barefaced lie when questioned, but also a track had been discovered by the gate behind Mr Kemp's manor house. The indentation formed by a single wheel made it appear that a wheelbarrow had come along the path from the fields and gone through the gate and into the grounds. There, unfortunately, the marks vanished into the shrubbery, though no abandoned wheelbarrow had been found.

The Blind Beak, listening to the report of his Runners, had ordered that all the barrows used in maintaining the Peerless Pool gardens be searched and, sure enough, one of them, when the grass it contained had been tipped out, bore indications of dark brown stains. John had examined them, his quizzing glass to his eye.

'Blood, I'm sure of it.'

'So it would appear that this is the way Hannah was brought in.'

Joe Jago had spoken. 'It seems more and more likely that someone working within these grounds assisted the killer.'

The Magistrate had stroked his chin. 'Or was the killer.'

'Things are looking black for Toby.'

'Black – but not black enough. However, I shall have him brought to Bow Street for further examination. He might not be quite so confident away from his own territory.'

Samuel had asked a question. 'As there seem to be no relatives or friends, what are you going to do about identifying the body, Sir?'

'I shall call upon Forbes the warder, as Mr Rawlings suggested.'

'I don't think he's going to be very happy about that.'

'It is not a happy task,' the Beak had replied without cynicism.

The final undertaking before the four men went to Mr Fielding's carriage was to ascertain which of Mr Kemp's servants was responsible for locking the back gate at night. This proved to be a gardener called William, who swore that he had locked up on the night of the crime.

'At what time would that have been?' Joe Jago had asked, Mr Fielding sitting quietly in his usual solemn pose.

William had rubbed his hands on his breeches. 'At sundown, Sir. I tends to lock up when the other gates are done.'

'But what happens if Mr Kemp or any member of his family, or any of the servants come to that, want to go out that way?'

'The family all have keys, Sir. And the servants shares one. It hangs with the household keys in the kitchen.'

'It couldn't have been easier,' Joe had commented as the door closed behind the man. 'The way I see it, the murderer either let himself in, or was assisted by his accomplice. All they had to do was take the key off the hook.'

'The field narrows and widens,' was the Magistrate's only comment as they walked through the grounds to the Old Street entrance, where his coach awaited them.

Taking leave of Mr Fielding, John and Samuel had gone their separate ways; the Goldsmith to his shop, the Apothecary to his home in Nassau Street, Soho, the thought of dining with his father and discussing the morning's events too great a temptation to be overcome. However, such pleasurable notions were driven straight from his mind by the sight of a carriage just leaving his front door and going round to the stables in Dolphin Yard, where Sir Gabriel Kent's own equipage was housed.

Guests, John thought, and made a point of going to his room and not only washing away the smell of the lunatic asylum but also changing his clothes for something far more elegant than he had worn for the morning's business. And as he entered his father's library, from which the buzz of lively conversation could be heard from halfway down the stairs, the Apothecary was glad that he had dressed up, for the place seemed full of people.

The first person to catch his eye was a tall, thin grandee, with dark lustrous eyes, a hawk's nose, and black eyebrows which contrasted interestingly with the full white wig that the man wore. Beside him stood a woman that John took to be the grandee's wife. Encased as she was in lilac taffeta, with eyes of an almost identical colour, the Apothecary thought for a moment that she, too, was wearing a wig, until he realised that it was the woman's own hair, swept up and adorned with fashionable feathers. The fact that she was white-haired surprised him, for he had taken her to be not much more than forty-five. Just for a moment the woman's eyes rested on him and she smiled, transforming herself into a beauty, regardless of age.

There were two other couples in the room, one of whom John knew slightly, the other very well indeed. The first, a round and jolly physician by the name of Dr Drake and his lanky wife, Matilda, who towered over him, he greeted with a polite and formal bow. The second, Comte Louis de Vignolles and his marvellous wife Serafina, John saluted then embraced. Indeed, he would have spent time talking to them had not his father summoned him to his side.

Addressing the violet-eyed woman, Sir Gabriel said, 'Lady Dysart, may I present my son, John Rawlings?'

She gave the Apothecary a warm glance, replied, 'How dee do,' and held out her hand for a kiss. Brushing her fingers with his lips, John smiled up at her and she lowered her lids, thus betraying what a flirt she once had been.

Turning to the grandee, Sir Gabriel, with a certain ring of pride in his voice, said, 'Anthony, this is the son of whom I have spoken. May I introduce him to you?' The grandee nodded his striking head and Sir Gabriel continued, 'John, this is my old friend, Lord Anthony Dysart.'

The Apothecary gave his deepest bow and said, 'An honour, my Lord,' feeling rather than seeing Sir Gabriel's smile of approval.

'Your father and I were at school together,' Lord Anthony remarked. 'My parents were particularly progressive and disliked the idea of tutors beyond a certain age for their sons. Consequently, I was sent out into the world, and look into what company I fell.'

He and Sir Gabriel laughed uproariously and John was left to consider that money bought everything. For Sir Gabriel's father, a minor baronet but an extremely wealthy one, had been able to send his son to Winchester, the great public school and the oldest in England, founded in the fourteenth century. There he had mingled with the sons of the aristocracy, a fact that had done Sir Gabriel no harm at all when he entered the world of commerce in order to enlarge his fortune.

Lord Anthony interrupted the Apothecary's train of thought. 'Your father was senior to me, of course, but was kind enough to help me read Ovid's Metamorphoses and Entropius. I fear that Latin and Greek were never my strong suit. I was always more interested in learning how to measure the stars.'

Lady Dysart joined in. 'There is a general laziness in all Englishmen about studying a foreign tongue, which is something I deplore. I attended the French Boarding School for Young Ladies in the Broadway, Westminster, and there we were obliged to speak the language in its purest form.'

'What else did you study, Ma'am?' asked John, surprised that she was so well educated and something more than a vapid member of the upper class.

'English, writing, drawing and accounts, to say nothing of needlework and dancing. In fact it was the claim of our headmistress that all her pupils went from her establishment knowing everything that was needed for life as a lady.' The beautiful eyes twinkled. 'Of course, the one thing that nobody told us about was men.'

Her husband smiled broadly. 'And where did you learn about those, my dear?'

'Attending balls, playing cards, and in the bedchamber,' she replied with spirit, then added, 'But only yours, of course.'

Sir Gabriel, who for this dinner-time was clad in black satin breeches with white stockings, a black full-skirted coat and a white waistcoat intricately embroidered with black threads, turned to his son.

'Will you escort Lady Dysart into dinner, my dear?'

The Apothecary, thoroughly intrigued by their attractive, outspoken guest, answered, 'It will be my pleasure to do so.'

They formed into a line, Lord Anthony offering Serafina de Vignolles his arm, and the Comte walking with Matilda Drake. The fat physician and Sir Gabriel came last of all. In this way, John found himself seated beside Lady Dysart and opposite Serafina, a most fortunate arrangement as far as he was concerned. Looking across the table at his old friend, with whom some years previously he had thought himself madly in love, the Apothecary caught her eye and they exchanged a knowing look. They had come through much together and had been involved in some interesting escapades. Yet even while they were staring at one another with awareness, Serafina slowly winked her eye, leaving John wondering what it was that she wanted to tell him. His gaze slid round to her husband, the handsome Frenchman, Louis, who had also been caught up in certain intrigues in his time, but it seemed that nothing was amiss there, for the Comte was chatting animatedly to his neighbour Matilda, who was flushed with all the attention.

Lady Dysart addressed herself to the Comtesse de Vignolles. 'Of course, we are relative newcomers to town life, having until recently divided our time between Paris and Somerset.'

Serafina looked interested. 'Oh, why was that, Ma'am?'

'My husband was the French Ambassador and had been so for many years, but at the outbreak of war two summers ago we were recalled. We have spent the intervening months looking for a town house but now we have had one built in the new development of Mayfair. You must call on me, my dear Comtesse, I could do with a little female company.'

'I should be delighted for I, too, have connections with France. My husband, as you know, is of Huguenot extraction and speaks French fluently, even though he was born here.'

'Better and better,' answered Lady Dysart, and effortlessly changed languages, addressing herself to Louis in his native tongue. 'I was just saying to your charming wife that I hope we can become friends. I need to enter the social scene once more and can think of no more delightful companion.'

'The only difficulty might be,' answered Serafina, also in French, 'that I shall be retiring from public life shortly. I am with child.'

John and Sir Gabriel, who could follow French with relative ease, both burst into delighted applause, much to the astonishment of Dr and Mrs Drake, who did not speak the language at all.

'When?' said the Apothecary in English, permitting himself to ask such a personal question because of his long and intimate association with the Comtesse, to whose other child he was a godfather.

'In February.'

'And what does Italia think?'

'She does not know yet but I am sure she will be mightily put out. She has had three years of my undivided attention and now a rival in the camp is sure to displease her.' Serafina turned to Lady Dysart. 'Do you have any children, Ma'am?'

It was an innocent enough question but, for all that, a strange quiet suddenly fell over Sir Gabriel and Lord Anthony, even though the other guests seemed unaware of it, for Matilda chattered on inanely and Dr Drake boomed a laugh at Louis. John, though, close to his father as he was, sensed that something had gone badly wrong and wondered what it could possibly be.

Eventually Lady Dysart spoke, her face expressionless, though her voice was full of pain. 'Anthony and I had only one child, a daughter, our son and heir having died at birth. Alice was very beautiful, a lovely girl in many ways and all that we could hope for, but she disappointed us by eloping with the son of one of our servants. Anyway, we put that scandal behind us and shortly after that we were posted to Paris and shut up the Somerset home. Then a message came from England that we were to return at once. Alice and her husband had both been killed in a coaching accident, leaving behind a baby boy of only two years old. Naturally, we rushed home to fetch the child and took him back with us to France.'

Her voice broke and, shaking her head, Lady Dysart relapsed into silence, then rose from the table and left the room. Her husband stared after her mournfully.

'Forgive her, please. My wife was foolish to embark on such a tale over the dinner table.'

Serafina looked fraught. 'It is my fault entirely. I should never have asked such a personal question.'

'You were not to know, Comtesse,' Lord Anthony answered sombrely. 'No blame can be laid at your door.' He stared down at his plate then cleared his throat, obviously coming to a decision. Eventually he said, 'I think you should know the rest of the story, terrible though it is to relate. Meredith, our grandson, lived with us until he was three, then one day, with no warning whatsoever, he vanished from the garden in which he had been playing and was never seen again.'

Everyone gazed at him in horror, and there was a long silence before John found himself asking, 'But how could this be? Was the child dallying in a public place?'

'No. The garden was situated behind the Ambassador's residence in the Marais district of Paris, a mansion protected by a high brick wall. After we reported him missing, the officers of the law searched the premises high and low, and further afield we employed our own people to look for the child, but all to no avail. It was just as if Meredith had been spirited off the face of the earth.'

'What did you do? Whatever did you do?' asked Matilda, with a sob.

'We went on looking, first in Paris, then further and further away. We followed every lead. Our quest took us to remote villages, to Spain even, seeing boys who answered Meredith's description. But each time we were disappointed. They were either beggars, or tricksters, or just poor homeless creatures who were wandering the streets. In the end I begged Ambrosine to give up the quest, assured her that too much time had elapsed, that we would no longer recognise Meredith even if we were to find him. But still she went on. I think one could fairly say that the hunt for her missing grandson became an obsession with her.'

'Anthony, my dear, I had heard about Alice but had no idea of this,' Sir Gabriel said quietly. 'What a grim burden for you to have carried all these years.'

Just for a second Dysart's dark eyes welled with tears, then he firmly controlled himself. 'Even worse than losing the boy has been watching the anguish eat away at Ambrosine. Believe me, she has only returned to anything like a semblance of normality since we came back to England.'

John stood up. 'I feel I should go to her. The very least I can do is mix her a concoction.' Suddenly remembering that there was a physician present, he looked contritely in Dr Drake's direction. 'As long as that is agreeable to you, Sir.'

Somewhat reluctantly, the doctor also lumbered to his feet. 'Yes, I think we should see the lady. Perhaps a word of cheer and a strengthening mixture might restore her good humour.'

Lord Anthony looked doubtful. 'Ambrosine prefers to be left alone when she is in low spirits.'

Sir Gabriel interjected, 'My son's compounds are excellent and Dr Drake is most experienced, my friend. Let them try to help her.'

'Very well. If you wish.'

Feeling that he ought to walk on tiptoe, so restrained was the atmosphere round the dinner table, John followed Dr Drake from the room, horribly aware that he had never seen Serafina so wretched with guilt.

They found Lady Dysart in the library, staring out of the window at Sir Gabriel's garden, the droop of her shoulders exquisitely sad and somehow more heart-rending than if she had been weeping. She turned on hearing their footsteps and regarded the two men with sorrowful eyes.

'Madam,' said Dr Drake, 'your husband has told us everything. I grieve for you as a grandfather myself.' He spoke very sweetly and the Apothecary's admiration for him rose mightily. 'My young friend, Mr Rawlings,' the physician went on, 'would be most happy to make you a concoction to restore your spirits. I do hope that you will agree to him doing so.'

Ambrosine smiled sadly. 'Nothing can ever take away the pain of losing a child — and I have lost three; my baby son, my beautiful daughter, and then Meredith. It is hard to see how a glass of physick could put matters right but I am most happy to try if it would please you.' She made a little gesture with her hand, so downhearted a movement that John found himself taking it between his own.

'Be brave, Lady Dysart,' he said. 'I will do all that I can to help you.'

He turned to fetch his bag of pills and potions but she stopped him, misunderstanding what he had said.

'You will look for Meredith for me?'

The Apothecary shook his head. 'I can hardly do that after all these years.'

'But say you will. Say that you will keep your eyes and ears open. You must meet so many people through your profession. One day somebody might say something that could put you on the right trail.'

'It really isn't very likely.'

Dr Drake's voice drowned his. 'Of course we will look out, Madam. Both Mr Rawlings and I will stay alert. But you must prepare yourself for disappointment. The chances of either of us hearing anything are very remote.'

'I understand that,' she answered dismally, 'but there is always a faint hope.'

Handing Ambrosine a glass of physick to which he had added a purgation of black hellebore, also known as Christmas rose, a sure cure for melancholy, John asked, 'How old would Meredith be now?'

Lady Dysart frowned slightly. 'He was three when he was stolen and that was eighteen years ago.'

'And, forgive me, no body was ever found?'

'Not in Paris, no. The city was combed, including those dangerous areas where civilised men hardly dare set foot. But as to the rest of France, who can say? It is, as you know, an enormous country.'

'Your husband raised the point, my Lady,' Dr Drake said tentatively, 'that even if you were to come across Meredith, you would no longer recognise him. Surely this must be true. By now, a young man would have taken the place of the child.'

'Meredith bore a birthmark,' Ambrosine answered defensively. 'He had a red patch, often described as a port wine stain, on the left-hand side of his chest. I would know him anywhere by that.'

'Such marks have been known to fade with age.'

'None the less.'

John shook his head. 'Lady Dysart, I wish you success, I truly do. But do not set store on finding and recognising him.'

Ambrosine set her lips in a firm line. 'My faith will not be shaken by anything you say. Now, to the present. I feel much recovered. If it would not be considered impolite I would like to join the others. Sir Gabriel suggested that we should play whist when we had dined and I would so enjoy a game.'

Dr Drake peered earnestly into his patient's face. 'You are sure you are up to it, my Lady? This is not just a show of bravado?'

Ambrosine shook her head. 'No, I really do feel greatly recovered. I think this young man's concoction has truly done me good.' She flashed a brilliant smile in John's direction.

She was very slightly hysterical, he felt sure of that, but really there was little he could do to stop her playing cards. Besides, to have to concentrate on something other than her tragic life would undoubtedly do her good. With an answering smile, the Apothecary bowed, then offered Lady Dysart his arm.

Serafina, who had once been renowned as the greatest gambler in London, the notorious Masked Lady, no less, was clearly suffering from a combination of guilt and pregnancy, for she threw her game of whist away, allowing

Ambrosine Dysart to execute a brilliant Bath coup, a move designed to deceive the other players which Serafina would normally have countered at once. Thus Ambrosine had stylishly won the rubber.

'Well played,' said her husband, clapping his hands at his wife's skill. John, highly suspicious that his old friend might have lost deliberately, did likewise. 'You are a fine player, Lady Dysart.'

'We got a lot of practice in Paris, of course. Even after Meredith disappeared we had to entertain as before.'

'It must have been a terrible strain on you,' said Serafina.

'It both destroyed and saved me,' Ambrosine answered truthfully. 'I think if I had not been forced to enact my role as ambassador's wife I would have broken down completely.'

There was a small silence, then Serafina, her equilibrium restored, asked the ultimate question. 'Why was he taken? Was it because of who you were?'

Lord Anthony answered for his wife. 'That was what was thought at the time but when no demand for money or favours arrived, the authorities began to reconsider the idea.'

'Then why?'

The people sitting at the other card table started to listen, Matilda already dabbing at her eyes with a large, sensible handkerchief.

'Slavery, possibly,' said Anthony, in a strained and quiet voice.

'Slavery?' echoed Dr Drake in shocked tones.

'Oh, yes. Perhaps you did not know that during the time of the Commonwealth, Irish men, women and children were snatched from their villages by English soldiers and shipped off in their thousands to act as slaves in the Barbadoes. They never returned, most of them being literally worked to death. They were treated far worse than the African slaves who were more difficult to come by. But in the case of the Irish, the plantation owners knew that for every one that died the government would send replacements. It was the most evil trade in human life ever recorded.'

'I was not aware of that,' Louis de Vignolles stated. 'Though I did know that the poor unfortunate bastards born to the wretched women of Bridewell were sent to the plantations to earn a living.'

Realising how distressing this discussion must be, Sir Gabriel tried to put a stop to it, but Ambrosine's voice rose above his.

'My grandson was beautiful, a truly handsome child. I cannot believe that he was taken merely to act as a slave.'

'Then why?' asked kind but tactless Matilda.

'To satisfy the whim of some terrible creature,' Lady Dysart answered, blanching as white as her hair. 'It is my heart's belief that the child was taken either to work in the brothels or become the plaything of some evil pederast.'

'For God's sake!' exclaimed Lord Anthony, still unable to listen to such words.

There was a stunned silence round the table before Lady Dysart, her attempt at rallying at an end, burst into long and raking sobs, quite terrible to hear.

It had still been bright, a fine summer's early evening, as John had journeyed by coach in the direction of the newly built houses of Mayfair, that exciting development lying behind Berkeley Square where all the most elegant members of the beau monde were choosing to make their home. He had accompanied Lord and Lady Dysart from number two, Nassau Street, in order to give Ambrosine a sleeping draught once she was safely in bed, Dr Drake having a professional call to make. Supported by her husband, the bereaved grandmother had not spoken during the journey back, had not said a word as she alighted from the coach and went straight indoors and up the stairs, a maid running along the landing to assist her.

As soon as she was out of sight, Lord Anthony turned a desperate face to the Apothecary. 'Come and have a brandy with me, there's a good fellow. And perhaps you could give me a draught of something while you're about it. Having to live with this situation is wearing away at my nerves.'

They had gone, then, into a book-lined library, obviously used as a study from time to time, and there sat down on either side of the fireplace, only to be joined a moment or two later by a footman, come to put a tinder to the wood.

'Begging your pardon, my Lord,' the man said, as he knelt before the grate, 'but Mr Gregg presents his compliments and asks if there is anything he can do.'

Lord Anthony looked up over the rim of his glass. 'Tell him that I am engaged for the moment but that I'll see him later this evening.'

John said nothing, merely sipping his brandy, watching the flames begin to rise and thinking about the terrible fate that might well have befallen his host's grandson.

Almost as if he could read them, Anthony broke in on his thoughts, his voice harsh and almost unrecognisable. 'Do you think our poor boy was taken as a catamite?'

The Apothecary shook his head, his face very serious. 'Sir, I have always been led to understand that child abduction rings have been at work since time immemorial, though as to their exact purpose I have never been quite certain. Yet, being honest, I cannot credit that all the children taken are destined just to be plantation slaves. Though I hate to say it, I'm sure some of them must end up in a life of prostitution, in one form or another.'

The older man nodded, his dark brows furrowing into a harsh line. 'You're right, of course. What vile times we live in!'

'Times have always been and always will be vile.'

Lord Anthony let out a grim laugh. 'Then there's little hope for us.'

'Come now, Sir, for every evil act one usually comes across a good one. Perhaps the boy was kidnapped by a childless couple who had fallen in love with the look of him and are now acting as his parents, giving him much love and affection.'

'Even that would not make his abduction any easier to bear.'

'No, it wouldn't. But it would give you a great deal more hope.'

'Aye, that it would, my Lord,' said a voice from the doorway, and John turned in his chair to see that a hulking creature with shoulders broad enough for two men and a shock of iron-grey hair, uncovered by a wig and crowning the man's ruddy complexion like a cock's comb, had entered the room.

'Ah, Gregg,' said Lord Anthony wearily, 'did you not get the message that I was engaged?'

'That I did, my Lord. But what with her ladyship near to collapse upstairs, and demanding that the young apothecary should give her something to make her sleep all night without so much as a dream, I thought I'd best act on my own initiative.'

'You're an insolent hound,' growled Anthony, without rancour.

'Yes, my Lord,' answered Gregg and, advancing into the room, he stood at attention before the fireplace as if he were awaiting orders.

'Mr Rawlings,' his lordship said with just a flicker of amusement, 'this is my steward, Gregg. He has been in my service for ever and a day; in fact he entirely ran the Somerset home while we were in France. But now, with it closed down most of the year, I have brought him here to be close to us, though I must be losing my reason to do so for he is as authoritarian as if he were master.'

'Take no notice, Sir,' answered Gregg, directing his remarks at John and winking an enormous blue eye in a most familiar manner. 'I'm as obedient as the hound his lordship just called me.'

That they were on extremely familiar terms was more than obvious, and even though it was wildly unconventional, the Apothecary was not at all surprised when Lord Anthony Dysart invited his steward to sit down and drink brandy with them.

'Gregg came out to Paris to help me search at the time of the abduction,' his lordship announced by way of explanation, and suddenly everything was crystal clear. Though deeply divided by class, by the unwritten laws governing servants and their masters, these two men were intimate friends, united by a common tragedy in which both had shared.

'It is a pleasure to meet you, Gregg,' John said.

The steward rose and bowed. 'Anyone who helps Lord and Lady Dysart can expect my friendship in return.'

The situation was getting more unusual by the second, but there was something refreshing about it for all that.

'Did you say that her ladyship wanted me?' the Apothecary asked the newcomer.

'Aye, Sir. She's ready for her sleeping draught now. I'll get one of the footmen to show you the way.'

So, accompanied by a servant, John mounted a new sharply curved staircase, built in the modern style, and went into a fine bedroom which looked out over Hyde Park. Though most of the curtains were closed against the evening sunshine, the sensational view could be glimpsed through one, only partly drawn. Opposite this window, in a draped bed which stood against the far wall, Ambrosine lay, her face and hair as white as the linen. Only her eyes, deep mauve in the shadows, added any colour to her immense pallor. She held out one of her lovely hands.

'My dear young friend, you have not seen the best of me today.'

He kissed her fingers, thinking how attractive she was and how very much he wanted to help her.

'Madam, you were forced to recall a most painful episode in your life. Everyone who met you at dinner can do nothing but admire your enormous courage in overcoming your suffering as greatly as you have.'

She smiled. 'How kindly put. Now give me my sleeping potion and let me rest. Tomorrow I will wake up strong once more.'

Opening his bag of physicks and pills, John drew out a dose of laudanum, derived from the white poppy, the most powerful opiate he carried.

'Will I dream?' asked Lady Dysart as she swallowed it.

'You might.'

'Will the dreams be pleasant if I do?'

'That I cannot say.'

She was falling asleep already. 'Mr Rawlings,' she whispered.

'Yes?'

'Don't forget your promise to me.'

'What was that?'

'To help me find poor Meredith.'

'I won't forget,' John answered, and left the room, his heart heavy within him at the thought of such a terrible delving, and what might be revealed if by the merest chance such a task should prove successful.

Chapter Seven

A sudden wild whim to do something exciting and unplanned overcame John Rawlings as he journeyed back from his visit to Lord Anthony Dysart's splendid new home. Indeed, so much did it have him in its grip that he lowered the carriage window and called up to the coachman, 'Would you be good enough to take me to the King's Theatre in the Hay Market. I should just have time to see the start of the play.'

'Very good, Sir,' came the reply, and the driver changed direction, turning right off Piccadilly instead of going straight on to Nassau Street. But it was a little more than love of the theatre which drew the Apothecary to a new production of Twelfth Night, now in the first week of its run. In truth, as soon as his eye had alighted on the poster advertising the play, he had determined to see it. For playing the part of Viola, that Shakespearean heroine who spends most of her time on stage dressed as a boy, was the woman who had haunted him ever since he had met her four years earlier, in 1754; none other than the rising young actress Coralie Clive, younger sister of the famous Kitty. Suddenly most anxious to see her again, John jostled his way into the pit, where sat the professional classes; young merchants of coming eminence, barristers and students of the Inns of Court, physicians and apothecaries. The critics also sat in this part of the theatre and denoted their status by smearing their upper lips with snuff. With only a few minutes to spare, John took his seat and looked around him.

The stage, as ever, was half filled with boxes, packed with exquisites and fine ladies, all decidedly tipsy, or lounging footmen reserving places for their late-coming masters. Even with the play about to start, a blood swung a high leg over a box's ledge, staggered slightly, and accidentally sat down hard upon his privy parts, causing him to wheeze with pain and rendering him incapable of further movement. To assist him, one of the two sentries posted upon the stage, a ridiculous custom frequently dispensed with by David Garrick of Drury Lane, heaved the wretched fellow over the edge, where he sprawled in a chair, quite done in. At this, the occupants of the gallery showered the box with oranges until the poor recipient, still bent double, was compelled to leave through a door at the back. Competing valiantly with this chaos, the sounds of the orchestra were lost, and the actor playing the part of the Duke was forced to repeat the immortal words 'If music be the food of love, play on' twice, in order to make himself heard. The Apothecary felt his stomach tighten with anxiety at the thought of the fate that awaited Coralie, due on stage next. But she took it all with quiet calm. Dressed from head to toe in a hooded black cloak, she stared out at the audience as if they were the waves of the sea Viola was meant to be regarding. Raked by those beautiful green eyes, even the rowdiest gallery-goer fell quiet, and Coralie began her scene in silence.

She was as attractive as ever, John thought, her dark hair shining in the lights, her lashes black against her roses-and-snow complexion. Watching her, the Apothecary wished, as he had so very many times before, that Coralie did not have the power to move him to such vivid fantasies about loving her. For truth to tell, though he had enjoyed the favours of several young ladies during his lifetime, he had never for one moment forgotten Miss Clive, nor stopped caring for her in a very deep and special manner. In fact, John had one great wish: that Coralie would put aside her burning ambition to be as great an actress as her famous sister and love him in return.

Her opening scene done, the gallery, who obviously adored her, burst into wild cheering, and were only stopped by the entrance of Sir Toby Belch and Sir Andrew Aguecheek, the latter tremendously well played by a famous queer-garter who minced about the stage on such tremendously high heels that John wondered how on earth the actor kept his balance. To further add to the general hilarity, one of the sentinels guarding the stage, by day no more than a common soldier, became overcome with laughter at the sight of Sir Andrew's strut and visibly clutched his sides.

Coralie appeared dressed as a boy, her costume deepest violet, and received a wild cheer from her supporters in the gods. John would have joined in had it not been for the intellectual company amongst whom he sat. Speaking her lines in a clear, carrying voice, with just the merest attractive catch in it, the actress took her part with great skill, far outshining a very stilted Miss Hippesly, struggling to give some sparkle to Olivia. Unable to help it, John felt himself falling in love with Coralie all over again.

The first two acts over, there followed a short interval during which the Apothecary was tempted to go backstage. However, he resisted, and went instead to take refreshment with the rest of the audience. And it seemed that not only the spectators had consumed wine, for, the interlude done, the outrageous Mr Sparks attacked the role of Sir Andrew Aguecheek with even more verve than he had in the first half, obviously enjoying the benefits of alcoholic liberation. The sentry who had laughed so heartily in the opening acts was now so overcome with mirth that he actually fell convulsed upon the boards, much to the amusement of the rest of the house, who roared alongside him. They also guffawed at the ill-treatment of Malvolio, something that the Apothecary had never found in the least amusing, considering that this revealed a dark, cruel element to the play which he did not care for at all. However, everything else was redeemed by the performance of Miss Clive, a grave and serious as well as beautiful Viola.

Entranced, John sat in the darkness of the theatre and listened to the plaintive voice of the Clown as he sang the closing words of Twelfth Night: 'When that I was and a little tiny boy, With hey, ho, the wind and the rain.'

Outside the theatre there was the usual throng of people waiting for their coaches, summoning hackneys, or rushing to find sedan chairs. The Apothecary stood amongst them, longing to see Coralie but afraid that she might be otherwise engaged, or no longer wish to speak to him. Then he chided himself for being faint-hearted and strode round the building to the entrance used by the actors and actresses.

'Yes, Sir?' said the doorman.

'Could you take this to Miss Clive, please.' And John wrote in pencil on the back of one of his cards, 'May I take you to a late supper and renew our acquaintanceship?' He handed it to the man together with a tip, then waited nervously for something to happen.

A great crowd of people surged forward as Mr Sparks, arrayed in canary silk, sallied forth, leaning on a beribboned great stick and announcing his intention of going off to sup at the Old Black Jack in Lincoln's Inn Fields, lovingly known as The Jump. His admirers duly piled into hackney coaches and followed in the wake of his carriage, grinning and chattering like a troop of merry monkeys. The Apothecary stared after them, much amused, and thus missed the very thing he had been waiting for. It was only a waft of her distinctive perfume which told him Coralie Clive was standing beside him. He turned to look at her and in his eyes she had grown even lovelier in the year since he had last seen her.

Her emerald gaze sparkled. 'Mr Rawlings, we meet again.' She curtseyed politely.

The Apothecary gave his very best bow. 'Miss Clive, it has been too long a time.'

'It has indeed been quite a while. Tell me, how have you been faring?'

John smiled crookedly. 'May I answer that over supper? I hope you will do me the honour of joining me.'

She tortured him for a good half-minute. 'Well...'

'You have another appointment?'

'I promised my sister, Kitty, that I would go straight home and play cards with her.'

Despite the fact that he attempted to control it, the Apothecary could feel his face falling. 'Oh, I see.'

Coralie smiled, and John's heart lurched. 'But as it has been such an age since we met, I am quite sure she will understand.'

The grin was on his lips before he could stop it. 'I am the happiest man in London.'

Coralie's cool green stare had a hint of mordancy in its depths. 'Oh, surely not.'

Momentarily, the Apothecary showed his real feelings.

'Oh, surely yes,' he said, bowing very slightly. He became incisive. 'Now,

Madam, where would you care to sup? I had thought of The Rose in Covent Garden, but if that is not acceptable to you...'

Coralie gave him a ravishing look, fair set to steal his heart. 'It would be most acceptable. We are bound to see the leading dramatists of our day at its tables.'

'To say nothing of our leading actresses. Your performance tonight was sovereign, if I may speak so boldly.'

Like all in her profession, Miss Clive glowed. 'Do you really think so?'

'I think, Madam, that you have now reached the high mark set by your sister, and that one day, not so far away, you may well surpass her.'

Coralie looked modest. 'Kitty is the leader of our field, despite the pretensions of Miss Woffington, who has risen to the heights of her fame in the prone position, in my view.'

John's elegantly mobile eyebrows rose. 'You refer to Mr Garrick?'

'Indeed I do.'

The Apothecary laughed. 'There's mischief in your look, Miss Clive.'

'Is there really, Mr Rawlings?'

'There certainly is. Now let me hail a hackney coach before I tell you how beautiful you are and make a complete fool of myself.'

Miss Clive lowered her eyes. 'I thought your interests lay elsewhere.'

'Who told you that?'

'Your long absences.'

'Last time we met you called me a positive ruffian.'

'Well, so you were; unshaven, unwashed, a veritable vagabond.'

'I had just come straight from the Romney Marsh to London with not a moment in which to do anything about my appearance.'

Coralie smiled. 'I know, but in my defence I was not aware of it at the time.'

'Then you forgive me?'

'Let us forget the whole incident.'

'Gladly,' said John, and kissed her hand.

It was at that moment that a hackney appeared round the corner and dropped off a passenger. Hurrying, the Apothecary managed to secure it and made much of helping Miss Clive up the step and into its somewhat odoriferous confines. And, once inside, he snuggled as close to her as he possibly could without appearing extravagant in his behaviour. To his relief, Coralie did not move away.

John cleared his throat. 'I read that Richmond married last year,' he said with a bold attempt at being casual.

The actress raised her chin. 'Yes, I went to the wedding, and a very fine affair it was.'

'His bride is very beautiful, I believe.'

'Her nickname is The Lovely, she is so blessed with looks. Do you know what Walpole said about the pair of them?'

'No.'

'The perfectest match in all the world; youth, beauty, riches, alliances, and all the blood of all the kings from Robert the Bruce to Charles II. Isn't it sickening?'

'Nauseating.'

Coralie turned a brilliant glance in the Apothecary's direction. 'I take it you are much relieved that the Duke is finally spoken for.'

His attempt at nonchalance became pitiable. 'I've always been fond of Richmond. He and I have never fallen out.'

'That is not what I said. John, you glowed green every time the poor man's name was mentioned. Confess it. You were convinced that he and I were lovers, weren't you?'

'I admit that I believed that last time we met.'

The actress gave a scornful laugh. 'You openly accused me of it, you mean.'

'I thought we were going to put that incident behind us and start afresh.'

Coralie nodded, her expression softening. 'You're right, let us not rake over old ground. And the answer to your question is no. Richmond had a hundred conquests but I was never one of them. I preferred to be his friend rather than his creature. Do you understand?'

John longed to say that should she ever become his mistress she would be adored, not regarded as a creature, but could not get the words out of his mouth. Miss Clive, not noticing his silence, went on speaking.

'Anyway, that said, tell me about yourself. What have you been up to in the time since we last met?'

'Precious little. That is until a few days ago.'

Coralie's green eyes rolled. 'Not Mr Fielding again?'

'I fear so. There has been a mysterious death at the Peerless Pool which I am helping to investigate.'

'One of these days,' the actress predicted weightily, 'you will find yourself in trouble, my dear Sir.'

'You mean that I'll get too close to a killer for comfort?'

'Yes, I do.'

'But surely that has already happened, and it was you, if memory serves, who saved my life on that occasion.'

'Just as you once saved mine.' Coralie laid her gloved hand in his. 'Does that not mean that we are bound together in some way? Or have I already asked you that?'

'Yes, you did at the time and I replied that I did not know. But I have been making enquiries since and the answer is that, as a result, your life belongs to me and mine to you.'

Miss Clive laughed but did not withdraw her hand. 'Surely not. It sounds so dramatic.'

'It was a dramatic thing we did.'

She turned to look at him, her profile a mere silhouette in the dimness. 'Yes, it was, wasn't it?'

'Certainly,' John said, and would have kissed her had the hackney not rumbled to a halt and the driver called out, 'The Rose Tavern'. Cursing his luck, the Apothecary got out to pay the fare, wondering if the day would ever come when his wish would be granted and he would make love to the elusive Coralie Clive.

'So, my dear,' said Sir Gabriel Kent, picking delicately at a piece of fruit while his son devoured eggs and great hunks of gammon which he had carved off a side set upon the table.

'So?' John answered, innocently raising his eyes from his breakfast.

'You stayed late at the Dysarts'?'

'No. I left early and on a whim went to the King's Theatre and there saw Miss Coralie Clive in Twelth Night. Then I renewed my friendship with her by taking her out to supper. Afterwards I escorted her home to the house she shares with her sister, and that, alas, was that. I returned to Nassau Street as chaste as when I left it.'

Instead of smiling one of his whimsical smiles, Sir Gabriel laid down his fruit knife and leant on the table, looking at his son in a penetrating manner.

'Naturally you confide in me only what you want me to hear, but I have, none the less, drawn certain conclusions over the years, one of which is that you have held a deep tendresse for Miss Clive for some time.'

John smiled wryly. 'There have been other people too, Father.'

'I am aware of that, my dear, and I would have thought it very odd if there had not been. Still, I think Coralie is queen of your heart.'

'She has never gone completely from my thoughts, if that is what you mean.'

'Have you considered wooing her formally, then asking her to be your wife? After all, you were twenty-seven in June, not too young to enter into matrimony.'

The Apothecary sighed. 'Father, as I have told you several times – Miss Clive is wedded to the theatre. She has no wish to marry at this stage of her career.'

Sir Gabriel attacked a pear, rather savagely, John thought. 'I fail to see why she cannot have both,' he said with acerbity. 'Many great ladies of the theatre are married women.'

'Perhaps she is afraid that a child might come along and spoil her chance of success.'

'But you are an apothecary, John, and obviously know a great deal more about the prevention of such an occurrence than does the average male.'

His son nodded. 'Thanks to that gallant soldier, Colonel Cundum, there really is no longer any need for men to go forth and multiply.'

Sir Gabriel smiled wickedly. 'But is Miss Clive aware of such an invention?'

For the first time during their conversation, John looked embarrassed. 'How would I know? She is a woman of our times, so I presume so. After all, the Colonel created his device over a hundred years ago. It is hardly anything new.'

Sir Gabriel lifted an elegant hand. 'Enough of that. The question of your future can be decided only by you. As to the present, a Runner from Bow Street called last evening with a letter from Mr Fielding. Would you like it brought to the table?'

The Apothecary nodded, and his father gave instructions to a footman. A few minutes later the letter bearing the seal of the Public Office was delivered on a silver tray. Breaking the wax, John scanned the contents.

My dear Mr Rawlings,

Much of Interest has occurred in the last Few Hours. Forbes, the Warder from the Hospital for Poor Lunatics, has been to the Mortuary and Identified the Dead Woman as Hannah Rankin. He was Sore put about at the Duty and in Much Need of Brandy due to the Ordeal of It.

Further, the References presented by Hannah Rankin when She made Application to the Hospital have now Been Located. They give Two Addresses in Bath. Sir, may I Trespass Yet Again on your Good Nature and ask if You might go there to make Further Investigation. Though I could send the 'Flying' Runners I feel that You might Succeed more Greatly with Society Folk. All Expenses will be met by this Office.

I remain, Sir, your most Sincere Friend,

J. Fielding.

A couple of addresses were enclosed on a separate piece of paper.

'A summons?' said Sir Gabriel.

'To Bath, no less.'

'That should prove amusing. It will be the height of the season.'

Thinking that he would rather stay in London and pay court to Coralie, John nodded. 'It will indeed. Ah well, I had better get to the shop and warn Nicholas that he will be in charge once more.'

'Will you send for Master Gerard?'

'He is getting very old and frail. I think I shall ask him to attend only on alternate days. Nicholas has been apprenticed three years now and his area of knowledge is considerable.'

'Perhaps that is one of the advantages of signing indentures with an older boy.'

'You may be right at that.' John stood up. 'I'll get to my packing. I shall catch a flying coach from the Golden Cross, Charing Cross, late this afternoon, and so go straight from the shop.'

Sir Gabriel looked very slightly put out. 'That is a blow. A footman of Lord Anthony's came earlier this morning with an invitation for us to dine today.'

'A pleasure I shall have to forgo, though please present my compliments.'

John's father looked reflective. 'What a terrible tale they had to tell us yesterday; about the abduction of young Meredith. Do you think that by any chance the boy is still alive?'

The Apothecary's expression was grim as he answered, 'If he is, you can depend on it that it is better by far they never find him.'

Chapter Eight

The early morning rush of custom, generally made up of those attempting to cure the excesses of the night before — nausea, a pounding head or fear of the clap — was clearly well and truly over. As John Rawlings walked into his apothecary's shop in Shug Lane, it was to find the place unnervingly quiet, not a soul being visible on either side of the counter. As part of his duty as an apprentice, Nicholas Dawkins would have risen early and gone to sweep and clean the premises before his Master appeared, and, sure enough, the place was glistening, but of the young man himself there was no sign whatsoever. Slightly puzzled, the Apothecary stood looking around him, then his lively eyebrows rose as from the compounding room at the back of the shop came the distinct sound of a suppressed giggle.

'Good morning,' he said with considerable emphasis, and waited to see what would happen next.

Nicholas, his pale face unusually flushed, appeared like a jack-rabbit out of a burrow. 'Good morning, Sir.'

'You have company?' John asked pleasantly, then drew in a breath of surprise as in Nicholas's wake, walking with her nose tilted saucily and a mighty confident expression on her face, came none other than Mary Ann Whittingham, the Blind Beak's niece, adopted by him as a daughter and brought up as such.

'Well, well,' said the Apothecary, too confounded for words.

She made a charming curtsey. 'Mr Rawlings, how pleasant to see you again.'

Inwardly he could do nothing but smile at the barefaced gall of the little witch, at fourteen quite one of the most ravishing creatures in town. Outwardly, John looked severe, his mind racing over the exact nature of the relationship between his apprentice and John Fielding's kin.

Nothing daunted, Mary Ann spoke up. 'I see you are startled at my presence but, if you recall, I have known Nicholas for an age. Remember that he lived in our house until he signed indentures and went to live with you, Sir.'

'Of course,' John answered lightly. 'How foolish of me to forget.'

Mary Ann smiled, her expression pert, but there could be no doubting the look of guilt in Nicholas's amber eyes. They had been in the back of the shop toying and kissing, John felt sure of it. However, there was little he could do until he got his apprentice alone, and even then other than thundering on about the pledges of indenture, one of which was that the apprentice would not fornicate, a vow broken by many as they got older, there was not a great deal to be said. Mary Ann, after all, was over twelve, the age of consent, and Nicholas was not far off his twenty-first birthday, having been apprenticed later than most.

Knowing full well that the girl was more than aware of his dilemma, the Apothecary gave a pleasant smile. 'Is Mrs Fielding shopping with you, my dear?'

'No. My aunt sent me out with a servant to get a few physicks, so naturally I came to your shop. Nicholas was just showing me how you compound your simples. It was truly fascinating.'

'I'm sure it was,' John answered smoothly, controlling a strong urge to put her over his knee and give her a smart smack to remove her smug expression.

The youthful flirt looked up at him from beneath her lashes. 'Well, I must be on my way, Mr Rawlings. Do you think that Nicholas might carry my parcels for me?'

'No, Mary Ann, I do not. He has work to do and I cannot spare him. Did you walk here or come by chair?'

'By chair. That is how I managed to get rid of the maid. I bribed my chairmen to dodge down an alley and thus avoid hers. Isn't it amusing?'

'Not in the least,' answered the Apothecary with much feeling. 'I shall hail a sedan for your return. You must not go about unaccompanied.'

'Oh, don't let me bother you; Nicholas can escort me.'

'Oh no, Nicholas can't. He has wasted enough time already this morning. Young man, go and pound me a mortar of vervain while I escort Mr Fielding's niece to a chair.'

'Yes, Sir,' answered the apprentice, peony-faced, and went into the back of the shop, the limp that became worse whenever he was distressed showing badly.

Taking the wayward minx firmly by the arm, John marched her into the street and hailed two passing chairmen, who looked relieved at the prospect of carrying so light a load.

'To the Public Office in Bow Street,' he ordered, 'and no stopping on the way, whatever the pretext.'

'Very good, Sir.' And picking up their burden they hurried off at a jog trot.

John did not waste words. Striding into the compounding room, he said, 'Nicholas, what is going on between you and Miss Whittingham?'

The young man looked doom-laden. 'Nothing untoward, Sir, I promise you. I respect Mary Ann. However, she is over twelve, Sir, if you take my meaning.'

'I take it all too clearly. But that aside, she is still very young and unversed in the ways of the world, whereas you have reached years of discretion.'

Nicholas gave him a sudden bitter look. 'I have experienced a great deal, if that is what you mean, Sir. But none of it has been particularly pleasant. In fact most of it has been harsh and terrible. But as to the promise I made when I was apprenticed, I have kept it, though it has been difficult indeed to do so, especially in recent times.'

John nodded, his expression less severe. 'It is not an easy constraint to put on any young man, I am more than aware of that. In fact I would say to you that I would turn a blind eye to what you do in your private time were your choice of sweetheart any different. But Mary Ann, Nicholas, is the Magistrate's niece! I have known her since she was a little girl. She must be treated differently.'

'Everyone has to grow up some time,' the Muscovite answered dourly.

John shook his head. 'But not her, not yet. Mr Fielding would flay you within an inch of your life if you laid one finger on her.'

Nicholas's eyes suddenly filled with tears of pure wretchedness. 'Then what am I to do?'

The Apothecary leant towards him and lowered his voice. 'I am no killjoy, my friend, believe me, and therefore I am prepared to take a risk and rely on your discretion. For what I am about to say to you is not fitting for a Master to tell his apprentice and must never be repeated. But overriding conventional behaviour is my concern for your physical and mental well being, so listen to me.'

And then John explained to Nicholas Dawkins about the house discreetly hidden amongst the trees in Leicester Fields, a house visited exclusively by gentlemen, a house where a young fellow might learn about life and come out none the worse for it.

'And you think I should visit there?'

'I do.'

'But what about my pledge?'

'I would consider you to have broken that if you began an affaire with Mary Ann.'

The Muscovite looked knowing. 'You are very protective of her, aren't you?'

John nodded thoughtfully. 'There has been much on my mind recently about the dangers children face, from the mad girl at St Luke's, found working as a prostitute, to a little boy abducted in Paris and never seen again.'

'But...'

'Do not protest, Nicholas. Miss Whittingham is too young for love. You know it and so do I. It would be the ruin of her if she were to enter into a liaison with you at this stage of her development.'

The apprentice sighed gustily. 'Are you forbidding me to see her?'

'I most certainly am not. The moment something is prohibited, the more attractive it instantly becomes. See your friend, kiss her if you must, but take your pleasures elsewhere.'

Nicholas shot him a penetrating look, 'You'll say nothing of this to Mr Fielding, will you, Sir?'

'My lips are sealed,' John answered, and found himself the subject of a very warm handshake which ended in an affectionate hug. 'I thank you for that, Sir. You are wise beyond your years.'

The Apothecary smiled crookedly. 'If that were true, my friend, I think my life would be a great deal simpler than it is turning out to be.'

* * *

Discovering the times of departure from the Golden Cross not convenient to him, the coaches leaving too early to give him a full afternoon in the shop, John caught the 8 p.m. flying coach departing from the Gloucester Coffee House, Piccadilly, having first dined and answered the call of nature before he got aboard. Booking a place before he went to eat, the Apothecary ended up travelling in company with two others, whom he met when he went to take his seat, businessmen from Exeter, both determined to get a night's rest. Agreeing that this suited him well John settled down to sleep after the short stop at Brentford, and did not wake again until the coach pulled in at Thatcham at three o'clock in the morning. There, the passengers went to take refreshment and relieve themselves, having been allowed twenty minutes in which to do so. And though they grumbled about the shortness of the break, everyone was happy when Bath was reached at ten o'clock the following morning. Alighting at The Bear to take breakfast, John's fellow travellers bade him farewell. as he went inside to book himself a room in the coaching inn, a pleasant hostelry well used to catering for the needs of visitors to the spa.

The addresses given on the two references which Hannah Rankin had presented to the board of St Luke's Hospital were both of places fashionably situated, according to the Apothecary's guidebook. Having studied the locations carefully, John slept for a while in order to sharpen his reactions, then washed and shaved before setting out for Queen Square, that elegant creation of John Wood, whose houses were the chosen resort of the beau monde. However, this first avenue of enquiry immediately presented a mystery. The number given simply did not exist. Eventually, having walked round for a good quarter of an hour, John knocked at a door, the number of which most closely resembled the fictitious number, and asked for Lady Allbury, whose name was signed at the bottom of the testimonial. He was met with a blank stare.

'There's no Lady Allbury here, Sir. This is the house of Mr Humphrey Bewl.'

'Has Lady Allbury moved away, do you know?'

'There has never been a Lady Allbury here, Sir,' the footman intoned frostily. 'Mr Bewl's father owned this house before him and came to it when it was newly built.'

Highly suspicious of this latest turn of events, John retired to Sally Lunn's Coffee House, where he demolished a bun oozing with butter and considered his position. It would seem obvious, he thought, that the reference was a forgery and that Lady Allbury was probably a figment of Hannah Rankin's imagination. None the less, it would be well worth asking about the mysterious titled woman just to see if anyone at all knew the name. Wondering what he was going to find when he got there, John made his way to the second address, which was given as Welham House, Bathwick, a suburb of Bath lying across the Avon to the east of the city. Crossing the river by ferry, the Apothecary made enquiries of a man sitting on a wall close by, watching the various craft as they plied the Avon's expanse, and was relieved to hear that Welham House actually existed. Climbing the hill pointed out to him, he toiled to the top to find himself standing before a pair of wrought-iron gates leading on to a straight drive lined by an avenue of trees, at the end of which could be glimpsed a Palladian house, superbly proportioned. John guessed that it might also be the work of John Wood, the architect, a disciple of the great Italian master, Palladio. Patting the letter of authorisation signed by Mr Fielding, now residing in his pocket, he called to the lodgekeeper to open the wicket gate.

Hannah's reference, headed with the Welham House address, was signed Vivian Sweeting, and the Apothecary's enquiry as to whether Mr Sweeting was at home was met with the reply that Sir Vivian was in residence but had left instructions that he was not to be disturbed for the next two hours as he was working on his correspondence. Leaving behind his card and the Magistrate's request for cooperation, John had no option but to retire to the nearest ale-house, a ramshackle establishment built close to the River Avon, called The Ship. Always a great believer in talking to the locals, the Apothecary struck up a conversation with an ancient fellow who announced that he had once been the ferryman, a post he had held for more than fifty years.

'So you've seen a few people come and go in that time, I imagine.'

'I have, Sir, indeed,' the old fellow answered, in the soft-toned accent of a native of Bath.

John assumed his honest and confiding face, simultaneously ordering the gaffer a tankard of ale. 'Truth to tell, I'm down here trying to trace a female who used to work for my aunt. She went off to London and was never heard of again.'

'Oh, and who might that be?'

'Hannah Rankin was her name. I believe that she worked at Welham House at one time.'

The old man shook his head. 'Don't mean nothing to me, Sir. What was the other lady's name?'

'What other lady?'

'Your aunt, Sir.'

'Lady Allbury,' answered John, with a flash of inspiration.

The old man's face underwent an amazing series of changes. 'Lady Allbury, Sir? But surely you know, Sir, being her kin and all.'

Realising that he was treading dangerous ground but not certain quite what kind, the Apothecary immediately looked concerned. 'I know nothing, my friend. I have been abroad for several years and have only just returned to this country.'

The ferryman appeared more distressed than ever. 'Then it is hardly my place to tell you, Sir.'

John hastily ordered another refill of ale. 'But I must beg you to do so. There is no one in the family left alive to give me the news.'

Even as he lied, the Apothecary caught himself wondering about the ease with which he could spin yams and not suffer from a guilty conscience. In the line of duty, he reassured himself

'Lady Allbury — what happened to her?' he prompted.

'She drowned herself. Jumped into the Avon just below the ferry. I was one of those who helped drag her out.'

'Where was she living at the time?' John asked, thinking to have put the question rather well in view of the fictitious address.

The old man's eyes widened. 'Nobody knew, Sir. She really did go mad, in the true sense of the words, after Lucy was taken. She abandoned her home in the Grand Parade and people saw her wandering the streets of town, her garments stained and filthy and her person not much better. Eventually, Lady Chandos, who was down for the season and had been at school with her — but then you'd know that — took Lady Allbury back with her to London in order to care for her. But Lady Allbury escaped and came back to Bath to end it all.'

Realising he had to be very careful, John said, 'I have been away so long and have forgotten so much. Remind me, Lucy was her daughter, wasn't she?'

The ferryman drank a vast draught. 'Yes, Sir. Born to her late in life, when she was well in her forties in fact. Her other three children had grown up and left home long since. But Lucy came along after Lord Allbury had been dead many a year, if you understand me.'

John nodded. 'I do indeed. A sad tale but not uncommon. Anyway, what happened to the child?'

'She vanished, Sir. Taken by the Romanies, some said.'

With his flesh creeping at the prospect of hearing a tale that was already reminding him vividly of the Dysart tragedy, John said, 'Go on.'

'She was out playing in the grounds of Prior Park, having a picnic with Mr Ralph Allen, the owner, and his family. Her mother was there and her nursemaid and all was well. Then the children played hide-and-seek and that was that, Sir. Lucy never came back.'

'Dear God!' said John, very shaken. 'And was nothing heard of her again?'

'Nothing, Sir. The constable was called but he could do little. Then Lady Allbury hired a man, an ex-soldier, wounded so living on his wits but with a good reputation for finding things out, and though he searched high and low he came up with no result. That's when Lady Allbury lost her mind. The shock was too much for her.'

The Apothecary hastily ordered more ale, abstaining himself in view of the interview that lay before him. 'This man,' he said, watching the ferryman effortlessly pour the liquid down his throat, 'the fellow who finds things out, you don't know his name by any chance?'

'That I don't, Sir. Never did.'

'Does he live in Bath?'

'I believe he does, though where I couldn't say.'

The old man's fund of knowledge was clearly running out. John got to his feet, pressing a coin into his informant's hand. 'If you remember anything else, I am staying at The Bear. I'd be grateful for any fact that could help me find out more about poor Lucy.'

'She was snatched, in my opinion, and in the belief of most others as well.'

'Why do you say that?'

'Because she was a winsome little thing with her great mass of hair. Like spun gold, it was.'

'How old was Lucy when she disappeared?'

'About seven or so.'

'And how long ago was that?'

'Roughly ten years.

The Apothecary fell silent, considering the similarities with the Dysart case, appalled, yet again, at the terrible danger in which the young were placed daily; aware, horrible though the thought was, that there were brothels in many of the larger cities staffed entirely by children. Eventually he shook himself out of his reverie and turned to the ferryman.

'You have been very kind. Don't forget to look me up if you hear anything more.'

The old man raised his finger to his forelock. 'I'll remember, Sir. You can count on me.'

'Thank you,' said John, and sensible of a mood of growing depression, he tackled the hill once more and arrived at Welham House at the appointed time.

On this occasion he was ushered straight into the receiving salon where Sir Vivian sat at ease, scanning a book, one exquisite silk-hosed leg crossed over the other. He looked up as the Apothecary came in, his brows raised in question.

'Mr Rawlings from the Public Office, Sir,' intoned a footman.

Sir Vivian nodded. 'Do take a seat. How may I assist you?'

Without replying, John sat down opposite his host, having first given a bow that would not have disgraced a member of the beau monde. 'By answering a few questions,' he said as he settled into the chair.

Sir Vivian waved a white hand. 'By all means. Pray continue.'

'It is a little difficult to know where to begin.'

'Well, tell me why you have come. I am a busy man, Sir.'

There was the merest edge of irritation in his voice and, studying him, the Apothecary could well imagine that Sir Vivian's temper was on a short rein, for he had the look about him of one whose emotions seethed beneath an implacable exterior. Very dark eyes with a strange dead glitter in their depths looked piercingly from beneath black brows that knitted together in the middle, not a physical characteristic that John liked very much. But the rest of his appearance seemed unremarkable enough, except for the man's extreme thinness. Beneath Sir Vivian's skin, somewhat pallid, as if it were rarely exposed to the sun, the bones of his face seemed almost skull-like, while his body bore the same emaciated look. The Apothecary thought that slenderness at this level was very far from becoming. In fact he shuddered inwardly at Sir Vivian's teeth, large and white, giving the impression that they were far too big for his thin and slightly snarling lips.

On Sir Vivian's hollow cheek, just below his right eye, was stuck a black beauty spot in the shape of a ship, at which he unknowingly picked as he waited impatiently for the Apothecary to speak. 'Well?' he said.

'I'll come directly to the point,' answered John.

'I wish you would.'

'Does the name Hannah Rankin mean anything to you?'

Sir Vivian considered, repeating the name a couple of times under his breath. 'No, I don't think so,' he said finally.

'A letter purporting to be from you and bearing your signature recommended her as a suitable employee to those whom it might concern. Is it a total forgery?'

'Not necessarily,' said Sir Vivian. 'My secretary often signs letters on my behalf, and as it is the duty of my steward to employ staff it is quite possible that he gave her a testimonial which my secretary subsequently endorsed.'

Thinking that the interview was going to be difficult, John asked politely, 'Would it be possible to see your steward? Might he remember her name?'

'Why do you want to know all this?' Sir Vivian replied, his dead eyes boring into his visitor's. 'Before I waste the time of one of my employees, I would have to be given a very good reason as to why I should do so.'

'As Mr Fielding stated in his letter, Sir, we are trying to learn all we can about Hannah Rankin's past.'

'And what care I what is going on in Bow Street, London? What is Hannah Rankin's past to me?'

'Nothing, except for the fact that she has been murdered and it is the duty of all citizens to help track her killer down.'

Sir Vivian raised a heavy brow. 'Is it? Is it really? In a perfect world no doubt everyone would be public-spirited. But this is Bath, not London, Sir, and therefore what happens in the capital is really of little concern to us.'

'Then you cannot help me further?'

'No, Mr, er...' He glanced at John's card... 'Rawlings, I cannot. Hannah Rankin might have worked for me, the testimonial could have been signed by my secretary. That is the most I can tell you.'

John stood up. 'Then I'll bid you good-day, Sir.'

'Good-day,' said Sir Vivian, and returned to the study of his book.

Inwardly, John seethed with anger at his abrupt dismissal, but there was little he could do. Bowing very briefly, he turned on his heel and left the room. Yet even on his way to the front door he decided somehow to approach one of the servants, however difficult it should prove to be. He turned to the footman who was escorting him out.

'A glorious place this. Have you worked at Welham House long?'

'No, Sir,' came the stony reply.

'Then you probably wouldn't have known Hannah Rankin, who was a servant here at one time.'

'No Sir.'

'Oh, that's a pity. I have a reward for information about her. You could have stood to gain there.'

'No I couldn't, Sir,' answered the footman as he closed the door in the Apothecary's face.

Chapter Nine

There still being two hours to occupy before the time to dine, John crossed the river back to Bath and, after a brief call at his lodgings to tidy himself a little, made his way to the Pump Room to take the waters. It being well beyond the hour for bathing, which usually began at six in the morning and continued until nine, there were few people about, most having gone to change for dinner or to pursue their various afternoon recreations. Thus, other than for a handful of infirm folk, the Apothecary found himself alone as he was served a glass of the hot Bath water by the pumper.

It was disgusting, there could be no doubt of that; sulphurous and horrid and made all the worse by the fact that it was warm. However, John, fascinated by water as he had always been, poured a little sample into a phial to take back to The Bear and analyse as best he could with the equipment he had brought with him. This done, he turned his attention to the others present, wondering if any of them might be able to give him some more information about Lady Allbury. For though her terrible tale had nothing to do with the death of Hannah Rankin, it was clear from the forged reference bearing Lady Allbury's name that the murdered woman had at least known of the bereaved mother.

A gouty old man in a Bath chair snoozed by one of the long windows, and two elderly ladies, both looking on the point of dropping off to sleep, conducted a desultory conversation. A husband and wife made much of the foulness of the water but declared that it had been most efficacious in treating their respective colons and phlegmatic humours to anyone who cared to listen. Meanwhile, the only person in the Pump Room who came within a dozen years of John's age drank glass after glass of the filthy stuff, clutching his guts as he did so. The wretch looked to the Apothecary to be on the point of vomiting and thus, when he started to retch, John was ready and heaved the man out of the door so that the harmony of the graciously pillared room should not be disturbed.

Puking hideously, the beau, for so he appeared to be from the extravagance of his make-up, stunningly white with a hint of base verdigris, ruined the state of the cobbles, then gasped for breath, wiping his mouth with a lace-trimmed sleeve. 'An excess of brandy,' he explained.

'Really?' said John, fully sarcastic.

'Yes indeed,' the other replied without apparent shame, though a drawn-in black eyebrow looped in the Apothecary's direction.

Suddenly anxious to get away from him, John began to move on, but unexpectedly an arm shot out and grabbed the Apothecary's sleeve with wiry fingers. 'Don't go. I owe you a favour, if you would care to name it. My name's Orlando Sweeting, by the way.' And stepping out of the heap of vomit, the beau made a bow.

John was instantly alert. 'Sweeting, did you say? Are you by any chance related to Sir Vivian?'

'He's my uncle. Why, do you know him?'

'I've only met him once, this morning to be precise. I called at Welham House.'

Orlando twitched his pencilled brows. 'I escaped last night. The Countess of Burlington was holding a circle at Hayes's. I was not invited but managed to make an entrance despite. I wore my pea-green frock which probably swayed the balance in my favour.'

He was as vapid as a gushing girl and clearly brainless, but quite amusing for all that.

'I made a bid for the affections of Patty Weymouth but as she would have none of me I turned my attentions to the Hon. Robert Sawyer Herbert instead,' Orlando prattled on. 'But, upon my life, he would have none of me either, so what's to do?'

John stood silent, wondering what kind of relationship one with the other, the grim Sir Vivian and this popinjay, could possibly conduct beneath the same roof.

As if reading his thoughts, the beau continued, 'Anyway, having escaped, for he's a hard taskmaster is my revered uncle, I decided to spend the night in town and drank till dawn with young Robin Sidmouth. Do you know him?' John shook his head. 'Ah, pity. I'll make a point of introducing you at dinner tonight.'

'But...'

'Nonsense, you will come as my guest. I insist. And afterwards we shall go to the ball. Mrs Cibber, the actress, is in town with some daughter of hers, though who is the father is anyone's guess, God be our guide. Anyway, they are bound to be there, and though the girl is ugly, all sidles and squints, the mother's a damned handsome creature. It will all be exceptionally fine.'

'But really...'

'I'll not hear another word. Your protestations grow tiresome. Where do you stay?'

'At The Bear.'

'Then hurry back and change into something of immense elegance. I'll go to young Sidmouth's and dress in my pink frock. I do believe my pea-green to be ruined.' And he pointed at a vomit stain soiling his violently coloured coat. 'I'll meet you back here in exactly one hour, then we can go to dine at Lyndsey's and on to the Assembly Rooms to dance.'

The Apothecary gave in, merely answering lamely, 'Then may I present my card, Sir?'

Orlando glanced at it, said, 'An apothecary, eh?', then hastened off down the street, shouting over his shoulder, 'Here, in one hour. Don't be late.'

Thinking that fate had clearly delivered him the chance to find out more about Hannah Rankin, John, tired after all his hill-climbing and wanting to save his legs for the evening's activity, took a sedan chair back to The Bear.

His love of high fashion, combined with the knowledge that to go to Bath in the season without a dazzling array of evening clothes would be an act of pure folly, served John in good stead. Decked out in plum velvet embroidered with silver leaves and flowers, an ensemble that would not have disgraced the most recherché ballroom in the capital, he arrived by chair at the appointed meeting place exactly one hour later. Much as to be expected, there was no sign of the beau, but within five minutes, during which John eyed the passing parade making its way to dine, Orlando appeared with another languid creature, who made a great show of bowing to John. His small feet, clad in their high-heeled shoes, minced over the cobbles as formal introductions were made.

The Apothecary's heart sank at the prospect of an evening in the company of two such butterflies, and he decided that only a wealth of information about the mysterious Hannah would make it worth while.

'You have dined at Lyndsey's before?' asked Orlando, taking John's arm in the most familiar manner as they walked along.

'Once, when I visited Bath with my father.'

'It can be very dull, of course. Full of femmes formidables drinking tea till it fair gushes from their every orifice. One is bound to see old Lady Westmoreland holding court. She likes me, though. In fact I do believe she runs a speculative eye over my person, considering whether or not I would make a good rum boy.'

Robin Sidmouth, clad from head to toe in powder blue, his face that of a petulant cherub, pealed with laughter. 'And would you consider being so, Orlando?'

His friend cocked a thin dark brow, painted well above the level of his own, and said, 'I've told you before, Rob. I would do anything that suited my purpose.'

'Which is?' asked John.

Surprised, the beau turned to look at him, and just for a second somebody else peeped out from beneath his fantastic maquillage. 'To get away from my uncle and make my own way in the world,' he stated bitterly.

Catching his mood, the Apothecary said, 'Is Sir Vivian that hard to live with?'

Orlando became himself again and executed a nimble dance step. 'La. how I do prattle on. I'll trip over my own tongue at this rate. Come, my friend, we are almost there. Believe me, I would not have suggested we walk lest Lyndsey's be just around the corner.'

And indeed, a few moments later, John, slightly daunted by the company he was keeping but putting a brave face on it, entered one of Bath's several sets of rooms where the beau monde met to dine and take tea. Lyndsey's, one of the more famous places of assembly, consisted of a long room set with tables of varying sizes, together with a small room leading off it, where more intimate gatherings could be held. Bowing to all and sundry, raising his quizzing glass to examine the many pretty girls present, to say nothing of the boys, Orlando made an entrance and headed straight for a table for three.

'Reserved,' he announced to the waiter grandly. He waved to an elderly woman. 'Cuckoo, Duchess. Your servant, Ma'am.' He bowed and she inclined her head. 'There,' he whispered to John with a note of triumph. 'I told you she fancied me.'

'I take it that's Lady Westmoreland?'

'You take it right, my dear.' Orlando looked thoughtful. 'She's a widow, you know. Perhaps...'

Robin shrieked. 'Oh, you couldn't! Even you would baulk at that, surely.'

Orlando shook his graceful head. 'I baulk at nothing.'

For no reason at all, John found himself saying, 'Not even murder?'

The beau shot him an unreadable look. 'No, not even that, were it to suit my designs.'

His friend appeared shocked. 'That is a terrible thing to say, Orlando. People might take you seriously.'

'I am very serious,' the beau answered quietly, then took to looking at the menu and deciding what he would eat.

If he hadn't been so smothered in enamel, he might have been quite handsome, John thought, studying Orlando covertly from behind the bill of fare. Strong, shapely features and large eyes, probably blue, though it was hard to tell in the midst of so much kohl, were clearly there. His carmined mouth, too, though drooping at the corners with the elegant air of discontent that the beau adopted as his constant mien, seemed liberally proportioned. He was not very old, John guessed, probably in his early twenties, no more. Though that, too, was hard to tell, camouflaged as he was by so many layers of powder and paint.

Orlando looked up, feeling the Apothecary's eyes on him. 'Champagne, my friend. Let us drink till the world glows golden.'

John smiled cynically. 'Or until we heave it all up.'

The beau pulled a face. 'Don't remind me. Thank God you spared me public humiliation.'

'What? What's this?' buzzed young Sidmouth, his face cracking into grins.

'Nothing. I felt queasy in the Pump Room, that is all. Our new friend John helped me outside. He is an apothecary.' This last being said as if it explained everything.

'Are you?' exclaimed Rob, the gleam of the hypochondriac in his eye. 'I suffer enormously with distempers. What would you recommend?'

'A simple diet and no wine,' John answered with a straight face.

Young Sidmouth's little mouth twisted with disgust. ''S'life! I'd rather be in agony than have to eat so.'

'That is your choice,' the Apothecary answered gravely, and heard Orlando chuckle to himself.

The meal passed pleasantly enough in view of the odd assortment of companions, and it was with a certain amount of anticipation that John, in company with the two beaux, who shrilled and waved at everyone they passed, made his way to the Assembly Rooms for the ball which, this night, began at eight o'clock. The Rooms had been built some years earlier at the behest of Richard Nash, known to all as Beau, the man who had literally transformed Bath from a somewhat rustic spa into the fashionable watering place frequented by the beau monde it had become. In his heyday, the Beau had been an autocratic Master of Ceremonies, laying down rules of behaviour and running activities as the supreme arbiter of taste. But now age had turned against him and he had become a rather shabby figure, wheeled into the Assembly Rooms in a Bath chair, from which he still attempted to run things through the new Master of Ceremonies, Mr Collet.

This night, sure enough, with the season at its height and many people of high rank in town, at a few minutes to eight there was a stirring in the doorway and the aged man, approaching eighty-four and frankly grown into a wearisome old fool, was wheeled in by an attendant. John, who had not seen the Beau for many years, took a good look at him.

His nickname was a misnomer if ever there was one. Even in his youth, Richard Nash had not been handsome, but in old age he looked a positive fright. Still wearing the battered white hat that was his trademark, the Beau slumped in his wheelchair, large and shapeless, while his poor face, with its many chins, seemed as huge as a ham. Tired eyes stared out from pouches reminiscent of fried eggs, and John's heart ached that such a vital creature could have deteriorated into so decrepit a wreck.

'Looks a nightmare, don't he?' murmured Orlando, close to the Apothecary's ear.

'It's a pity he doesn't retire from the scene with good grace.'

'Should have done so long ago, but some of 'em just won't relinquish power. Poor Collet's a mere puppet with the ancient dodderer pulling his strings.'

'An unpleasant situation.'

'Just you observe.'

With the time now fast approaching eight o'clock, Beau Nash stared fixedly at his watch, then poked the Master of Ceremonies in the back with his stick, which he proceeded to wave vigorously at the orchestra. There were frantic sounds of tuning up before the music started in earnest. Collet, jabbed painfully in the back once more, walked across the room with great state to lead out the most noble lord and lady in the minuet to begin the dancing. All this would have been extremely impressive had not the Beau been wheeled along just behind the Master of Ceremonies, which rendered the whole effect ludicrous.

However, despite the aged bore, the evening was very jolly, and John thoroughly enjoyed the country dances. He also derived a great deal of amusement from watching Orlando and young Sidmouth, who whirled about like a couple of wasps, zooming in and out of the set figures with great élan. Though foppish to a degree, there was something quite likable about them, and John, watching their outrageous cavorting, found himself laughing with honest enjoyment.

'Phew!' said Orlando, flopping down on to the bench as the interval came. 'I could drink a bottle of champagne to myself. Fine figures like me are entitled to take refreshment more than most.' He dabbed at his upper lip with a lace-trimmed handkerchief and John saw that beads of sweat were forcing their way through the thick enamel.

'Shall we step outside to cool down?' he suggested.

'That, and to get drunk.'

'But the Beau has strict rules about drinking,' shrilled young Sidmouth.

'Bubs to the Beau,' answered Orlando and, taking John by the arm, hastened him to an anteroom where tea and wine were being served.

'A drink, my friend?' he asked.

Feeling like an elderly schoolmaster, John said, 'Orlando, you vomited earlier today. Have some respect for your guts, I beg you.'

The beau's expression was like that of a disappointed child, even his lower lip trembling as he said, 'Oh, don't turn into a spoilsport. I want you for a friend and simply won't be able to abide it if you prove to be boring.'

The Apothecary shrugged. 'I was trained to tend the sick and it seems to me that you are drinking somewhat heavily, but your constitution is yours and yours alone. I can't stop you doing a thing.'

Orlando turned away. 'I hate that sort of lecture. It always make me feel guilty.'

'I'm sorry for that.'

'No, you're not. It's what you intended.' Orlando's manner brightened. 'However, I shan't let you spoil my fun. Nor will I let your killjoy attitude ruin a new association. I intend to remain close to you until either you become as debauched as I am or you cure me of all my many and various evils.'

John's brows rose. 'Are they that numerous?'

The strange expression that the Apothecary had glimpsed earlier, briefly swept Orlando's face. 'My dear, I am steeped in sin,' he said.

The moment seemed as opportune as any other. 'Talking of sin, do you remember a servant of your uncle's named Hannah Rankin?' John asked casually.

Now the beau's features really did transform. Just for a moment his face became a mask of hatred and his eyes glittered dark and serpent-like in his head. Then he controlled himself. 'I never mix with servants,' he said, flapping a hand in John's direction. 'I mean, can the lower orders even converse?'

But he was patently lying. Not only had the name Hannah Rankin been familiar to him but it had also produced a violent reaction. John decided to remain relaxed. 'Well, if you should remember anything about her, be good enough to let me know.'

'Why? What is this being to you?' Orlando asked, not quite flippantly enough.

'I am trying to trace her family,' John answered smoothly. 'She was found dead in London and I have been given the job of informing her relations, if there are any.'

Orlando's look of relief was unmistakable. Not only had he known the dead woman but he was glad that she no longer walked the earth. But the beau still had his wits about him.

'By whom?' he said.

'What do you mean?' the Apothecary asked, not understanding.

'If she was known to none, who gave you the job of finding her people?'

'The asylum at which she worked, St Luke's Hospital for Poor Lunatics.'

'I see,' said the beau. He winked an eye. 'It all sounds very sad and sordid to me. If I were you I would have nothing further to do with it. Now, my dear, bumpers all round.'

'And for me,' said a petulant voice, and they both turned to see that Robin Sidmouth had come looking for them.

'And for you,' Orlando said fondly, and jigged a series of solo dance steps, much to the consternation of a party of elderly ladies drinking tea.

Chapter Ten

At six o'clock in the morning the huge, dark, cavernous cistern situated beneath the Pump Room, known to bathers as the King's Bath, was full of steam and dim with shadow. Indeed, it so resembled a dragon's lair that John Rawlings felt a decided twing of apprehension as he clambered down one of the four series of steps leading into its black, vaporous depths. The surface of the bath, the largest and the hottest of the five that the city had to offer, curled with mist to an extent whereby the water itself was invisible, and the Apothecary, clad in drawers and a turban and nothing else, felt his nervousness grow as he descended through the steam into the boiling water and felt it close in up to his neck.

At that hour of the day there were few dippers present. Staring about him, John glimpsed one or two heads bobbing through the vapour, but other than for them the place was deserted, adding to the air of eeriness. Unnerved, he made his way through the water, telling himself that he was a man of medicine and as such should have his imagination under control. Yet the stories he had heard since he had arrived in Bath had done nothing to put his mind at rest.

The tale of Lady Allbury's missing child, so similar to the calamitous experience of the Dysarts, together with Orlando Sweeting's extraordinary reaction to the name of Hannah Rankin, had made the Apothecary positive that there was something dark and terrible at work in the city. Something that might be better left unearthed. And yet his instinct to go on seeking the truth had never been stronger. Clearly, the murdered woman had at one time in her life lived in Bath and been known to Orlando at least. But it was John's guess that Sir Vivian Sweeting and Lady Allbury were also involved with the victim, though what the connection had been was at this stage obscure. Wading slowly and thinking that this water treatment was so awful it must be doing him good, the Apothecary proceeded through the Dragon's Lake, as he fancifully thought of the King's Bath, not enjoying himself at all.

He had arranged to meet Orlando at a public breakfast to be held at the Assembly Rooms, occasions at which people of fashion met and invited their acquaintances to join them after the rigours of bathing. The beau would not be dipping, he had firmly informed John on the previous evening, intending instead to lie in a darkened room until the inevitable hammering in his head had subsided.

'My dear, I shall get there when I can. But I have a regular table so just make your way to it. There is to be a concert so you should keep amused.'

'Will young Sidmouth be present?'

'No. I believe he intends to fornicate with someone or other later tonight and will be well exhausted until dinner-time.'

Shaking his head, very slightly aghast and feeling elderly because of it, John had left the two younger men to their own devices and taken a chair back to The Bear. And now he planned to do the same. Rising like Neptune from the waters, the Apothecary made his way to the changing rooms, where he wrapped himself in a robe-like garment before calling for a sedan to return him to his lodgings, in which he intended to lie and sweat for an hour, then feel thoroughly virtuous into the bargain.

So it was, dressed very finely and mightily pleased with himself, that John walked into the Pump Room as eight o'clock struck, to find the place as crowded as yesterday it had been empty. In fact the room resembled a Welsh fair rather than a spot for taking health-giving waters. The world and his wife were there, from the beau monde, attired with negligent ease, to wrecks of humanity, more dead than alive, shuffling towards the bar from which the pumper served, as if it were the very last step they would ever take. In the gallery above, a band of enthusiastic musicians thundered away with more zeal than skill, so that everyone was forced to yell in order to be heard. Filled with a sudden zest for life because of the general uproar, John joined the queue of people waiting to drink the water.

Much to his surprise, standing just ahead of him, painted but fit-looking, was Orlando. The Apothecary called his name and the beau turned.

'My dear, how nice to see you. Forgive my deshabillé. I thought I would heed your advice and do something healthy for a change. Et voila!' He downed the metallic brew in one, then shuddered delicately.

'I am flattered to think my words were heeded. I thought you might consider me an interfering busybody.'

'A busybody, yes, interfering, no.' Orlando leant closer. 'I have changed my mind about the public breakfast. Let us repair to Mr Gill's, the pastrycook's, where we can take a jelly or a tart or a basin of vermicelli, or all three come to that.'

John nodded. 'In my case it probably will be all three. I am a firm believer in a severe repast to start the working day.'

Orlando shuddered again. 'My dear, you have mentioned two words that I detest. One is work, the other breakfast. I shall pick at a blancmanger and pray God that it slips down without effort.'

The Apothecary chuckled. 'You dined quite heartily last afternoon.'

'I toyed with a wing of fowl and a sliver of salmon, if that is what you call hearty.'

'Well,' said John determinedly, 'I could eat a mountain and can't wait much longer. To Mr Gill's.'

'His shop is near the river, and just to defy you I'll walk.'

'Good,' John answered, beginning to feel more and more like a middle-aged schoolmaster with every passing moment.

But the real reason why the beau had abandoned the public breakfast, where all was orchestra and prattle, became clear as soon as they were seated in the pastrycook's shop and had given their orders. 'I've remembered something about Hannah Rankin,' Orlando said, blurting the words as if he must get them out before he thought better of it.

'Oh yes?' John answered, looking up sharply.

Behind his mask of enamel, it was not easy to read the beau's face, but there was an air of determination about it which made the Apothecary think that Orlando had considered long and carefully during the night and had decided to come up with a story that would silence the investigator, at least for the time being.

Staring at his blancmanger, wobbling it to and fro on the end of his spoon, Orlando said, 'She was employed by my uncle, I recall it now. I think she was a skivvy of some kind, not a personal servant. Anyway, she left for another position and we never heard of her again. I'm afraid that's all.' He smiled artlessly at John. 'Tell me, how did you know that she was connected with Welham Hall?'

'Very simply. She gave references when she applied to St Luke's. One of them purported to be from your uncle, the other was signed by a Lady Allbury.'

'And have you found this Lady Allbury?' Orlando asked carelessly.

'She's dead,' answered John. 'She killed herself after her young daughter, born to her late in life, was abducted from a garden in which she was playing and never heard of again.'

The blancmanger fell plopping on to the tablecloth below. 'Oh yes,' said the beau after a fractional pause, 'it all comes back to me. I was only a child at the time but I do remember my uncle speaking of it.'

'He and Lady Allbury were acquainted?'

'The quality folk of Bath all knew one another — and still do.'

John considered in silence, then asked, 'When did Hannah Rankin leave your employ?'

'Oh, I don't know. Twelve years ago, perhaps. As I said, I was scarcely aware of the woman's presence.'

If he asked any more questions, he was going to lose his quarry completely, John could see that. So instead he said, 'I quite understand. It is hard to remember what one did last week, let alone a dozen years back. I think I can safely conclude that Hannah Rankin has no living relatives, at least not in this part of the world. Tomorrow I shall return to London and report my findings – or lack of them!'

Orlando hesitated, then said in a rush, 'If you want to ask the other servants about her I could arrange for you to call when my uncle is out. One or two of them have been there a while and might be able to tell you something.'

Wondering what could possibly have brought about this change of heart, the Apothecary answered matter-of-factly, 'That is very kind of you. It would certainly be better for me if I could tell the authorities that I have talked to all concerned and still come up with nothing.'

'Yes, yes, of course.' Orlando stared into the middle distance. 'Would this afternoon be convenient? My uncle goes to Bristol to dine and does not return till late.'

'It would be very convenient indeed, for I really must get back to London soon.'

'A pity, that,' Orlando said with a touch of sadness.

'Why?'

'Because you make such a change from the usual parade of fops and flaps. Steeped in sin I might be, but I still have something left of my brain, I believe.'

The Apothecary could not help himself. Looking at Orlando earnestly, he said, 'What is all this sin you keep mentioning? Are your sexual preferences for other men? Or do you sleep with both male and female alike? Are you a drunken debauchee? In God's name, what is it?'

'A joke, that is all,' the beau answered, and smiled such a terrible smile that John sat aghast to see so much horror on the face of another human being.

He crossed the Avon at half past two and slowly wended his way up the hill to Welham House. The weather was oppressively hot, and thunder rolled in the seven hills that surrounded the city of Bath. The sky was dark as lavender and the air unbreathable. It was, John thought, an unbearable day on which to be doing anything other than sitting in the shade sipping cold drinks, and he was never more grateful than to find a carriage waiting for him when he reached the lodge gates. A young coachman sat upon the box, and he raised his hat cheerfully as John approached.

'I would have come down to the river to fetch you, Sir, but Master Orlando had to go out and I wasn't sure what you looked like.'

'That's all right,' John answered, wiping the dirt and sweat from his face. 'I'm grateful that you've come at all.'

'Master Orlando's orders, Sir. He said you were to be treated as an honoured guest until he returned.'

'How very kind of him.' John mounted the carriage step. 'May I know your name, please?'

'It is Jack, Sir. I believe it was originally spelt the French way, with a "c" and a "q", but now it's just plain Jack.'

John paused. 'Why is that? Are your parents French?'

The coachman shook his head. 'I don't know, Sir. I never met them.'

'But surely…' John started.

The conversation was at an end however. Jack shouted, 'Get ye up there,' and the smart horses obeyed instantly, leaving the Apothecary no option but to take his seat and quickly close the carriage door as they set off up the tree-lined drive.

This day Welham House brooded in the sultry atmosphere. Similar in appearance to Ralph Allen's mansion, Prior Park, with its pillared entrance and two vast wings, Sir Vivian's home seemed to lack the light, airy quality of the other building, and stood dominating the surrounding countryside with a dark, mournful air. Feeling decidedly uncomfortable, John climbed the steep flight of steps leading to the front door and presented himself as being a guest of Orlando.

The footman who answered said, 'If you would follow me, Sir, Master Orlando said you wished to interview certain servants. The people concerned have gathered in the west-wing salon and await your arrival.'

Amazed that the beau had gone to so much trouble, the Apothecary walked in the man's footsteps through scores of vast rooms, all classically furnished with busts and paintings, until, at last, they came to a cosier part of the house. Here, forgathered in a comfortable anteroom with couches and cushions, were an elderly couple who looked like husband and wife, and, surprisingly, the young coachman, Jack.

John came straight to the point. 'Thank you for assisting me. As Master Orlando may have told you, I am trying to trace any friends or relatives of Hannah Rankin, now deceased. I presume by asking you to come here he thought that one of you might have known her.'

The old man spoke up. 'She didn't work here that long, Sir, and it must have been twenty years ago that she did, but I do remember her, yes. I was an under-gardener in those days. Now I'm head gardener and tell the others what to do.'

The woman chimed in. 'I'm Doris Cotter, Sir, and this is my husband, Thomas. I remember Hannah Rankin because I was working in the kitchens then as a cook. I used to see her when she came down to order the children's meals.'

John stared at her. 'Children's meals? What do you mean? I thought she was just a skivvy.'

'No skivvy she,' Jack put in quietly. 'Hannah used to be in charge of the young people.'

'What young people?'

'There were children living here then. I was one of them, Orlando was another. As well as us, there were two other boys and two girls.'

Still amazed, the Apothecary said, 'But who were they?'

A shadow crossed Jack's face. 'Sir Vivian's nieces and nephews. That is all but me.'

'Are you telling me that Sir Vivian was guardian to a group of children? But why? What had happened to their parents?'

'All dead, Sir,' answered Doris. 'Out of the goodness of his heart he took them in. And so he did for quite a few years, looked after orphans that had nowhere else to go.'

'What a Christian and charitable thing to do.' John turned to Jack. 'And you? Where did you come from? Were you an orphan too?'

The coachman shrugged and shook his head. 'I have no idea, Sir. I can remember little before this house. Just a large garden, that is all. Yet I have a recollection of Hannah bringing me here by coach. More than that I cannot tell you.'

Still hardly able to believe this strange new twist in the dead woman's tale, John said, 'Then Sir Vivian brought you up with his nieces and nephews?'

'Not exactly, Sir. I was…' Jack paused very slightly. '…badly behaved, and so he sent me to work as a stable boy. I shovelled dung for many years, and only by hard work did I get to be second coachman.'

'What happened to Hannah?'

Thomas answered. 'She went back to London when the children were grown a bit. We never heard no more of her after that.'

Jack spoke again. 'She used to visit Sir Vivian occasionally.'

The two Cotters looked surprised. 'Did she?'

'Yes. I used to pick her up from the coaching inn and bring her here. And once Sir Vivian asked me to drive her to Bristol where she was buying a Negro slave child to take to a lady in London for employment as a black boy.'

'So Hannah's main concern was with the young?'

Jack dropped his gaze to the floor. 'Oh yes, Sir. She was very interested in them.'

Was the coachman trying to tell him something? John wondered. Could the unpleasant notion that had just now crossed his mind possibly be right? With a courteous smile, the Apothecary turned to the elderly couple.

'Tell me, did you live in the house at this time?'

Thomas answered. 'No, Sir, we didn't. We had a cottage on the estate which we have still.'

John nodded. 'I see. Well, thank you for your time. Everything you have said has been most useful. I take it that you know of no relatives or friends of Hannah's that I should contact?'

'No, Sir. Not a one for a lot of friends was Hannah.'

They all three made to go but John said, 'If I might have another word with you, Jack, in view of the fact that you were one of the children concerned.'

Jack's eyes, an arresting shade of iris blue, almost mauve in fact, glanced piercingly in John's direction, but he merely said, 'As you wish, Sir.'

The Cotters looked uncertain. 'You won't keep Jack long, will you, Sir? He'll be wanted soon to go and fetch Master Orlando.'

John looked at them reassuringly. 'Don't worry. Just a few minutes, that is all.'

Looking duly relieved, the old couple left the room and the two young men were left facing one another.

'Jack,' said the Apothecary tentatively, 'forgive me asking this, but the plight of certain children has been much on my mind of late. Tell me, were Sir Vivian's motives in adopting so many orphans as truly Christian…'

But he got no further. The noise of pounding feet drowned his words, then the door was flung open to reveal Orlando panting in the entrance.

'He's back,' he gasped. 'Sir Vivian has returned. He must find neither of you here. Jack, out of the window and leg it to the coach house. John, into this cupboard and don't make a sound.' And without ceremony he bundled the Apothecary into a cupboard containing candlesticks and candles, where he crouched uncomfortably beneath the bottom shelf.

There was the sound of someone else coming in and approaching the chair into which Orlando had thrown himself, picking up a book at random.

'My dear,' said Sir Vivian's voice, 'you seem out of breath. Have you been running?'

'I hurried back from the grounds when I saw your coach coming through the gates.'

'Taking the air? How very unlike you.'

'The weather is oppressive, don't you think? I stepped outside in order to breathe more freely.'

There was something sarcastic and sharp about the way in which Sir Vivian addressed his nephew, almost as if he didn't believe a word he said. With a sinking heart, John hoped that Jack hadn't been seen sprinting towards the coach house.

Orlando spoke again. 'I had not expected you back, Uncle. I thought you had gone to dine in Bristol.'

'That was cancelled, my dear, and so I would have informed you had you been good enough to put in an appearance at breakfast this morning. But I was told when I enquired of your valet that you had risen with the lark and gone into Bath to take the waters. Such strange behaviour I can hardly credit. It is almost as if you have reconsidered your avowed intent to kill yourself by the time you are twenty-five.'

There was a noise from the chair, and through the door crack John saw that Orlando was stretching and yawning in his usual languid pose. 'Damme, no. Nothing will shake me from that resolve. If drink don't get me, then the pox surely will.'

'You bloody little fool…' Sir Vivian started, but Orlando cut across him.

'Don't worry, Uncle dear. I haven't got it yet. The creatures I corrupt are still as pure as snow.'

Sir Vivian breathed an audible sigh of relief. 'Make sure it stays that way.'

'You can count on it.'

The beau got up and disappeared from John's eyeshot, but he heard him move across the room.

'And what would my beloved uncle like to do now that he finds he has the afternoon to himself?'

There was a reply but the words were uttered in such a low tone that John could not hear them.

'Very well,' Orlando answered with just the slightest edge to his voice. 'If that is your pleasure.'

'It will be a pleasure indeed,' Sir Vivian said glutinously. 'It is quite some considerable while since we went there.'

'Then allow me to escort you,' Orlando replied, and John heard him lead the older man from the room.

The Apothecary cautiously opened the door and, seeing the window through which Jack had departed still open, stepped through it and into the garden. Then, by means of dodging from tree to tree, he made his way to the gates, only stopping once to listen to the distant sound of voices coming from a little temple which stood in the gardens. But he was too far away to identify who was speaking, and as thunder was now rolling overhead, the Apothecary decided that to make a hasty retreat was the wisest course. Indeed he did not stop again until he had reached the city of Bath.

Chapter Eleven

Much put out that there was no seat available on the overnight flying coach to London, John was forced to take a place on the slower conveyance which stopped for the night at The Pelican near Newbury. Setting off again after breakfast, a hearty affair which he much enjoyed, the Apothecary finally arrived at St Paul's late in the afternoon, irritated that the journey had taken a full twenty-four hours but pleased that he was not exhausted through lack of sleep. Taking a hackney coach, John went straight to the Public Office in Bow Street to report his somewhat extraordinary findings to Mr Fielding.

The court was still in session, and John stood at the back of the public seats to hear the final cases, one in particular catching his attention. Mr Fielding was evincing every sign of not being trifled with by a thickset young man who stood at the examination bar staring truculently around him.

'This is a pack of lies,' he shouted, even before Joe Jago had opened his mouth.

The Magistrate ignored him. 'Read the charges,' he boomed, his voice drowning all other sound.

Joe cleared his throat and with a long finger scratched the red curls that peeped out from beneath his wig.

'That the prisoner, William Barnard, a former employee of the Duke of Marlborough, did make threats against the person of the Duke and sent him threatening letters. Further, he called upon several occasions at the Duke's London residence where he threatened the male servants and made indecent proposals to the female.'

There was a stifled giggle which the Blind Beak quelled simply with a movement of his head.

'Is the Duke in court?'

'No, Sir. He made a verbal charge to the Public Office which I have here in the form of a statement.

'That will suffice,' replied Mr Fielding, which surprised John, who knew how particular the Magistrate normally was about the complainant being present at the hearing. The Beak turned his eyes, hidden by the familiar black bandage, in the direction of Barnard. 'How do you plead?'

'Not guilty. The old fool bears a grudge against me.'

'I would rather take the word of a peer of the realm to that of someone who is not even a gentleman,' John Fielding answered in a highly elitist manner. 'Six months in Newgate.'

Somewhat startled by the peremptory fashion in which the Beak had administered justice, John turned his attention to the final case.

A complaint had been lodged by an extremely brave member of the public, a young man called Joshua Merryweather, who openly admitted to frequenting brothels, against Mother Cocksedge, an infamous brothel keeper with an equally disgusting nickname, always used because nobody knew what she was actually called. Mother had premises right next door to the Public Office and, as if this weren't enough, it was now alleged that she had employed a girl of eleven as a prostitute, and by doing so had broken the law.

'And you admit to seeing this child while you were actually in the brothel?' asked Mr Fielding in ringing tones.

'I not only saw her, Sir. I witnessed her going to a room with a man for the purposes of having sexual intercourse.

There was a stunned silence in court which John felt certain was hypocritical in many cases. Children were exploited ruthlessly by parents too poor to keep them. The sons were turned out of doors to become pickpockets, the daughters whores. He was absolutely certain that there was not one person present who did not know it, and further that many of the men in court had taken advantage of under-age girls.

'This kind of criminal activity must stop,' replied Mr Fielding sombrely. 'Half the females working in brothels are aged between twelve and eighteen. As some members of the public here present may well be aware, the appeal for support of my plan to set up a refuge for these defenceless creatures is under way. In fact the first batch of youngsters was admitted to the Female Orphan Asylum on July fifth this year. I ask anyone present who would care to make a subscription to this worthy cause to contact the Duchess of Somerset, who heads the list of benefactors.' The Magistrate paused in order that his words might sink in, then he turned once more to young Mr Merryweather. 'I must ask you one final question, Sir.'

'And what is that?'

'How did you know the girl was under twelve years old?'

'Because Mother Cocksedge had offered her to me, Mr Fielding, but thinking she looked so terribly young I asked the child her age, and she told me eleven.'

'Remember, Mr Merryweather, that you are on oath.'

'I do remember, Sir. Indeed I do.'

The Magistrate turned his blind gaze on Mother Cocksedge, who stood where young Barnard had, facing Joe Jago and John Fielding, the Beak raised above her on a dais. 'What have you to say for yourself, woman?'

'I didn't know her age, I swear it. Why, she said to me she was fifteen.'

'I don't believe you. If the child told Mr Merryweather the truth why should she not tell you?'

'Because she wanted the work, see. These girls will say anything to get into a comfortable establishment like mine.'

Mr Fielding lost his temper in a spectacular manner. 'How dare you utter such words. It is you and your evil kind who are ruining these children. Whether the girl is eleven or fifteen makes no difference whatsoever in this sordid case. You should not have employed so tender a creature in the first place. Now, get you gone to Newgate for a year. You are not fit to walk the streets with decent citizens.'

A Runner moved forward to take the woman down, but not before she had shot one contemptuous look at the public gallery and shouted, 'How fine, Mr Beak, to punish me for the sins of all those gallant gentlemen sitting there. Why, if they were not so obsessed with the delights of young flesh I would not have to cater for their lewd and jaded tastes by providing it.'

There was so much truth in what she said that John, brim full of all the things he had recently heard, shivered. But Mr Fielding would have none of it. Rising to his full height of over six feet, he shouted, 'Take that woman below.' Then he swept from the court, clearly indicating that the day's business was concluded. Joe Jago, looking somewhat flustered, announced officially that the court had risen, while the spectators, excited by all the scandal and drama, hurried out in a throng, jamming the doorway. John, thinking better of reporting to the Magistrate in his present state of mind, followed on behind, wondering what he ought to do next.

The urge to chat to someone was strong, and the urge to see Coralie Clive even stronger. Almost acting of their own accord, the Apothecary's feet set off down Bow Street in the direction of The Strand and the house in Cecil Street that Miss Clive shared with her famous sister, Kitty. Not wishing to arrive empty-handed, he called into a shop famous for its chocolate and there procured some sweetmeats to take with him.

Quite the lovelorn suitor, he thought to himself, and had to smile at the memory of the number of years he had spent hankering after the actress, even though there had been dalliances in other directions in the interim. Rather sadly remembering his last liaison, an affaire with a girl who had lived close to the Romney Marsh, John felt an overwhelming desire to make love to Coralie, then wondered how he was ever going to achieve so difficult an objective.

The individual houses of Cecil Street differed somewhat in date, though most appeared to have been built within the last fifty years. At the bottom of the street was an archway, from which a flight of steps led to a passageway running down to the river. The last house but one before the arch, on the left-hand side as one walked down from The Strand, belonged to the Clive sisters, and was one of the oldest in the row. Built during the reign of William and Mary, it was recognisable by its mellow brick facade, its wide square windows, and the generous proportions of its front door.

A footman answered the bell, not the usual glum kind but quite a friendly chap, who looked as if he might at one time have been an actor, perhaps not too successfully, and had therefore decided to cut his losses and become the trusted servant of two young actresses. He also had the appearance of someone perfectly used to dealing with admirers hopefully calling to visit one or other of the beautiful and talented sisters Clive.

'Yes, Sir?' the man said cheerfully.

'I wondered whether Miss Coralie was at home. I am an old friend of hers, John Rawlings.'

'Is she expecting you, Sir?'

'No, I'm afraid not. I just wanted to have a brief word with Miss Coralie and give her these.'

And John rather lamely held out the box of sweetmeats.

The servant inspected them with a practised eye. 'Miss Coralie is at home, Sir, but might well be resting. I shall go and make enquiries. Do kindly take a seat in the anteroom. You will find a copy of today's newspaper to look at.'

He gave John an extremely knowing smile, took his card and placed it on a silver tray, then ushered him into a small room, comfortably furnished and with copies of various journals scattered about upon a table. The Apothecary took a seat, wondering how many other gallants had sat there before him, nervously turning the pages of The Gentleman's Magazine, and imagining themselves in love with either Kitty or Coralie. For it was an irresistible combination; two beautiful women, gifted and famous, adored by the theatre-going public, and neither of them married.

The manservant returned, dark eyes twinkling. 'Miss Coralie will see you in the upper salon, Sir. Miss Kitty will join you later.'

'I am honoured,' John answered, meaning it, and followed the footman up a flight of gracefully curving wooden stairs.

The interior of the house was charming. Wooden floors glowed with wax, and the Clive sisters had decorated with a great deal of style. The room in which Coralie awaited him had been painted a charming shade of deep blue, its furnishings, other than for the wooden pieces, harmonising in a darker shade of the same colour. Almost as if she had done it deliberately, the actress was dressed in iris-blue satin, a colour that enhanced her dark beauty to the point where John could have made a fool of himself and declared his feelings there and then. Instead he bowed formally.

'How kind of you to receive me. It was unpardonable of me to call without an appointment but I just happened to be passing your door.'

Coralie laughed and indicated the chair opposite hers. 'Really? What a happy coincidence, for I was on the point of writing you a letter.'

John's face lit up. 'Were you? What was it going to say?'

'That as it is Bartholomew Fair fortnight and the theatres are consequently closed, I felt like a little frivolity and wondered whether you would care to escort me out on the town.'

'Gladly, Madam. Where do you wish to go?'

'Why, to the fair itself. Kitty is acting there at Mr Timothy Fielding's booth. Mrs Cibber will also be taking part.'

'She was in Bath a few days ago.'

Kitty smiled. 'Do I take it that that means yes?'

'Of course it does. I'm sorry, I wandered off at a tangent. I have just returned from that city.'

'Where you had travelled at the behest of the Blind Beak. Am I right?'

'Perfectly. By the way, is Timothy Fielding any relation?'

'A cousin, I believe. Now, may I offer you some refreshment?'

'I would adore a sherry. A crisp, pale, nutty sherry.'

'Then you shall have one,' said Coralie, and rang the bell.

The empathy between them had never been better. So much so that John felt yet another rush of relief that, despite the actress's many denials that there had been a tendresse between herself and the Duke of Richmond, the attractive young peer was safely wedded and bedded and no longer posing a threat. It was at that moment in his deliberations that Kitty Clive, as dark as her sister but with brown eyes rather than green, entered the room, expressing surprise that her sibling had a visitor, though John had a strong suspicion that the redoubtable manservant must already have informed her.

She swept a curtsey that would have done credit to the stage at Drury Lane. 'My dear Mr Rawlings, how very nice to see you again. What brings you to our home?'

'John is taking me to Bartholomew Fair, Sister. We are resolved to see how you proceed in Mr Fielding's booth.'

Kitty gave a tinkling laugh, the kind that sounded as if it had been practised long and hard. 'Timothy's booth, let me hasten to assure you, is lined with green baize and lit by many lamps. It is a superior place of entertainment and not some cheap fairground stall.'

'I spoke in jest,' said Coralie soothingly. 'It is a well-known fact that the main attraction at the fair is the theatrical performances. They alone draw the town.'

'You are a silken-tongued flatterer,' Kitty answered, and once more laughed charmingly.

She was behaving delightfully, but all the time John had the feeling that she was regarding him shrewdly, ready to tell her sister exactly what she thought of him when they were alone together. Longing to make a good impression, John said, 'I am currently working with Mr Fielding, investigating a mysterious death which took place at the Peerless Pool.'

Kitty arched her brows. 'How unfortunate. Did somebody drown?'

'In a way, yes.'

'What do you mean by that?'

'The woman concerned was weighted down and thrown into the Fish Pond while she was still alive.'

The actress shuddered. 'How frightful. I simply don't know how you can bear to delve into these sordid cases, Mr Rawlings.'

Slightly impatient with her attitude, John answered, 'Because I like to see justice done, Madam. And if I can be instrumental in bringing a villain to book, then I will gladly give my services.'

'That is all very noble,' Kitty answered with just the slightest note of acerbity, 'but what of the danger? When my poor sister offered to help over that unfortunate affair at The Beggar's Opera, she nearly met her end at the hands of a madman.'

'John saved my life on that occasion,' Coralie put in quietly.

Kitty persisted. 'Indeed you did, Sir. But if you had not been there, what then? I truly believe that Mr Fielding should use his Runners to search for thieves and murderers and not involve ordinary members of the public like yourself.'

'Even though it is my wish?'

'Even though it is your wish.'

John gave one of his eloquent shrugs. 'Then there is nothing more to be said.' He turned to Coralie. 'May I take you to dine before the fair?'

'No, let us eat there. It will be amusing to observe who is present, despite their protestations that it is not the place to be seen at.'

'Quite so. Then let me suggest we leave shortly so that we can get ourselves a good table.'

'As soon as we have had our sherry,' said Coralie, and gave the Apothecary a look that raised both his spirits and his hopes.

Miss Kitty taking her carriage for herself, John hailed a hackney coach, helped Coralie into it with some unnecessary hand-squeezing, then sat back to enjoy the ride from The Strand to Smithfield, where the Bartholomew Fair was held every August. Proceeding at a good pace, the hackney entered Fleet Street, passing through the spiked Temple Bar, rebuilt by Christopher Wren in the 1670s. Going down Fleet Street, the coach crossed the River Fleet at Fleet Bridge. To the left, the waterway had been completely covered over, but to the right it was an open sewer, its smell overpowering and putrid. Coralie put her handkerchief over her nose and John did likewise. The actress also averted her eyes from the dead dogs, the floating excrement, the rotting vegetables and all the disgusting detritus of human life. The Apothecary, however, stared beyond Fleet Ditch, as the sewer was known, to one of the two terrible prisons that lay on either side of it. On the left bank was Bridewell, the gaol specifically for women accused of sexual offences. John, his mind still mulling over the disappearance of various children, thought again about the fate of the bastards born therein, shipped off to the plantations to work as soon as they were old enough. He turned his head and gazed towards the river's right bank, and there loomed the Fleet Prison, considered preferable to Newgate, though that said very little. It was a relief when the hackney ascended Ludgate Hill and turned into The Great Old Bailey, which led to Gilt Spur Street, then on to Smithfield and the fair.

Held annually and lasting two weeks, pitched on the site of Smithfield Market, the fair consisted of a great conglomeration of stalls and booths, merry-go-rounds, sideshows, tents and platforms, not to mention the many taverns adjoining the market, each and every one of them making an effort to contribute to the general rowdiness. Taking Coralie firmly by the arm and joining the crowd trying to make its way in, which was driving hard against the crowd attempting to get out, John entered the fairground.

The racket was unbelievable, a great cacophony of fifes and fiddles, trumpets, drums and bagpipes, all playing different tunes, attempting to drown out the raucous sounds made by the fairground's population. Fists crunched on bone as drunken fights broke out; barrow girls screeched their wares; women squeaked as strangers fondled their buttocks; children burst into tears at the sheer monstrous tumult of it all. Glancing around, John saw that all the human parade was present. Fat landladies jostled pimps; pawnbrokers nodded to jockeys; sailors and thieves rolled their eyes at jilts; strollers and tailors passed the time of day. Sideshows abounded: learned pigs, jugglers, tightrope dancers, acrobats, fire-eaters, giants and dwarves were quite literally falling all over one another. A dog that could read the alphabet had drawn an audience of admirers, while others were grouped around a hornpipe dancer, others still circled a rather saucy 'showing of postures'.

'Well?' said John.

'Well!' answered Coralie, and they laughed and held each other more tightly as the crowd pressed in.

A man thrust a leaflet into the actress's hand. Leaning over her shoulder, John read the following:

'At Mr Fielding's Great Theatrical Booth in The George Inn Yard in Smithfield, during the time of Bartholomew Fair, will be acted a diverting Dramatic Opera called "Hunter, or the Beggar's Wedding", with Alterations, consisting of a variety of English, Scots and Irish Ballad Tunes, with additional Songs never perform'd therein before. NB. the Booth is very commodious, and the Inn Yard has all the conveniences of Coach Room, Lights, Houses of Easement, etc. for quality and others. Performances will be hourly during the time of the Fair, and continuing every hour till Eleven at Night.'

'Would you like to dine there?' John asked.

'Very much. Then we can get a good seat.'

All tastes were being catered for at The George. The smell of hot black and pease puddings, strong beer and even stronger ale competed with the delicate aroma of oysters and champagne, wine and fruit tarts. In no mood to stint with the girl who had never been far from his heart since the moment he met her, John ordered the best of everything, then watched with pleasure as she ate and drank with obvious relish.

Coralie looked up. 'Are you enjoying yourself?'

'Very much.'

'You've hardly eaten a thing, I always believed you a trencherman.'

'I'm sorry. My mind has been elsewhere.'

'With a woman?'

'How did you guess?'

'By the slightly crazed expression in your eye.'

The Apothecary shouted a laugh. 'I didn't realise I looked mad when I thought about the female sex.'

'Most men do.'

'Oh, 'zounds! What transparent creatures we must be.'

'Transparent indeed.'

'Then, Madam, you will no doubt know the woman I was thinking of.'

Coralie gazed at him earnestly, green eyes glowing beneath the sweep of long black lashes. 'I cannot be certain, I fear. Rumour reached my ears that recently you were much enamoured of a lady living near the Romney Marsh.'

'If recently is eighteen months ago, then, yes, I was.'

'What happened?'

'She was in love with someone else. I think she used me to try and forget him.'

'Not an unknown thing for a female to do. So it was her that you were dreaming about.'

Leaning across the table, John took the actress's hand in his. 'No, Coralie, it was you.'

'Me?'

'Don't pretend to be surprised. Ever since I met you, that time when you took the part of the girl murdered in the Dark Walk at Vaux Hall and ended up saving me from being shot, I have been in love with you.'

Coralie's eyebrows rose. 'That is hard to believe in view of your other women.'

'I must admit that there have been one or two, but that was only because I believed you hardly noticed me.'

'Oh, I noticed you all right, do not be mistaken about that.'

'Then my heart is light.'

Coralie squeezed his hand, which was still holding hers. 'Are you truly in love with me, despite your other...diversions?' She said the word deliciously, her eyes smiling as she did so.

'I have never stopped. That last time, with the Romney Marsh affaire, I had to make a conscious effort to banish you from my thoughts.'

'Did you succeed?'

'Never.'

'Oh, my dear John.'

'Will you marry me?' said the Apothecary, wonderfully and wildly, full of passion and champagne.

Coralie looked at him very seriously. 'One day, perhaps.'

He pulled himself together. 'I suppose you are about to say, yet again, that you are married to the theatre.'

'For the time being I am, yes.'

'What does that mean?'

'That at some point in the future, heaven alone knows when, I shall be satisfied with what I have achieved and then seek a fascinating husband, the sort who will always keep me interested, and with him raise some large-eyed children with hair the colour of mine and wits sharp as his.'

The Apothecary felt sweat break out beneath his shirt. 'Coralie, might I be their father?'

'It's possible, I suppose.'

'So you are asking me to wait until you are ready?'

She shot him an unfathomable glance. 'Actually, my dear Mr Rawlings, I am ready now.'

He stared at her. 'What are you saying?'

'You know my history, John. You know that I am not a creature of convention. Why don't we make love to one another while time passes?'

The Apothecary drank an entire glass of champagne in one swallow. 'Do you mean...?'

'Sample the delights of marriage without the tie? Yes, I do.'

'My God, Coralie.'

'Are you too much of a prude to countenance such unusual behaviour?'

'You know damned well that I am not.'

'Then let us drink to our future.'

'There is only one bar to this arrangement.'

'And that is?'

'Having shared your bed I would be cut to the quick if you met another.'

'And so would I, my dear. But that is a chance we have to take. Life can never be pre-planned. One never knows from one moment to the next which way the whole mad whirligig is going to lead us.' Coralie's expression changed. 'And talking of that, take me on the merry-go-round, John. I have always adored them and on this occasion the spin will symbolise something about our relationship, would you not agree?'

Weak with the realisation that at long last he had won the woman of his choice, John gave Coralie a look in which he expressed all that he had felt for her since first they met.

'In what way do you mean?'

'We have got on the roundabout and been close, then we have got off again and drifted apart. Now we are getting on once more, possibly to remain together for the whole long ride.'

Summoning the waiter so that he might pay the bill, John said, 'I shall be an ardent lover, you know that.'

'And you will not care that every night of my life a hundred men fall in love with me?'

'I'll care not a whit nor a jot provided that it is my bed you get into when the evening's performance ends.'

She leaned across the table and kissed him, and John would have done more by way of response had the waiter not arrived at that very second. But finally, and at long last, the account settled, they wandered off hand in hand through the crowd of people in painted masks and merry-andrew tawdry dresses until they came to the roundabout. There, John lifted Coralie on to one of the painted horses, then mounted the one next to hers.

'You are certain about this?' he said, as they started to whirl round. 'It is not all too sudden for you?'

'We have known each other four years, have we not?' she answered.

'Yes.'

'Then where's the suddenness in that?'

And leaning across the space that divided them, Coralie Clive kissed John Rawlings full on the lips, and continued to kiss him as the merry-go-round gathered momentum.

Chapter Twelve

At five o'clock in the morning, John Rawlings quietly left Coralie's house in Cecil Street and walked back through a sweet-smelling shower towards his home. Beneath his feet the cobbles were washed and clean, and it seemed to him as he proceeded along The Strand, then turned left up St Martin's Lane, that though he had walked this way on a thousand occasions, this time it was all new. For he felt renewed too, seeing the world with a kindlier eye, a different, more understanding outlook, because at long last, after so many years of longing for her, he had become Coralie Clive's lover. What it was that had made her change her mind so suddenly he could not be sure. Whether the Duke of Richmond's recent marriage had had any bearing on the situation he could not tell. But the fact was that he did not care. Not one damnation. They had spent the night together and it had been as wonderful as he had always imagined.

They had watched the eight o'clock performance of Kitty's play and then had left Bartholomew Fair, walking a little way, taking a hackney coach for the rest of the journey. But though he had wanted her urgently, the Apothecary had bided his time once they were hidden from the world in her house; drinking wine and laughing in Coralie's bedroom, wooing her with sensuous kisses, then finally taking the actress to bed and experiencing a passion far beyond any he had felt before. Every other woman he had made love to had been banished from his mind for good as he had gathered the dark red rose of her beauty into his arms and mingled his essence with hers.

And now he walked the streets, his mind still unable to grasp what had actually taken place, yet his body as alive and alert as he had ever known it. Bursting into song, John hurried through Leicester Fields, and back to the house in Nassau Street in which he had been raised from boyhood, an age of innocence left behind for ever.

Sir Gabriel had not yet risen, but Nicholas Dawkins, a much calmer air about him, the Apothecary was relieved to see, was just about to leave to open the shop in Shug Lane.

John gave him a beaming smile. 'Nicholas, how is everything with you, my friend?'

The Muscovite returned the discerning gaze of a young man come to wisdom. 'Very good, Master. I took your advice.'

The Apothecary stared at him blankly. 'What advice was that?'

'To visit a certain house in Leicester Fields. I did so and I promise you, Sir, that my course is set. Mary Ann will be wooed honourably and with propriety from now on.'

An irrepressible grin crossed John's features as he suddenly saw himself as a wanton youth and his apprentice as the controlled man of the world. But putting on the most serious expression in his repertoire, the Apothecary answered gravely, 'Then my mind is at rest, Nick. I shall exercise a Master's discretion as to your private affairs as long as you continue this sane and sensible plan.'

Then he ruined the whole effect by letting out a wild and lunatic laugh as he proceeded indoors.

As angry and turbulent as the Blind Beak had been on the previous day, this morning he was calm and tranquil as the ocean after a storm. He sat behind his desk in the Public Office, to which John had walked after first going to see that all was well with his shop, his head bowed, listening intently to the Apothecary's account of what had taken place in Bath. Occasionally he nodded, sometimes the black bandage that covered his eyes turned in John's direction, but for the main he sat stiff, taking in every word that was said to him. Eventually he asked a question.

'So is it your opinion that there was something amiss regarding Sir Vivian Sweeting and the children he cared for?'

The Apothecary shook his head. 'I'm not certain. I was on the point of hearing the truth from Jack the coachman when Orlando burst in and further conversation became impossible. But yet, Sir, it is the other story which haunts me.'

'Other story?'

'The disappearance of Lady Allbury's youngest child. It is so similar to that of Lord Anthony and Lady Dysart.' And John recounted the tale of how Meredith had vanished in Paris.

The Magistrate became even more silent, adopting that pose which often made John wonder whether he had fallen asleep. But, finally, he spoke.

'I remember hearing about that case. My brother Henry told me of it. It seems that Lord Anthony wrote to the Public Office and enlisted their help to look for the boy in London. I need hardly say that no trace of him was ever found.'

'What do you think happened to him?'

Mr Fielding became motionless. 'It is highly unlikely that the child wandered off on its own. Particularly as it has always been known that rings of child abductors have been at work for decades. Consider the Spiriters; those creatures who, particularly in the reign of Queen Anne, prowled the streets of London, often dressed in the cast-off clothes of the fashionable, to seduce young people to go beyond the seas. Those who would not leave willingly were taken by force, their final destination the plantations, where they were sold into slavery by the Masters of the Ships.'

'Do you suspect that Meredith Dysart…?'

'I do not know. As I said, it is hardly possible that a child could take itself off without a body being found. Perhaps he and Lucy Allbury both fell into the hands of a kidnapping gang. Perhaps neither.'

'Yet one vanished in Paris, the other Bath.'

'There are certain evidences that the Spiriters were at work in other great European cities besides London.'

The Apothecary cleared his throat, 'So what moves should be made now, Sir? Hannah Rankin obviously lived in Sir Vivian's house for a while. Should I pursue that avenue further or follow her trail in London?'

'I think you should start by confronting the lying Toby. We called him into the Public Office while you were away, but he stuck with his story.'

'That I had stated the victim was female?'

'Just so. But it was clear from his manner that he knew more than he was prepared to admit.'

'Could he have killed Hannah?'

'Quite easily, I imagine. Yet something about Mr Swann's idea that one of the lunatics was responsible appealed to me so much that I instructed Runner Rudge to go to the Hospital and find out the background, as much as was possible that is, of the various inmates.'

'And?'

'One of them, a young fellow of twenty-odd, bears the same surname as Toby, namely Wills. So far nothing has been said about this. I think you should tackle him with it, Mr Rawlings. Tell him that you know he is lying, ask him why.'

'And what of Hannah's two mysterious visitors, the coachman and the Frenchman? Has anything further been discovered about them?'

'Nothing so far, but I thought an enquiry at the French Hospital might not go amiss.'

'It seems I have much to do.'

'So much so that you must have an assistant.'

'Runner Rudge?'

'No. I think Jago, though I am loath to spare him.'

A wonderful idea came to John. 'Would it be possible to call in someone else instead? That is if the person concerned is willing?'

'I presume you are talking of a personal friend? Somebody you can trust?'

'Oh, yes, I am. In fact I thought of asking Miss Coralie Clive, Sir. The theatres are closed for two weeks because of Bartholomew Fair and I believe that she has a certain amount of time on her hands.'

The Magistrate gave a very small chuckle but in no other manner revealed what he was thinking. 'I wonder,' he said slowly, 'if Miss Clive could be persuaded to take the waters at Bath. Women always have such a way with worming out secrets. Were she to get into the confidence of your friend Orlando, then we might learn a great deal more.'

'But Orlando is a self-confessed libertine. I wouldn't like to think of Coralie keeping bad company.'

Mr Fielding chuckled again. 'I am quite sure that Miss Clive is more than capable of looking after herself, my dear Sir. Is it not a fact of life that those in the acting profession come across all sorts and have to get along with them as best they can?'

'Yes, but…' John protested.

'I think she would be an ideal choice for someone to help you but, of course, the option to ask her must remain with you,' said the Blind Beak firmly, then laughed again at some private joke of his own.

In the event the decision was made for John. Longing to see Coralie again but dutybound to go home after he had closed his shop, not having set eyes on Sir Gabriel since he had returned from Bath, the Apothecary found his heart leaping high as he hurried through the front door and heard a female voice coming from the library. Rushing down the passageway, he flung the door open. And there she was, looking divine in an emerald-green gown. Throwing convention to one side, John's new love had daringly come to visit him.

'Coralie!' he said breathlessly.

'Good afternoon, Mr Rawlings,' she answered, but her smile said it all. She had missed him as much as he had her.

Going into the room, well aware of Sir Gabriel's quizzical gaze and determined to look calm and collected despite it, John gave a fanciful bow, to which Coralie, already on her feet, responded with a formal curtsey.

'Miss Clive, how pleasant to see you again.'

'May I return the compliment, Mr Rawlings. It seems like an age since last we met.'

'To what do we owe the honour of this visit?'

'I thought I would invite you and your father to dine with me while I have a short break from the theatre.'

John feigned a puzzled expression, loving the playful and very exciting act of deception. 'A short break?'

'It is Bartholomew Fair and the playhouses are closed, though my sister Kitty is participating in the event.'

'How kind of you to ask.' The Apothecary turned to his father. 'Sir?'

Sir Gabriel's look was unfathomable. 'I rarely refuse an invitation from a beautiful woman. I would be delighted to accept, Miss Clive.'

She flashed John a glance that made him go hot and cold. 'And you, Sir?'

'Your every wish is my command.'

Sir Gabriel's clock struck half past three, breaking the crackling atmosphere that was passing between the two lovers. Almost as if it were a cue, the older man rose to his feet. 'If you would excuse me, I need to have a word with one of the servants. Pray stay a while, Miss Clive. Indeed, if you wish to join my son and myself for a simple repast, then we would be more than delighted. Wouldn't we, John?'

'Delighted,' repeated the Apothecary, never taking his eyes from Coralie's face.

'How very kind,' she breathed.

The door closed behind Sir Gabriel's retreating back and they flew into one another's arms and kissed wildly. 'I've missed you,' he said.

'It's been all of twelve hours.'

'It seemed much longer.'

'John, we have to be sensible.'

'Why?'

'Because when we are both working we will inevitably be apart.'

The Apothecary smiled into her lovely eyes. 'I know. You are right. But it is all a bit too soon and a bit too beautiful for me to act rationally. Let us be mad for a few more days before we pass on to the next phase.' He frowned. 'And talking of that reminds me.'

'Of what?'

'I was with Mr Fielding earlier today and like a fool suggested that you might be able to help me with this investigation.'

Coralie held him at arm's length. 'Why like a fool?'

'Because it would mean our parting company almost straight away. He wants you to go to Bath and try to get into conversation with Orlando.'

'And who might he be, pray?'

'I will tell you everything as long as you promise not to go.'

Coralie's eyes narrowed. 'What? First of all you suggest I help you, then in the next breath you tell me not to. What do you want?'

'To marry you.'

Coralie brushed her lips against his cheek. 'My very dear John, let us start our relationship as we mean to continue it. I have already told you that the day is far distant when I take a husband. Now, to other, more important things. It is my express wish that I do help you and Mr Fielding. Remember that I was assisting the Blind Beak when we first met.'

'But we are investigating a murder. Recall what your sister said about putting oneself in danger.'

'I was in danger when I saved your life.'

'Is there nothing I can say to dissuade you from taking part?'

'Nothing at all. My mind is made up.' Coralie lowered her voice discreetly. 'Tell me, where are you spending tonight, my dear?'

'With you,' the Apothecary answered, and drew her close before they went to find Sir Gabriel.

Some two hours later, after the actress had gone, John and his father retired to the library to drink a measure of port, an occasion not as comfortable as it normally was. The younger man sat in silence, staring into the glass's ruby depths, wondering just how much he should tell Sir Gabriel about his love affaire with Coralie. In the event, though, the wind was taken completely from his sails by his father saying, 'I see that you two have finally become lovers.'

Totally startled, the Apothecary looked up. 'What did you say?'

'That you have flown in the face of convention, as do so many young people nowadays, and taken the woman of your choice to bed.'

John simply could not help himself. He laughed at the sheer audacity, the sublime shrewdness of the man, now over seventy years old, who had adopted him as a child.

'How did you know?'

'It is written over both your faces for all the world to see.'

'Father, if you are going to give me a lecture on morals...'

'Perish the thought!'

'Then let me simply explain that I have asked her honourably to marry me and the minx has refused.'

'Much as you imagined she would,'

'Yes. But meanwhile she offered me a situation in which we become lovers and remain so until she achieves her ultimate ambition in the theatre and is finally ready to settle down to family life.'

'Is this, then, the coming thing? O tempora! O mores!'

John looked serious. 'It may well be. I am sure Coralie leads the way. However, who am I to argue with such an arrangement? To love her or to lose her; which would you have chosen?'

'As you have done, of course. But, my son, there is a flaw in this state.'

'Which is?'

'That if she keeps you dangling on a string too long you will tire of her.'

The Apothecary could not help but acknowledge the truth of what Sir Gabriel was saying.

'Then let us hope she is sensible and understands that.'

'I agree. For Coralie is beautiful and intelligent, witty, but not altogether wise. In other words, she would make a perfect daughter-in-law.'

'If she ever decides to enter the married state, that is.'

Sir Gabriel leant forward and kissed his son lightly on the cheek. 'Just enjoy the situation for what it is worth. Who knows where fate will lead one next. Now, my dear, let us be practical. All I ask is that you tell me when you are going to be at home so that I have no cause for concern when you are absent.'

'You are very understanding.'

'That is the duty of every parent to a good child, in my view.'

'You still consider me good?' Sir Gabriel nodded. 'You truly are one of the most remarkable men of our time,' said John, and raised his glass to the linchpin of his life, his father in all but the actual, Sir Gabriel Kent.

It was late when John's chair arrived in Cecil Street, but still Coralie waited up for him, dressed in a white nightrail trimmed with scarlet ribbons. She had ordered a light supper to be served before the fire in her bedroom, and they ate it lying on low cushions set in front of the flames. It was so romantic, so idyllic, that the Apothecary began to feel he had entered a dream world and refused to spoil it with tales of the murder he was investigating. Nor, indeed, by telling the strange story of Meredith Dysart and the children of Bath. Not, in fact, until the next morning when they breakfasted together did John recount all that had happened since Hannah's body had been discovered in the Fish Pond.

Coralie's eyes widened in shock, then she asked a very pertinent question. 'Is it possible that all of this is connected?'

'What do you mean?'

'Well, if these Spiriter people were working throughout Europe, could Meredith and Lady Allbury's daughter have been snatched by the same gang?'

'I suppose it's feasible. Yet somehow, and it's no more than a feeling, I do not believe that either child was destined for the plantations.'

'And what of Sir Vivian Sweeting's houseful of wards? Were they all abducted as well?'

'That is my point. If they were snatched to be slaves what were they doing living with him? If possible, Coralie, try to talk to Jack the coachman. If Orlando doesn't invite you to dine, then somehow you'll have to find an excuse to visit the house unofficially. Though for God's sake don't take any risks.'

'I shall be perfectly safe. Do you think Sir Vivian is the type to be impressed by a title?'

John considered. 'Quite probably, yes.'

'Then I shall pass myself off as the Marchesa di Spinotti, wife of some crumbling old Italian diplomat. The fact that they think me married will make me safe as far as the men are concerned, yet they will all still want to flirt with me, even seduce me perhaps.'

John looked askance. ''Zounds and zoodickers, Coralie! Don't go on with this mad scheme, I beg you. I do not want to think of my mistress being pawed by every old wretch in Bath.'

'But you said Orlando was young.'

The Apothecary threw his hands in the air. 'Are you doing this to annoy me?'

Jumping to her feet, Coralie came to stand behind him, putting her arms round his neck and kissing it. 'Yes, of course I am. My dear, I have been in the theatre eight years; since I was sixteen. I truly have learned how to take care of myself.'

'Still, I don't like the idea of it.'

'You are not going to become jealous and possessive just because we have shared a bed, are you?'

John looked at her with a straight face. 'I am only human, sweetheart. If the pangs of jealousy did not stir in my heart, then you would consider me callous indeed. I have no wish to live your life for you, but on the other hand I am obviously concerned for your welfare.'

He was rewarded with another kiss and Coralie saying, 'I really am very fond of you, you know.'

'So I should hope in view of our arrangement,' the Apothecary answered, and pulled her on to his lap so that he might take leave of her in proper loving style before, for the time being at least, the pair of them parted company and went their own separate ways.

Chapter Thirteen

When William Kemp, jeweller and renowned citizen of London, had taken on the task of turning a dangerous swimming pond into one of the capital's most enchanting hubs of leisure, he had overlooked nothing at all. As well as building himself a charming home and various structures in which to house the different baths and changing rooms, he had also created a lodge close to the main gates to act as both office and ticket bureau. And it was to a tiny salon contained therein, as delightfully furnished as if it were a genuine lodgekeeper's dwelling, that John was shown when he arrived at the Peerless Pool later that morning. Mr Kemp himself was on duty and had personally ushered the Apothecary on to the premises.

'You seem very busy,' John had commented, running an eye over the line of people waiting to show their subscription tickets as they passed through the entrance.

Agile as the dancing master he resembled, William had spun on his heel. 'It was just as Mr Fielding said. When we reopened for business after the murder, patrons formed a veritable queue. Indeed, the Fish Pond has been so crowded since that I have been forced to obtain more rods. The human race will never cease to surprise me.'

'There is certainly an unpleasantly morbid streak lurking in us all,' John answered as he went into the lodge.

'Alas, how true. Now, you wish to see Tobias Wills? Nothing wrong, I trust?'

John shook his head soothingly. 'No. I am merely clearing up one or two points and hoping to jog his memory a little.'

Mr Kemp looked relieved. 'I'm glad to hear it. A sound man is Toby.'

'Have you known him long?'

'Only about a year. But please be assured that in that time he has shown his worth. Why, it was he who helped you get the body up, if you remember.'

'How could I forget?' John answered, and wondered, as he had several times already, why it was that Toby had lied about how he knew the gender of the murder victim. But the ex-soldier's face as he marched into the room military-style, then stood rigidly at attention, gave nothing away, and the Apothecary mentally paled at the thought of the task lying ahead of him.

He adopted a pleasant approach. 'Toby, you will never know how grateful we all were for your help on that terrible day when the dead woman was found.'

The old soldier gave him a contemptuous glance. 'Well, scant reward I've had for my pains and that's a fact. I've been accused of being a liar by practically everybody, including yourself.'

John changed tack as swiftly as the wind at sea. 'As you now accuse me.'

'What do you mean?'

Half the size of the powerfully built Toby, John none the less brought his face to within an inch of the other man's. 'Because you know as well as I do I never mentioned that the body at the bottom of the Fish Pond was that of a woman. And no bluff or bluster on your part is going to make a ha'p'orth of difference on that score. Listen to me, Tobias...' John decided to take several wild guesses and see if anything he said hit home. '...it is my belief that you saw the murdered woman being brought into the grounds in a wheelbarrow. You may or may not have seen her being thrown into the Pond. I don't know. But whatever the case you decided to keep your mouth shut because you recognised her. How? Because you had met her before when you had gone to visit your young relative in St Luke's Hospital for Poor Lunatics.' The ruthless streak that was part of the Apothecary's make-up suddenly surfaced. 'That is the best construction I can put upon your actions. The worst is that you actually aided and abetted the murderer, perhaps even committed the crime yourself. Now, tell me the truth or I shall repeat this whole thing in front of the Blind Beak.'

Toby was tough, there was no doubt about that. His leathery face barely moved a muscle, though his eyes darted frantically. 'That's what you suppose. You've got no proof of it.'

'Then you leave me no choice but to order the Runners to take you to Bow Street — and bring along your relative from the asylum while they are at it.'

'You wouldn't do that.'

'Oh yes I would,' John answered nastily. 'The murdered woman, Hannah Rankin, has a strange past, one that has not yet been untangled. If ordering a lunatic to tell what he knows, cruel though that might be, is necessary to find out who and what she was, then so be it.'

Toby coughed and stared at the floor. 'Don't bring the boy into it, Sir. It wouldn't be right. He knows nothing.'

The Apothecary had a moment of inspiration. 'He's your son, isn't he?'

Tobias did not look up.

'I see. What a tragedy for you. How long has he been incarcerated?'

At last Toby stared him in the eye. 'Since the hospital was built. I used to pay for him to be looked after, but it stretched my army wage to the limit. I was a regular soldier, you see, and Tom was born to a camp follower, my woman of the time.'

'What became of her?'

'She was a bad lot. She took off with an officer and put Tom out to a baby farmer. I think something that happened to him in her charge unhinged him. He was born normal as a rosebud but had gone quite simple when I came back from fighting and went to find him.'

'Was any of this to do with Hannah Rankin?'

Toby looked genuinely surprised. 'No. I'd never come across her before I saw her at St Luke's.'

'Then why did you dislike her so much?'

'Because she used to beat my boy. That's what he told me, and though Tom might be an imbecile he has never lied in his life.'

'And that fault was sufficient to allow you to calmly watch her being wheeled in here, bleeding and beaten, then thrown, weighted down, into the Fish Pond?'

'No, there was something else,' Toby answered reluctantly.

'What was it?'

'Something somebody said, nothing I knew for sure.'

'Can't you give me any details?'

'No. It concerns other people. I swore to keep it to myself.'

'Mr Fielding could order you to tell him on oath what you know.'

More white than usual showed in Toby's eyes. 'Don't let that happen, Sir. I would be betraying a trust.'

'Then just give me the gist of it and I promise to say no more.'

'Somebody I know came to me when they heard my boy was in St Luke's. They asked me to find out if a Hannah Rankin worked there. Then they said a little about her past, that's all.'

'What did they say?'

'Simply that it was unsavoury. I can't go any further.'

'Very well. So you were not surprised when you saw her murderer wheel her body in through the gate from the fields?'

'No.'

'Who was it, by the way?' John asked casually.

Toby flung up his head. 'What do you mean?'

'Who was her killer?'

The old soldier gave the Apothecary a steadfast look. 'I don't know and that I swear to you. All I saw was a figure in a voluminous cloak that hung to the ground,'

'Was it a man or a woman?'

'That I couldn't tell you. The person wore a hat and mask, and a most eerie thing the mask was too.'

'What do you mean?'

'It was shaped like a bird's head, with a big beak sticking out at the front and slanting slits for eyes. It looked foreign, if you know what I mean.'

'A Venetian carnival mask?'

'Possibly.' Toby gripped John's arm tightly. 'It frightened me, Sir, and that's the honest truth. There was something terrifying about it.'

The Apothecary smiled at him reassuringly. 'Calm yourself. Sit down and tell me all that you saw. Start at the beginning.'

They took seats opposite one another and Toby, after a moment's hesitation, clearly made up his mind to unburden himself.

'Well, I was coming from Mr Kemp's, having delivered some vegetables to his kitchen. I was just about to let myself out of the gate in his garden – all the trusted employees have a key – when I heard the sound of something approaching. Don't ask my why I drew back, Sir, because I'll never know the answer myself. Anyway, draw back I did, and by the light of the moon, quite faint but enough, I saw this terrible figure pushing its wheelbarrow. It came into the garden and immediately took the path heading towards the Fish Pond.'

'And Hannah?'

'She was lying in a pool of blood in the barrow. I thought she was dead, Sir, and that's a fact.'

'There was enough light for you to recognise her?'

'Yes. You see, when this person told me what they had to say about Hannah on that other occasion, she was present and I had time to study her.'

'Where was this?'

'In The Old Fountain, a tavern which stands at the east end of the Gardens. I met my friend, and Hannah Rankin was sitting just round the corner. That's when he asked me if she was at St Luke's and informed me of her past.'

'And you are quite certain that it was not him pushing the barrow?'

Toby's battle-torn face looked sad. 'No, Sir, I am not certain. I could not truthfully say who it was or who it wasn't, and I swear that on my son's life.'

'Toby, you've got to tell me who your friend is. He might be able to help me enormously.'

The old soldier shook his head. 'That I'll never do. I've already said more than enough. The rest you will have to discover for yourself. From now on my lips are sealed.'

'Then let me ask you one more thing. What time of day did this occur?'

'It would have been about nine o'clock, Sir. Whoever brought her along waited for darkness to protect them.'

'And they definitely came across the fields?'

'Yes, Sir. Either from Islington or the French Hospital or Ratcliff Row, for the path forks three ways, remember.'

'I think,' said John, more to himself than to poor Tobias, who was by now shaking with the sheer effort of the tale he had decided to tell, 'that the French Hospital must be my very next place of call.'

'Aye, Sir. Look for the painted old Frenchman,' answered the soldier unexpectedly. Then, with a salute, he was gone, before the Apothecary could ask him another thing.

More as a matter of curiosity than in the hope of finding any additional evidence, John took the route that the killer must have taken. Going from the entry lodge to the Fish Pond, walking through the Garden's pleasant vistas, admiring the shrubs and flowers, the Apothecary traversed the perimeter, raising his hat to the various anglers standing there, then took the path to the right of Mr Kemp's house. To his left stood the proprietor's private garden, a high wall protecting it from the fields that lay beyond, a tall hedge shielding it from the gaze of visitors. Within this hedge a small wooden latched gate marked 'Private' gave access to William Kemp's property, but the gate to which Toby had referred lay straight ahead. Much larger, it stood in an arch in the brick wall, its black latch at hand height. Trying it, John discovered that it was locked. Undeterred, he proceeded to Mr Kemp's front door, protected from the Peerless Pool by yet another brick wall, and rang the bell. A saucy maid answered.

'Yes, Sir?'

'Good morning. Is Mrs Kemp at home?'

'No, she's taken the carriage into town, Sir.'

'Well, Mr Kemp is busy about the Gardens — I know because I've seen him. The thing is I need to borrow the key to the back gate. I..."

But the girl cut John's explanation short, smiling and somehow contriving to wriggle her pert breasts and nose simultaneously. 'Help yourself, Sir. It's hanging on a hook in the kitchen. Over the fireplace. You can't miss it.' And with a further impudent look, she was gone, leaving the Apothecary free to wander through a small outbuilding and take the key, meeting no one other than a skivvy shelling peas, who waved a skinny arm at him and did not challenge him at all.

'Only too easy,' the Apothecary said to himself as he unlocked the gate and passed through into the fields beyond.

Three paths, all leading from one track, spread out before him. To his right the path went off into the distance, heading towards Islington, while the track ahead veered left and ended in Ratcliff Row. The path going sharp left went round the outside of the Pleasure Garden and directly to the French Hospital. Locking the gate behind him and dropping the key into his pocket, John set off.

The fields were bleached by the sun and full of wild summer flowers, and he would dearly have loved to have walked that way, looking for simples. But the Apothecary stuck to what he must do and strode briskly on, crossing Pest House Row and going in at the hospital entrance, admiring, yet again, the fine architecture and beautiful garden of this most gracious building.

The Hospital was built round three sides of a square, the imposing front door lying in the middle of the right-hand wing, complete with a flight of wide steps and a pillared entrance. Not quite sure how he was going to conduct the interview, John climbed to the top step and rang the bell. An imposing maid, tall and graceful and very French, answered.

'Yes, Monsieur?'

With not an idea as to what he ought to say, John took a chance and asked, 'Is Monsieur le Marquis in at the moment?'

The maid frowned. 'Monsieur le Marquis? Do you not have his name?'

The Apothecary put on his buffoon's face. 'No need of a name when he is around. One would know him anywhere by his maquillage. Le visage blanc, les grains de beauté noir. Ha, ha, ha, quel homme!'

The servant stared at him as if he were utterly crazed. 'Do you mean the old Marquis?' she asked cautiously.

John winked a solemn eye. 'Old, perhaps. Mais un renard sage, n'est-ce pas?'

The woman looked more unsure than ever. 'And what is your business with him, if you please?'

The Apothecary produced his card, bowed so low that his hat brushed the top step, and said with a knowing look, 'I have a message from one of his friends, Miss Hannah Rankin.'

'I will see if Monsieur is in,' the maid said, snatching the card from John's fingers and shutting the door in his face, all in one ill-tempered movement.

'Pray do,' he said to the closed door, and wondered whether the man he sought really was a marquis or whether that was merely the old fellow's nickname.

He was still considering when the door opened again to reveal the Frenchman himself.

'Monsieur le Marquis?' John enquired, but the other just inclined his head, giving no indication as to his status.

He really was extremely ancient, and the careful application of cosmetic enamel only served to make him look even older, for each line and wrinkle was filled with white substance, a repulsive effect, particularly when he grimaced, which the Marquis did now.

'Who are you?' he asked, his voice coming from some bronchial area deep within his chest, as if he had smoked a pipe from the moment he was born.

'I have some information about Hannah,' John answered, never taking his eyes from the Frenchman's.

'Hannah who?'

'Hannah Rankin. My understanding is that you know her, Sir. Her landlady told me that you called at the house; another informant says that you are her recognised associate.'

Ringed by black dye, the Marquis's reptilian eyes did not so much as blink. 'I know many people, young man. Hannah Rankin could well be one of them. But now you answer me a question. By whose authority do you come to this place of refuge and interrogate me? Your card says that you are an apothecary. Since when have herbalists had the power to pry into private lives?'

Anticipating this attack, John did not falter. 'I represent Mr John Fielding of the Public Office, Bow Street, Monsieur. The fact is that your companion Hannah was brutally murdered a few days ago. Everyone with whom she had contact is being questioned. However, if you do not wish to talk to me I can easily arrange for you to be taken to Bow Street and there to speak to the Principal Magistrate himself.'

The old lizard face remained impassive, but the Marquis shrugged a world-weary shoulder. 'It is of little consequence to me where I tell my story.'

'Then if you would care to ask me inside we may as well get the business done now.'

'As you wish,' answered the Marquis, and opened the door wide enough to allow John to step within and take stock of his surroundings.

La Providence, as the French Hospital was known to its residents, was certainly as elegant on the inside as it was on the exterior. From the beautiful and spacious hall rose a graciously proportioned staircase, obviously leading to apartments situated on the first and second storeys, while corridors to the right and left extended the length of the wing, giving access to the rooms on the ground floor. With a humourless smile, the Marquis turned left, cocking his head for John to follow him, and they proceeded down the corridor, the stamp of their feet on the polished wood floor breaking the immense calm of the place. Eventually they reached a door to which the Marquis produced a key, and the two of them stepped into a large room full of sunshine. Yet despite the light and warmth, John shivered.

It was strange. The room itself was clean, not a speck of dust on the floor or furniture, the window panes shining in the sunlight. Yet an overpowering smell — of clothes saturated with a scent grown stale; of thick white face enamel allowed to harden; of a chamber pot used in the night and not yet attended to — made the atmosphere unbearable. There was also, John thought, a distinct aroma of rot coming from the old man himself.

'Sit down, please,' said the Frenchman, indicating a wing chair.

The Apothecary sat gingerly, not liking the atmosphere of the place at all, while the Frenchman took a seat opposite, crossing one leg over the other. As he moved, small clouds of powder rose into the air, adding to the generally fusty aroma.

The Marquis licked his carmined lips. 'Now, how can I help you?'

'By telling me, Sir, your full name and title, that is if you have one.'

The Frenchman laughed deep in his smoke-filled lungs. 'I am the Marquis de Saint Ombre, and my estates and properties were originally in Gascony. However, religious persecution of the Huguenots made me seek sanctuary in this country, and now I own nothing.'

Congratulating himself on guessing the elderly wretch's title correctly, John continued, 'Now, Sir, I believe you are connected with a woman called Hannah Rankin. Just to jog your memory, she lived in the house of Mother Hamp in Ratcliff Row and she worked at St Luke's Hospital for Poor Lunatics. It is thought by some that you were her suitor.'

The Marquis tapped the side of his nose and a flake of enamel fell on to his coat. 'I recall the woman now. Yes, of course. Her suitor, eh? Are you suggesting that she granted me her favours?'

'I am not suggesting anything, Monsieur le Marquis. Instead I would prefer you to tell me all that you can remember about her. For example, where did you meet Hannah, and when?'

The Frenchman looked vague. 'Let me see now. I fled to this country some twenty years past and came to live directly here in La Providence, remaining ever since. As a gentleman, I do not have a trade and was therefore unable to become part of the London working community. I met Hannah some years ago in The Old Fountain where I sometimes go to take refreshment. That is all there is to it.'

'You visited her in her home, I believe.'

'Oh, yes. She occasionally obliged me with a feather-bed jig, as you English would say.'

'You were Hannah's lover?'

'Hardly that. But even old men have needs and Hannah catered for mine quite adequately.'

The Marquis leered unpleasantly, exposing his yellow teeth.

'In that case I must comment that you do not seem particularly upset about her death.'

'I already knew about it. Word spreads quickly in this community. Would you care for a glass of canary?'

'Not at the moment, thank you.'

'You have no objection to my partaking?'

'None at all.'

John sat silently, watching the old man go to a decanter and pour himself a deep glass, his hand shaking very slightly as he did so. Taking the opportunity while the Frenchman's back was turned, the Apothecary snatched a quick look around the room. Other than for the usual books and furnishings there was little of interest to see, but through the open bedroom door John caught a glimpse of a painting, a painting that seemed a little unusual to say the least. Unable to resist, he got to his feet and sauntered towards the door.

It was the sort of picture that could, at first glance, be thought of as perfectly innocent. A female child, naked but for a wreath of flowers in her hair, stood in a field surrounded by fairy folk. But there all semblance of innocence ended, for each and every one of the immortals was engaged in salacious behaviour of one kind or another. Ghastly grinning gnomes raped a screaming fairy; a satyr bestrode an elfin boy child; a ring of goblins indulged in homosexual intercourse; Oberon displayed magically enlarged privy parts. It was one of the most brutal paintings the Apothecary had ever seen.

Behind him, the Marquis laughed. 'I see you like my picture.'

'I wouldn't say that like was quite the right word.'

'I bought it in Paris many years ago. The artist was young and struggling. I paid him a fair price and have treasured it ever since.'

'Personally I find it disturbing.'

'You are meant to, my young friend.'

John turned round. 'Monsieur le Marquis, eight nights ago Hannah Rankin was beaten almost to death, then she was thrown into the Fish Pond to drown. I must ask you to tell me where you were on the evening in question.'

The Frenchman frowned. 'Eight nights back? Would that have been a Friday? Gracious, I can hardly remember yesterday, time passes so quickly. But if I recall correctly I played whist with friends. Yes, I believe I did.'

'Where was this?'

'In town. In a house near Piccadilly. I took a hackney coach.'

'What was the name of your hosts?'

'Monsieur and Madame Menard. They are wealthy Huguenots who have become part of British common life.'

'Perhaps you would be good enough to give me their address.'

'But you have my word as a nobleman that I was there.'

'In a case of murder I am afraid that is not good enough.'

'You are impudent, Sir.'

'If so, then I apologise. But let me hasten to assure you that Mr Fielding would have said the same.'

The Marquis downed the canary with one rapid swallow and refilled his glass. 'Now, is there anything more I can tell you?'

"Yes. Did Hannah ever mention to you that she might have enemies of any kind? People from the past who could have known her when she lived in Bath? Or even earlier?'

There was a definite shift in the whitened features. Something John had said had struck a chord.

'What do you mean exactly?' the Marquis responded and the Apothecary knew that the old man had asked the question in order to gain time.

'I am simply enquiring whether Hannah, as your mistress, confided in you that she might be afraid of anyone. A burly coachman has been mentioned to me. Someone from whom she apparently said she might have to escape.'

The Marquis gripped the table at which he was standing. 'I cannot think what you are talking about. Somebody has been joking with you, I believe. Hannah had no enemies that I was aware of.'

'Did you realise that she once lived in Bath?'

'I believe she mentioned it.'

'Only mentioned? How long did you say you knew her?'

The Marquis waved a vague arm and the overpowering smell of stale scent filled the room once more. 'I didn't, but it must be two years or thereabouts.'

'Before she went to work at St Luke's, then?'

The lines in the white face hardened. 'No, I don't think so.'

'But she was only there a year. I learned that from the Hospital directly.'

'Then perhaps I am confused. Hannah is a relatively new acquaintance, let me hasten to assure you of that.'

Why? the Apothecary wondered. Why hasten to assure me? And he became instantly convinced that the relationship between Hannah and the Marquis went back much further than the Frenchman was prepared to admit. He attempted to pursue the idea.

'Are you familiar with Sir Vivian Sweeting, by any chance?'

A muscle twitched beneath the Marquis's pallid mask. 'No, I don't believe so. Is he a member of the beau monde?'

'Yes, I think one could say he is. In Bath, most certainly.'

'Then how would I know him?' The Frenchman sprang to his feet and began to pace. 'My dear Sir, I lost everything when I left France. I had nothing but what money and jewels I could carry on me. I live here on charity and conduct my life by means of my small investments and the kindness of my friends. I do not have the resources to sojourn at Bath, that is for certain.'

He was ruffled, and John was more than aware of it. He smiled his honest-citizen smile. 'I did not mean to pry into your affairs, my dear Sir. It just occurred to me that as you were an intimate of hers, Hannah might have introduced you when Sir Vivian came to town.'

The Frenchman shook his head. 'No, she did not. Now, Sir, will that be all?'

The Apothecary made a highly elaborate bow. 'Indeed it will, Monsieur le Marquis. For the time being that will most certainly suffice. Good-day to you, Sir.'

He bowed again and left the room, well aware of the Marquis's ravaged face turned towards him, watching his every move as he made his way back down the corridor.

Having returned the key to Mr Kemp's walled garden, John set off for St Luke's Hospital before taking a hackney coach home. The asylum being so close to the French Hospital, it seemed foolish not to seize the opportunity of making another visit, and yet there was no real reason for it. But still something lurked at the back of the Apothecary's brain, some reason, not yet formulated, why he needed to call and indulge in general conversation, if nothing more serious..

Warder Forbes was on duty and received John cheerfully once he had managed to get past the trembling individual who manned the wicket gate.

'And how are you today, Sir? I was wondering when we would see you again.'

'How are you is more to the point. Have you recovered from your unpleasant ordeal?'

'You mean identifying Hannah's body?' The Apothecary nodded. 'It took me several days to get over it, Sir, and I'm no coward. God's life, I've never seen such wounds. Whoever beat her put all his hatred into it and that's for sure.'

'You think it must have been a man?'

'Can't imagine a woman being strong enough, unless it were one of ours, of course.'

'Do you mean an inmate?'

'I do. When they're in a frenzy they've got superhuman strength. Do you remember me telling you about Petronelle?'

'Not liking children, do you mean?'

'Yes. Well, she saw one the other day. Child of a visitor, it was. Anyway, it took four of us to hold her down, she went so wild. Eventually we overpowered her and tied her up tight for her own good. Then the apothecary came and dosed her with laudanum and we didn't hear no more out of her for two days.'

'Where is she now?'

'Locked in her room.'

'Could I see her?'

'No, Sir. It's too dangerous.'

'I am a medical man, remember. And besides, I feel she might have some information for me.'

'About Hannah Rankin?'

'Possibly.'

Forbes shook his head. 'It's more than my job's worth, Sir.'

'Then should I ask Mr Burridge?'

'He's not on duty, Sir.'

'Then who is in charge?'

'I am.'

It appeared that they had reached an impasse, and John would have accepted the situation and taken his leave had it not been for the sudden sound of running feet. A second later a woman warder, panting and much out of breath, appeared, coming down the corridor at speed.

'It's Petronelle,' she gasped. 'I think she's having a fit.'

Without another word, Forbes beckoned the Apothecary to follow him and they sprinted along the passage until they came to an open doorway giving access to a small cell-like room. Inside, John could see the girl, tied to the bed but conscious, saliva flecking her lips, the pupils of her eyes so contracted that the brilliant blue which was their natural colour had almost consumed the rest, making her look like a demonic angel.

'How much laudanum has this girl had?' John shouted at Forbes, feeling for Petronelle's pulse as she slipped into unconsciousness.

'She's kept under with it constantly,' the woman warder answered.

'Dear God, she's had too much,' the Apothecary said, looking at his patient in horror.

'Should we try to get the medicine out of her?'

John shook his head. 'I don't think we can. It must be deep in her system for her pupils to react like that.'

'Is she going to die?' asked Forbes.

'I don't know,' the Apothecary answered. He lifted the girl into his arms. 'Petronelle, can you hear me?'

She opened her terrible, tortured eyes and gave a parody of a smile. 'She's gone, the wicked one, hasn't she?'

'Yes,' John said. 'She's gone and she won't come back any more.'

'She thought I didn't know her, but I did.'

'Who, Petronelle? Who are you talking about?'

'She said she would take me to see Minerva's head. It was lucky to touch it. Only a shilling, Sir. Just to pay for my lodging.'

'Be quiet, my dear. You are looked after now.'

'She told me I would see Minerva,' Petronelle replied faintly, then she lowered her lids and went very still.

Chapter Fourteen

Afterwards, when he was home, safe in his own surroundings, John had wept, struck to the heart by the futility of Petronelle's short life, by the sheer devastating waste of it. That so flawless a beauty should have had the greatest flaw of all seemed too terrible to come to terms with. And yet the fact remained. The lovely girl had lost her wits on the streets of London while little more than a defenceless child and had spent the rest of her time incarcerated in an asylum.

'May God have mercy on her,' John had said aloud, wishing for the hundredth time that he had got to her earlier.

Yet there was a part of his brain, a little icy sliver, that told him the poor creature was best out of her cocoon of madness, that death while she was still young and perfect was far preferable to life as a gibbering, slobbering wreck of a woman, made ugly by dementia. But even though he knew this logical, rational argument was right, still he grieved for the fact that she had been too far gone for him to administer the treatment of emetic and stimulants which might have saved Petronelle if he had found her in time.

With his usual tact and wisdom, Sir Gabriel had left his brooding son alone, but eventually there had come a tap at the bedroom door to which John, having washed his face thoroughly and taken a dose of reviving physick, had responded, 'Come in.' His father had appeared.

'My dear, you have a visitor.'

'Who?'

'The redoubtable Joe Jago clad in an emerald-green frock. He presents Mr Fielding's compliments and wonders whether you could spare time for a talk.'

The Apothecary instantly felt cheered, pleased as he always was to see the Magistrate's wily clerk. And today was no exception. As he walked into the library, Joe rose to his feet, scratched his red curls and gave a grin broad as a barge.

'Mr Rawlings, Sir, how goes it with you?'

'A mix of fortunes, my friend. And what of yourself?'

'I attended a funeral this morning, not a cheerful event at the best of times and this one worse than most.'

'Was it Hannah Rankin's?'

'Indeed it was. She went into a pauper's grave at first light at Tindal's

Burying Ground, with no one to see her off except me. Alone and friendless, as you might say.'

'No one at all? Not even from St Luke's?'

'Not even from there.'

'What about her lover? Surely he went?'

Joe's eyebrows almost hit his hair. 'A lover, did you say? Well, well. How the world goes on! And who might he be?'

'A decrepit old marquis from the French Hospital. You couldn't mistake him. He's all beauty spots and satin breeches.'

'There was nobody within a mile answering to that description.'

'Probably sleeping off the previous night's dissipations.'

'Could the Marquis be the man we are looking for?'

'Somehow I don't think so. Amazingly, the murderer was actually seen by Toby Wills.' And John went on to describe everything that had taken place since he had last reported to the Blind Beak. Joe sat silently, taking it all in, then said, 'So Petronelle is dead. How very tragic. Tell me, was it an accident in your view?'

'I believe so. Either an inept apothecary or, more likely, a member of St Luke's staff incapable of measuring out the right dosage of laudanum, killed her.'

'So there is no connection with the murder of Hannah Rankin?'

'I'm not sure about that. When I first encountered Petronelle she spoke about the wicked one who had come for her. Her dying words were of the same thing. It may be fanciful, but I can't help wondering if she was referring to Hannah, though of course I can never find out now.'

Joe looked thoughtful, his bright blue eyes clouded. 'The truth has a way of coming out in the end. Did Petronelle say anything else before she died?'

'Only that the unnamed wicked one, who was quite definitely female, had promised to show her the head of Minerva.'

'What?'

'No, I know it doesn't make any sense. Minerva was an ancient Roman goddess, patroness of arts and handicrafts. It really means very little.'

Joe sighed, then said, 'Mr Fielding has given me a week off court duties in order that I may help you. Where would you like me to begin?'

'I think the best place would be with the Marquis's friends, the couple who, according to him, entertained him for whist on the night of the murder.'

The clerk nodded. 'The times of his visit are all-important, for logically he is the most likely to have committed the crime. However ancient, he may have had a violent quarrel with his mistress, beaten her half to death, then drowned her.'

'But why?'

'Perhaps the mysterious coachman was not a threat but a rival. Perhaps the old man thought himself cuckolded. They say that age is no bar to strong emotions.'

The Apothecary fingered his chin. 'That wretched coachman keeps cropping up and yet I still have no idea who he could possibly be. I'll have to visit Mother Hamp again.'

'And try Toby.'

'Toby Wills? The waiter who saw the murderer?'

'He knew about the Frenchman, didn't he? I think he still might have more to tell you, Mr Rawlings.'

John sighed. 'Back to the Peerless Pool again.'

The clerk looked wise. 'Try to find him in The Old Fountain. He might be more relaxed in those surroundings, and I believe that most of the staff go there at nightfall when the Pleasure Gardens close.'

'I shall make a point of it. After I have plied Mother Hamp with gin, of course.'

Joe stood up. 'Well, I've plenty to report back, Sir, so I'll be on my way. Incidentally, Miss Mary Ann asked me to convey her compliments to you.'

'Impudent little madam,' John answered before he had stopped to think.

Joe raised a sandy brow. 'You're right there, Mr Rawlings. I've noticed her giving the eye to all and sundry, She's anxious to join the ranks of the women of the world, is that one.'

The Apothecary groaned. 'And her principal target is my apprentice.'

'Young Nick? Oh dear! He's at an age to bust out of his breeches, into the bargain.'

'Well, I've done my best with him.'

'Leicester Fields?'

'Yes.'

Joe looked sage. 'Ah well, one can only do so much, After that, what will be, will be.'

'Alas, yes.'

There was a twinkle about Joe Jago's eye. 'Mr Fielding tells me that Miss Coralie Clive will be going to Bath on behalf of the Public Office. It appears that he has received a letter from her.'

'I believe she is going to pretend to be the wife of an aged Italian diplomat and worm information out of all the gentlemen.'

'Then I wish her luck.'

'As do I, Joe.'

'That girl is something of a rum doxy, I must confess,' the clerk said with a grin.

'That,' answered John, 'she most certainly is.'

Exactly one hour later, the Apothecary lay in the rum doxy's arms, telling her about the death of Petronelle, his worst grief now at an end, his emotions beginning to sort themselves out.

'The old midwife,' said Coralie, when she had heard it all.

'I beg your pardon?'

'Did you not tell me before that a terrible old woman goes on duty at St Luke's at night? She would be the one who would have given the poor child an overdose, too full of gin to notice.'

'We can't prove that.'

'No, of course not. But the chances are very likely, would you not agree?'

Just for one wonderfully challenging yet comfortable moment, John had a vivid picture of what it would be like to be married to Coralie Clive: the excitement, the arguments, the discussions, the love.

'I agree, you rum mort, you.'

She laughed. 'Did Joe call me that?'

'No, he called you a doxy — and he's right.'

The actress changed the subject. 'I leave for Bath in the morning.'

'Where will you stay?'

'Where you did, at The Bear. It seems centrally placed and well thought of.'

'Has Mr Fielding written to you?'

'Yes. He suggests, as you did, that I find out all I can about Orlando, the coachman Jack, and Sir Vivian.'

'We must know what Sweeting was up to with those children.'

'I shall make the coachman my first target.'

'Be careful.'

Coralie undid a button. 'Why?'

'Because I care for you.'

'Why don't you come and join me there in a few days? Then you can rescue me from the clutches of all those wicked men.'

'That,' John answered gravely, 'is exactly what I intend to do.'

The Shepherd and Shepherdess hostelry and tea garden, built at the turn of the century, commanded a supreme view of the fields stretching to Islington. In fact, even though it stood at the top end of Ratcliff Row, it was really a country inn and a well-known place for convalescence, poorly people coming to stay there in order to benefit from the pure air of the neighbourhood. But for those fitter mortals who had no need to be residents, there was the attraction of cakes and cream and furmity, all served in the tea garden overlooking the attractive vista. Knowing the inn's reputation for good food, and anxious to see his old friend again, John had sent a message to Samuel to meet him there as soon as he could after both their shops were closed. Thus, at six o'clock, the Goldsmith strolled into the garden and found his friend tucking into an extremely severe high tea.

'Well met,' he said, thumping John on the shoulder. 'How goes it all? I expect there have been a lot of developments.'

'A mass,' the Apothecary answered, and brought Samuel up to date while another vast spread was ordered and attacked.

The Goldsmith's eyes widened over his fruit tart. 'So Toby admitted that he lied?'

'Yes, in the end he was very helpful. However, Joe Jago thinks he might know something further. Something about the mysterious coachman.'

Even as he said the words, John's voice trailed away, and he sat with his mouth wide open, a jam-laden scone, halfway to his lips, arrested in mid-air.

'Of course!' he exclaimed loudly. 'Why didn't I see it before? The coachman. Of course.'

Samuel stared at him blankly. 'What are you talking about?'

'Jack, the coachman. The boy brought up by Sir Vivian, the one who remembered Hannah Rankin. He and the coachman who called on her have to be one and the same.'

'How...?'

But Samuel's question was drowned as John rushed on. 'The man was seen sitting on the coachman's box by Mother Hamp. The conveyance was parked outside her front door and had a coat of arms on the side. It was obviously Sir Vivian's coach driven there by jack from Bath. No wonder Hannah was afraid of him. It must have been like the past coming back to haunt her.' He turned his gaze on Samuel. 'You must remember all this. You were there.'

'Of course I remember it. But not having met Jack I feel at something of a disadvantage.'

'Well, accept it from me, he fits the bill completely. I must write to Coralie at once and tell her.'

The Goldsmith's affable face took on a gossipy look. 'I take it, as much from what you haven't said as from what you have, that your relationship with her has passed the point of no return?'

John gazed at him blankly for a second, then burst out laughing. 'What a terrible euphemism. Why don't you come straight out with it? But the answer is yes, we have at long last been to bed together. And yes, my dear friend, before you ask, it was as wonderful as I had always dreamed it might be. And yes, yes, yes, I do want to marry her, but the little witch won't have me.'

'Oh, not that wedded-to-the-theatre pose of hers again?'

'Yes, again. But one day I shall marry her. Coralie is for me, Samuel. That fact is inescapable.'

'But does she know?'

'Deep in her heart I think she does. All I am waiting for is the moment when she admits it.'

'Then I wish you joy, my friend, with all sincerity.'

Samuel was so patently pleased that John flung his arms around him and hugged him over the tea table, dislodging a custard as he did so. Wiping his sleeve and dabbing at his cheek, the Apothecary could not help but laugh at the expressions on the faces of the other patrons, to whose sour looks the Goldsmith responded by throwing a cream bun high in the air.

'Champagne!' he shouted loudly, then looked duly remorseful as a child sitting close by burst into tears with the shock of it all.

As dusk fell over the flower-filled fields, above the distant sound of the lowing herds winding their way home to peaceful Islington, the noise of a bell chimed from the direction of the Peerless Pool.

'Closing-down time,' said John. 'This is where we make our way to The

Old Fountain and hope that Toby will come in for his usual nightly drink.'

'Indeed,' answered Samuel solemnly. 'There's work to be done.'

They were both very slightly inebriated and walked with care down the path leading from Ratcliff Row across the fields to the eastern corner of the Pleasure Gardens, where stood The Old Fountain hostelry.

'We should have called on Mother Hamp while we were there,' John commented, looking over his shoulder.

'Why don't I run back and invite her to join us for a gin?'

'Do you think she can stagger this far?'

'I see no reason why not.'

'Then we'll meet inside. I'll get hold of Toby — if he appears.'

'He will,' Samuel answered confidently. 'This is going to be a lucky night.'

He strode off, leaving John to pick his way in the moonlight, muttering a childhood rhyme beneath his breath.

'To The Shepherd and Shepherdess then they go
To tea with their wives, for a constant rule;
And next cross the lane to The Fountain also,
And there they all sit, so pleasant and cool,
And see, in and out,
The folk walk about,'
And the gentlemen angling in Peerless Pool.'

It was a little misleading, of course, as fishing was done in the Fish Pond, but John presumed, though he had never questioned the verse before, that the line referred to the Pleasure Garden as a whole.

His mind wandered, contemplating the beauty of the night, the exquisite surroundings of Old Street, its ancient Moor Fields to the right, the splendour of the Peerless Pool and the sweep of meadows to the left. He was unprepared, therefore, when a figure detached itself from a spinney of trees and took his arm. Instinctively the Apothecary's hand reached for his pistol, which he always carried when visiting strange parts of the metropolis, but a voice in his ear said, 'There's no need for that, Sir.'

'Toby?' he said into the darkness.

'No, Sir. It's Forbes, from the asylum. There's something I have to say to you and it's best said here, in private.'

John turned and saw in the fitful moonlight that it was indeed the warder who stood beside him.

'Go on.'

'It's about Petronelle.'

'What about her?'

'I feel her death somewhat on my conscience.'

'Because you left her in the care of Mother Richard and she subsequently died of an overdose of laudanum.'

'How did you know it was the midwife who gave it to her?'

'It didn't take a genius to work it out. Nor even an apothecary,' John added wryly.

'But there's something else too.'

'What is it?'

'As you know, St Luke's opened seven years ago, in 1751. Petronelle came to us four years later, when she was about thirteen. She was all right then. In truth, Sir, I think she might have recovered from her madness. Every day she grew in strength, both physical and mental. Dr Thomas Crow took particular notice of her and, by God, I swear he was on the point of curing her.'

'So what went wrong?'

'Hannah Rankin joined the staff and the girl became uncontrollable. I vow and declare to you, Sir, as I must answer on the blessed day of judgment, I had to tie Petronelle down to stop the girl killing herself when she first saw the new warder.'

'Forbes, what are you trying to tell me?' John asked, peering into the warder's face in the intermittent moonlight.

'That Petronelle was terrified, Sir. It was fear of Hannah that drove her crazy in the end. If that woman hadn't come to us, Dr Crow would have been able to find the child a place in society.'

'Christ's wounds! Are you saying that Petronelle had met Hannah before?'

'I'd give an oath that she had, Sir.'

'Then what I feared must be true,' said the Apothecary, shaking his head. 'Dear God, what sink of darkness is about to be revealed?'

It was in sombre mood that John entered The Old Fountain and ordered himself a glass of brandy wine. A mood so dark indeed that when Samuel pummelled a fist into his shoulder and he turned to see Mother Hamp's toothless grin, the Apothecary could barely raise a smile.

'She's here,' said the Goldsmith, but his eyes were already narrowing at his friend's lack of response.

'So I see,' answered John, and made a tremendous and half-successful attempt to rally.

'Greetings, lovely boy,' said Mother Hamp, drunk as a fiddler's bitch and jolly into the bargain.

Knowing that he would probably never again find her so affable, John responded in kind.

'May I say how bonny you look this evening, Ma'am?'

She simpered, a terrible sight indeed. 'I'm too old for you, young gentleman.'

Heaven forbid! thought the Apothecary, but still he maintained his charming smile.

'Ma'am, I have one more question to ask you regarding Hannah Rankin.'

'And what might that be?' Under the table she fondled his knee.

'It's about the coachman; the one who called on her, the one she was afraid of.'

'What about him?'

'Did you ever get a good look at his face? Could you describe him to me?'

'Well, like I said, he was a big man. Tall and broad and rather set of appearance.'

'What do you mean?'

'He seemed stern to me.'

'What sort of age was he?'

The old woman shook her head. 'That I couldn't say. He kept his hat pulled well down. He could have been anything between twenty and fifty.'

'Can you not be a little more specific?'

Mother Hamp downed her gin and turned to Samuel. 'He uses long words, don't he.'

'He means have you no idea of the coachman's exact age.'

'No I ain't,' the old woman answered crossly.

'Very well,' said the Apothecary, knowing a lost cause when he saw one. But then his attention was caught by Toby Wills, coming into the ale-house as if all the troubles of the world rested on his shoulders.

'Toby,' John called, and the waiter looked up.

'Yes, Sir?'

'Would it be possible to have a word with you?'

The man's entire visage changed and he looked as fierce as daggers. 'No, Sir, it wouldn't. I thought you and I said all there was to say when we spoke yesterday.'

John got to his feet. 'I thank you for the help you gave me then. All I wanted to find out further was how you knew about the ancient Frenchman and his association with Hannah Rankin.'

'It was common knowledge round St Luke's. Mother Richard, the old midwife who worked there from time to time, gossiped of it constantly.'

'And what about Hannah's other friend, the coachman? Was he the subject of gossip too?'

Toby returned a completely blank stare. 'What coachman might that be, Sir?' he said. Then he turned away to hide the fact that once more he was lying.

Chapter Fifteen

Early the next morning, after, for him, a very modest breakfast, John set out to walk to Bow Street, having first sent Nicholas Dawkins round with a note to say he was on his way. As the Apothecary trod the familiar route, he frowned in concentration, his mind teeming with all the facts with which it had been filled since he had last spoken to John Fielding. Uppermost was the vital information that poor dead Petronelle had recognised and been terrified of Hannah Rankin, followed by the extraordinary fact that the Marquis de Saint Ombre had been Hannah's lover. All this, together with John's certainty that the mysterious coachman who had visited her was none other than Jack from Bath, made the Apothecary long to hear the Blind Beak's opinion.

However, in the event, the pieces of intelligence had already been passed on. The Magistrate and his clerk were breakfasting together and the subject under discussion was the Frenchman. Joining them and taking a large slice of ham and bread at Mr Fielding's insistence, John entered the conversation.

'He really is a disgusting creature. Let me tell you about the painting on his bedroom wall.'

''Zauns!' exclaimed Joe, when he had listened. 'I reckon he must be a lecherous old goat.'

'The child in the picture is interesting,' said the Blind Beak thoughtfully.

'In what way?'

'Because wherever we turn in this case some poor benighted youngster seems to come to the surface.'

'What do you think about Forbes's statement that Petronelle lived in dread of Hannah Rankin?'

'It does not necessarily prove that the child had known her before.'

'That may well be true, Sir. But none the less I find it very significant.'

The Blind Beak nodded and steepled his fingers. He turned his head towards his clerk. 'What did you find out from the Marquis's friends?'

'Well,' said Joe, 'unless the beastly old bastard has mastered the art of being in two places at once he is certainly not our killer.'

'He was where he said he was?'

'All the evening until late, long beyond the time when Toby saw the extraordinary apparition in the bird mask.'

'Talking of Toby,' John put in, 'he has taken to lying again.' And he explained how the waiter had reacted to his question about the coachman.

'But I have a theory,' the Apothecary continued.

'Which is?'

'That Hannah's mysterious visitor was the young man I met in Bath.'

'Orlando?'

'No. Jack.' And John set out in detail his precise reasons for thinking so.

Mr Fielding became very still, a sure sign that he was absorbing everything, while Joe Jago nodded as the various points were made.

'Do you think Jack's motive was blackmail?'

John shook his head. 'He isn't that type somehow. Too honest a soul. No, I think he wanted revenge for all that had happened to him in the past.'

'But that is just the point,' boomed the Blind Beak. 'We don't know what happened in the past. We are only surmising that Sir Vivian Sweeting was engaged in something unsavoury as regards those children. Perhaps he looked after them out of the kindness of his heart.'

'Well, I shall be returning to Bath within the next few days and this time I am not leaving until I have discovered the truth: the truth about him, about Hannah, about Orlando, about them all.'

'Perhaps you will get there to find that Miss Clive has already done so.'

'I just hope she doesn't put herself in any danger while she's about it,' John repeated for the hundredth time.

'Miss Clive is more than capable of looking after herself,' the Magistrate reassured him, then rumbled his deep and tuneful chuckle, just as if he could see the look on the Apothecary's discomfited face.

The shop was unusually quiet that day, and John was just thinking that he would be quite justified in leaving early in order to attend his dinner engagement with Lord Anthony and Lady Dysart, an invitation issued to him via Sir Gabriel when he had returned home late the previous evening, when the doorbell rang. Coming round from the compounding room where he and Nicholas were working, the Apothecary was irritated to see the pert and pretty Mary Ann Whittingham, accompanied by a miserable-looking maid, come hobbling across the threshold, her face contorted as if every step hurt. Instantly suspecting a ruse, John went to meet her.

'You seem in some distress, young lady. What is the nature of your injury?'

'Oh, I've sprained my ankle,' she answered in a loud voice, obviously so that Nicholas could hear her at the back. 'Please can you, or Nicholas if you are too busy, treat it for me?'

Treating her to a glacial stare instead, John answered, 'Then be so kind as to remove your shoe and stocking. I will have to examine you.'

The little wretch had the temerity to reply, 'Is that quite proper?'

'You can take your choice,' John stated tartly. 'Either you go elsewhere for treatment or you allow me to look at the injury.'

Nicholas appeared, scarlet-faced. 'Do as Mr Rawlings says, Mary Ann. He cannot possibly help you unless you cooperate.'

She shot him a look from beneath a dark fringe of lashes. 'Oh, Nick, you took me by surprise. I didn't realise that you were in the shop.'

'And where did you think he would be?' John asked crossly. 'It is usual for an apprentice to be with his Master.

'I thought he might be running errands.'

'Well, he isn't. Now, let me see what you have done.'

Crouching down beside her, the Apothecary took the young but shapely limb in his hands, feeling round the delicate ankle for any indication of breakage. Needless to say there were none, nor indeed was there any sign of bruising. The maid averted her gaze, as if he were doing something intimate.

'So where is the pain?'

'There.' She pointed to an invisible injury.

'Well, I can't find anything wrong. Now, does this hurt?'

He gave her ankle a tight squeeze, watching her reaction carefully. Tears of apparent pain appeared in Mary Ann's eyes.

'Yes, it does. Very much.'

'I see.'

She was a clever little actress, the Apothecary had to grant her that. Totally convinced that she was faking, he stood considering what to do next. And it was then that Nicholas intervened and showed exactly the nature of the man that he was rapidly becoming.

'Mary Ann,' he said, his voice quiet and forbearing but extremely firm, 'you are not to try Mr Rawlings's patience nor waste his time any longer. I am sorry, but I do not believe that you have hurt yourself. I think you have come here to talk to me. And why? Because last night I told you that, for both our sakes, it would be better if our courtship were, temporarily at least, to end. As a mere apprentice I am not in a position to settle down and take care of you as you deserve. You must understand that, surely.'

The pretty little thing distorted her features into a terrible scowl and stamped her so-called injured foot hard upon the floor.

'It is because you don't love me that you finished with me. That's the truth of the matter.'

'No, it isn't. You know how I feel. It is just that at this stage of my career my hands are tied.'

'Of course they are,' put in John. 'As an apprentice, Nicholas is not allowed to marry until his indentures are at an end.'

Mary Ann wept genuine tears of distress. She was only a child, after all, albeit a precocious and advanced one.

'I wanted to be his sweetheart, not his wife.'

'Worse and worse. You are far too young for such things.'

'I am fourteen years of age.'

'Still not old enough.'

Mary Ann glared at the Muscovite from suddenly pouring eyes. 'How could you show me up like this in front of Mr Rawlings? I hate you for it.'

'I had to stop you making a spectacle of yourself. Don't you understand that?'

She shot to her feet. 'No, I don't, you disgusting wretch. I wish that I had never set eyes on you. I've a good mind to go into town and find myself a proper man. Come, Lizzie, let us go.'

'Don't you dare…' Nicholas began, but to deaf ears. Without a backward glance, Mary Ann hurtled from the shop at the speed of a greyhound, the downtrodden maid trundling behind, and disappeared down Shug Lane.

'I'll go after her.'

'No, don't,' answered John, physically blocking his apprentrice's path. 'The sight of you will make her even angrier.' And he hurried off after the girl himself, ignoring the fact that he was still wearing his long apron.

There was no sign of her in any direction, and after fifteen minutes of searching John could only presume that she had hailed a chair and gone home. Perturbed and anxious, he went back to the shop.

'Was I too cruel?' said Nicholas, his face suspiciously peaky.

'You weren't cruel at all. You did what had to be done.'

The Muscovite looked serious. 'I hope Mary Ann doesn't do anything foolish. I would hate Mr and Mrs Fielding to know how naughty she really is.'

'Well, I shall keep my own counsel on that score,' John answered, and wondered why a distinct chill of unease swept over him.

Forgetting the inauspicious events of the early afternoon, the Apothecary could not have enjoyed the dinner party, held at a fashionable four o'clock, more. Striving to widen their circle of London friends, the Dysarts had invited not only Sir Gabriel and his son, together with Louis and Serafina and the redoubtable Dr Drake and Matilda, but also half a dozen sparkling people, all of whom had something to contribute to the evening's success. Seated next to a charming young lady who turned out to be the daughter of one of Lord Anthony's old friends, John was both flattered and attracted by the brilliance of her eyes, and had to remind himself quite severely that he was currently engaged in a relationship with Coralie, albeit a somewhat unconventional one.

Yet despite the attractions of his dinner partner and the fact that general conversation never waned, the Apothecary was constantly aware of Lady Dysart's gaze upon him, and could almost feel her willing him to have a private word with her. The moment came as they made their way in to cards.

Drawing close to him, his hostess whispered, 'Can you spare me a moment, Mr Rawlings?'

He gave a slight bow. 'Gladly, Madam.'

'Have you by chance heard anything of Meredith?'

John shook his head. 'Of him himself, no. Yet strangely, when I was in Bath recently, I was told a story that was so similar to his it gave me quite a shock.'

'What was this story?'

'It was about the daughter of Lady Allbury. Apparently the child was playing in the grounds of Prior Park and vanished from there under her mother's very nose. Nothing has ever been heard of her since.'

Ambrosine Dysart's hand went to her throat. 'You realise that our Somerset home was only twenty miles from Bath?'

'No, I wasn't aware of that. Did you know Lady Allbury, by any chance?'

'The name is familiar. But after the scandal of our daughter eloping with one of the servants we socialised very little and hardly ever went into the city.'

'I am going back there in a few days' time. I wonder if I might have permission to visit your home.'

Ambrosine's eyebrows rose. 'Well, of course you may. Gregg, our steward, is there at the moment. He would be pleased to show you around. But, forgive me, what would be the point? After all these years. what could you possibly learn? When all's said and done, the disappearance took place in Paris.'

The Apothecary nodded. 'You're perfectly right, of course. But yet I can't deny a feeling that the cases of Lucy Allbury and your grandson were somehow connected, on different sides of the Channel though they might have been.'

'Why do you think that?'

'Because of the modus operandi. Two children playing in a garden, their guardians not far away. The facts are too similar to be a coincidence in my view.'

The beautiful eyes brimmed with tears. 'That is the first ray of hope I have had in ages.'

John took her hands in his, 'Please don't look on it in that way. It is a course of enquiry that will never bring them back. It is just my own curiosity that drives me to pursue the connection.'

Ambrosine wept in earnest. 'But you are the first person in a decade to take an interest in Meredith. Anthony gave up hope years ago, when the last of the searches was called off. It was only I who kept faith.'

'I admire you for it, Lady Dysart, but I do beg you to be realistic. It is my certain belief that Meredith has gone for good.'

But even as he said the words, something right at the back of the Apothecary's mind denied what he was actually saying. If Ambrosine's grandson had been sold into the world of child prostitution or slavery, there was really no reason why he should be dead at all.

They played cards well into the late evening, when Ambrosine, clearly delighted to see her guests having such a good time, ordered a cold supper to be served. Eventually, with the hour fast approaching eleven, the visitors called for their carriages and prepared to leave. Serafina, going to kiss John farewell, whispered in his ear.

'My dear, you must come and see me. Soon I shall be too large to go into polite society and will need all my friends to cheer me.' She looked at him with a smile. 'You appear very well, by the way. Does everything go smoothly in your life?'

Unable to resist sharing his secret with the woman he had always so greatly admired, John lowered his voice. 'Recently, Coralie and I have become very close.'

She pealed with laughter and pointed to the rounding of her body. 'I've been very close to Louis, too.'

The Apothecary hugged her tightly. 'If you had not been married.'

'But I was, wasn't I?'

'You were indeed.'

'Are you making love to my wife again?' said Louis, coming up to them.

'It is a habit I find hard to break.'

The Comte shrugged. 'Ah well, I shall try to overlook it on this occasion, but take heed.'

'I'd thrash the rascal,' said jolly Dr Drake, enjoying the joke.

'Trés bon, I will,' answered Louis, and started to remove his coat.

'Gentlemen,' said Ambrosine, full of some inner elation of her own, 'no fisticuffs, if you please.'

John and Louis bowed and politely shook hands, just as if they had acceded to their hostess's wishes, and the party broke up with much mirth and good humour, made all the gayer by the fact that everyone was slightly tipsy.

Yet the Apothecary's euphoric state began to pass as the coach turned out of Gerrard Street into Nassau Street, and he saw more illumination in Sir Gabriel's house than was usual at this hour of the night. In his corner seat, John's father slumbered and noticed nothing, but the Apothecary was wide awake and bounded down the carriage step even while the postillion was lowering it for him.

The footman who answered the door was solemn with import. 'You have a visitor, Sir. I have shown him into the library.'

'Who is it?'

'One of the Runners from Bow Street, Sir,'

'At this time of night? Oh dear, that does not augur well.'

'I think there could indeed be bad news,' the footman replied, shaking his head slowly and loving every minute of it.

John, not even stopping to remove his cloak, hurried through the library door only to find Benjamin Rudge, a familiar figure, standing uncomfortably before the fire.

'Mr Rudge,' the Apothecary said, frankly astonished. 'What are you doing here?'

'I've come with a message from Mr Fielding, Sir. He wants you to attend him at once.'

'Why? What has come about?'

'It's Mary Ann, Sir.'

John's heart plummeted, seeing again the angry little girl running off into the dangerous streets, her maid already several paces behind. 'What has happened to her?'

'She's gone missing. She went out shopping earlier today, accompanied by a servant. But somehow Mary Ann managed to elude her and the maid came home alone. There's been neither sight nor sound of her since.'

'Oh my God!'

'Mr Fielding wondered,' Runner Rudge continued, apparently not noticing the Apothecary's shocked expression, 'if you might have seen her.'

'She called into, my shop early this afternoon. But I'll tell him all that face to face. Do you have a carriage outside?'

'In the mews, Sir.'

'Then I'll travel with you, if I may. But first let me wake someone who should know about this.'

And without further explanation John left the library and hurried up two flights of stairs to the top floor, where slept the servants and his apprentice. In his small, neat room, its tidiness somewhat reminiscent of a ship's cabin, Nicholas Dawkins lay fast asleep, his pale face rosy with slumber. In order not to startle the young man, John did not shake him but simply repeated his name several times until finally the Muscovite opened his eyes. Instantly an anxious look came into them.

'Master?'

'Nick, you must get up and get dressed. We're going to the Public Office.'

'Why, Sir?'

'It's Mary Ann. She's disappeared.'

The Muscovite gazed at John uncomprehendingly. 'But she can't have done. We saw her only this afternoon.'

'And I imagine that we were probably the last to do so. Now get your clothes on and prepare for a night of searching.'

And so saying, the Apothecary left him and went downstairs to find Sir Gabriel.

Chapter Sixteen

Even though it was now past midnight, every candle in the Public Office had been lit and there seemed to be people everywhere. As John and Nicholas made their way up to Mr Fielding's first-floor salon, they passed innumerable persons going down, some of them so dirty and rough that the Apothecary guessed at once that the Blind Beak had called in the peachers, those shady members of the criminal class who made a living by informing on others. Inside the room itself there were more of them, some of the peachers sitting on the floor for fear of dirtying Mrs Fielding's elegant chairs. John was vividly reminded of a similar occasion when the Magistrate had called in the help of this brutal brigade whilst investigating a murder at the Theatre Royal, Drury Lane.

Mr Fielding was speaking. '...I regard this girl as though she were my flesh-and-blood daughter. No stone must be left unturned in the search for her. All the Runners are out, as are the Brave Fellows with the coach, so now I must rely on you chaps to assist me. There's a good reward for whoever brings Mary Ann in.' The Blind Beak moved his head slightly. 'Is it you, Mr Rawlings, who has just come into the room?'

'Yes, Sir.'

'When Mary Ann left the house she said something about calling in at your shop. Did she in fact do so?'

Realising that he was skating on very thin ice, and most anxious to protect both Nicholas and Mary Ann, John chose his words carefully. 'Your niece came in during the early afternoon, Sir. She complained of having ricked her ankle on the cobbles. I examined her and could find little wrong, just a minor injury perhaps. In playful spirit, Nicholas teased her with malingering and instead of seeing the joke, Mary Ann became angry and ran into the street, ordering the servant to do likewise. I pursued her but could not find her, so concluded that she had hailed chairs and gone home.'

There was a horrid silence during which the peachers and the two Runners who were present all turned to look at poor Nicholas, who turned the colour of a wild rose.

Mr Fielding cleared his throat, an ominous sound in that deadly quiet. Then he said, 'Did you upset my niece, Mr Dawkins?'

'I think I did, Sir. But no harm was meant. I am very fond of her.'

'You are saying to me that a jape went wrong?'

The Muscovite began to stutter a reply, but John hastily answered for him. 'They are good friends, Sir. And everyone knows how friends can fall out from time to time.'

'Yes,' said Mr Fielding, but his features were stem and severe. He turned back to the general assembly.

'Runners, peachers, do your best. Joe Jago has divided London into areas. Each of you, working in twos, will be allotted a district. I want every house searched, every room looked into, every alleyway combed. My niece must be found at all costs. We have the rest of tonight and all of the next day in which to do so. I suggest that we meet here again at six o'clock tomorrow night in order to compare notes.'

A ruffian spoke up. 'But what if she's not found by then, Beak?'

Mr Fielding looked exceedingly solemn, 'In that case I'm afraid that I would fear for her life.' He stood up, his cane tapping before him. 'Now, I must go to my wife, who is beside herself with grief and needs my company. Jago, the meeting is yours.'

'Very good, Sir.' The clerk turned to the assembled crowd of peachers, one of whom, John noted with interest, was a slatternly woman. 'If you will come downstairs to the Public Office I will allocate you your areas.'

They all trooped down, the smell of their unwashed bodies wafting before them.

'My God, Sir,' Nicholas whispered, clutching John's sleeve. 'What have I done? Surely I can't have driven Mary Ann to her death?'

'I cannot believe that you have. Now, concentrate. Joe's handing out instructions.'

'The area of Covent Garden,' the clerk was saying, 'being so difficult to search, I am giving that to Mr Rawlings and Mr Dawkins, together with Runners Rudge and Thompson. Little Will and Sukie, you are to go in as well and mingle with the crowd. See what you can learn just from keeping your eyes and ears open. If you get wind of the girl, don't try to do anything yourselves. Find a Runner. Is that clear?'

The slatternly girl and a most peculiar tiny man, no more than four feet high, nodded.

'Mr Rawlings, Mr Dawkins, you are to search as gentlemen would. Go to those places where the quality folk are to be found.'

'Very good,' said John.

He turned to leave, anxious to begin the quest, but the slattern pulled at his sleeve. ''Ere, d'ye want a word of advice?'

'Yes.'

She pulled his head down and cupped her hands to whisper in his ear. 'You've 'eard of Jack Harris, the procurer? Well, 'e might be worth having a word with.'

'Why?'

"Cos 'e can get girls — little girls — for those gallants who like that sort of thing. If the girl's been picked up for that work, 'e'll know where to find her.'

The Apothecary's blood ran cold. 'Do you really think...?'

'Yes, I do. Any child wandering the streets of London would be taken in five minutes, and don't you imagine otherwise.'

'And where will I locate this Jack Harris?'

The slattern grinned, displaying a set of rapidly decaying teeth.

''E doubles up as a waiter at The Shakespeare 'Ead. That's 'ow 'e makes 'is honest shillings. The rest, we don't talk about.'

John squeezed her ragged arm. 'Thank you for your help.'

'Fink nothin' of it,' the girl answered, and with a fine swing of her hips, went out into the night.

Despite the lateness of the hour, Covent Garden swarmed with people, for this, to use Mr Fielding's own words, was London's most infamous quarter, where every whim was catered for and total provision made for the desires of the flesh. There were more prostitutes per square yard in Covent Garden than in any other part of the capital, and every building was of ill repute; either a brothel, a seedy lodging establishment, a tavern boasting private rooms for assignations, a bagnio where depravity was the code, or a gaming hell. There were also some nefarious coffee houses, the most notorious of which was Tom's. Founded by the late Tom King, an old Etonian, it had been and still was the haunt of every buck, blood, demi-rip and choice spirit in London. Further, after Tom's death, the place had passed to a certain witty woman called Moll King, though whether she had ever been Tom's wife nobody seemed to know. Whatever, under her guidance the coffee house had become even more popular, and was frequented night after night by fashionable fops and noblemen, attired in swords and bags and rich brocaded silks, flocking there after they had left court in the evening, wishing to be entertained till dawn broke over the city. But it was not to Tom's, situated by the portico of St Paul's Church, that John led a pale-faced Nicholas. Instead he made his way to the Piazza, close to which stood The Shakespeare Head.

Women for hire abounded on every side of the square, encouraged by the fact that they were partially hidden beneath the shadow of the Piazza's arches. Fresh-faced girls from the country, unable to afford the fare home, offered themselves; milliners, seamstresses and other tradeswomen strove to enhance their meagre wages; bloated, savage whores, clap-riddled and poxy, promised customers a carnal experience in a dark alley for a shilling; wretched servants, dismissed from their employment because they had been seduced by the master or the footman — or both — begged for trade in order that they might eat.

Horribly fascinated, John could hardly credit the difference in their ages and was aghast that skinny little things of twelve, their meagre bodies not yet fully developed, should have to walk alongside raddled strumpets of seventy in order to ply their wretched trade. Producing a coin, he linked arms with a runt of a creature and took her to the door of The Shakespeare Head, where he paid her and let her go. Nicholas, who had not had the foresight to fend off the drabs, literally had to fight free of all the arms trying to grab him as he, too, stepped into the tavern.

It was a seedy place, thick with pipe smoke and the stench of stale ale and sweaty bodies. Set out in a series of boxes, in which blustering boys and blowsy buttocks sat drinking their fill before they moved to the private apartments above, the main room had a second leading off it where piquet was being played for feverishly high stakes. Lumbering between the two rooms, waiting on table, was, John felt reasonably certain, the man he had come to see, the arch-procurer himself, Jack Harris.

Tall and thin, Harris none the less had hunched shoulders and a flabby beer paunch. But it was his face which interested the Apothecary, who considered it one of the most unappealing he had ever seen. Wispy grey hair surrounded an enormous, moon-like, heavily chinned visage, in which bulging short-sighted eyes, a pitted nose and blubbery lips were the predominant features. Huge gappy teeth, badly chipped and brown with tobacco, appeared as the procurer opened his mouth to breathe, confirming John's theory that he was adenoidal.

'Is that him?' Nicholas whispered, following the Apothecary's gaze.

'I think so. I'll call him over.' He clicked his fingers, and the waiter looked up. 'Mr Harris?' The man nodded. 'Would you be so good as to serve this table.' John winked.

The other smiled knowingly. 'Straight away, Sir.'

The Apothecary fixed Nicholas with a look and lowered his voice. 'I am about to act out a role. Do not be shocked at anything you hear.'

'I was at sea, remember, Master.'

'Let's hope the experience stands you in good stead. And don't call me Master. You are a young debauchee. As depraved in thought and deed as I am.'

And with those words the Apothecary slanted his brows up at the ends, narrowed his eyes and put such a dark, evil look on his face that his apprentice was quite startled that the affable and friendly John Rawlings could command such a demonic countenance.

'How may I help you, Sir?' asked Harris, bowing as he approached.

'I think you know how,' John answered, once more winking an eye.

'You wish to see my list of Covent Garden ladies?'

'In a way, yes, I do.'

Jack Harris pursed his large, moist mouth. 'I don't quite understand you, Sir.'

'I would like to see your list of young ladies, my friend. Nothing over fifteen interests me at all. Besides which, I have a certain enthusiasm.'

'Most gentlemen have,' Harris answered thickly, leaning down so that he could whisper. Close to, it could be observed that his bulbous lower lip was also stained by constant use of a pipe. He had to be, John thought, one of the most unattractive specimens ever born.

'I'm sure they do. But only mine concerns me.'

Harris looked wise and tapped the side of his nose. 'May I guess at it?'

'By all means.'

'You are particularly excited by defloration.'

John's expression became lewd to the point of depravity. 'How clever of you to know.'

'Then I am right?'

The Apothecary nodded. 'What do you have on offer for tonight?'

Harris fingered his several chins. 'Well, I have a Nelly Blossom, so new to town her feet are still wet with dew. No man's been near her, I can assure you of that.'

John's eyes glistened. 'She sounds very interesting. How much?'

'Twenty guineas.'

'And her age?'

Jack Harris's myopic gaze glazed slightly. 'I'm not too sure, Sir.'

'Is she fifteen or more?'

'I think she could be.'

'Then I am not interested. What else do you have?'

'Well, there's little Miss Molly. Her teeth aren't up to much but she has incomparably fine legs which are yet to grip a saddle.'

'I can't abide poor teeth,' the Apothecary answered, with a dismissive wave of his hand. 'What else?'

There was no doubt that Harris was racking his brains. Virgins were specially prepared for those with defloration mania, but were not always in plentiful supply. John decided to help him out.

'I don't mind someone entirely new, untrained. Indeed, I quite like 'em raw.'

The procurer looked thoughtful. 'I believe Mrs Tredille had something brought in today. Something utterly unpolished, in fact with no instruction at all. Might be a bit of a handful, mind.'

The Apothecary twitched his brows. 'What fun!'

Harris's moon face grew surly. 'Pardon me for mentioning it, Sir, but what about your companion here? I hope that you weren't expecting two for the price of one.'

Nicholas blushed crimson but managed to mutter, 'I pay my own way.'

'Then that's all right then,' answered Harris, all smiles and winks again.

'That's as may be,' John put in. 'Tell me how old this unpolished thing is before I take a look at it.'

'Fourteen — or so she claims.'

The Apothecary stood up. 'Has she been put in a bagnio window yet?'

'She most certainly has. I'll get a boy to escort you.'

'Well,' said John, rubbing his hands together, 'this is obviously going to be a very exciting night.'

And he smiled at Nicholas, who had broken out in a sweat at the sheer stress of it all.

* * *

Since the Roman invasion of Britain, there had always been public baths of one kind or another, even though from time to time they had fallen out of fashion. Baths were forgotten after the Romans left, but the returning Crusaders had reintroduced the population to the benefits of a Turkish bath, as the warriors called them. Indeed, a famous and respectable bath establishment in St James's Street was still called The Turk's Head even after so many centuries. Commonly known as 'stews', the baths had thrived in earlier times, but immoral business done on the side had brought objections from the Church, and many had been closed down. However, in Covent Garden they flourished, the bath just a cover, the real function of the place, prostitution.

Every bagnio had a window, and from seven at night until five in the morning these windows were filled by whores of every size and shape who, in the most impudent manner, invited customers to come inside. Hoping that he was not going to see Mary Ann in such degrading circumstances, but fairly certain that he was about to, the Apothecary followed the lantern-carrying boy away from the Piazza and down a side street. Here, deviation was king. Every house was devoted to pleasure of one kind or another, and every sixth building had the familiar lighted window with a female sitting in it. Repelled but drawn, John could not help but stare at the flesh on display, some of it very beautiful, some repulsive: fat, thin, black, white, very fair, raven-haired. Every possible combination of female charms was on display, all tastes catered for.

'We're nearly at the young un's place now, Sir,' said the boy, calling back over his shoulder.

'What do you mean?'

'The stew we're coming to is the kinchen's. There's no one over sixteen as works there. Mrs Tredille runs it but she's the only one full-fledged in the place.'

'Except for the customers,' John put in drily.

The boy said, 'What?', then laughed and repeated, 'Except for the gen'lemen.'

'What do we do if it is Mary Ann?' whispered Nicholas.

'I say I want to hire her, then somehow we steal her away.'

'Isn't that going to be difficult?'

'We'll have to judge the lie of the land when we get there. If the worst comes to the worst, I'll have to send you to find the Runners.'

'Pray we can do it ourselves. I don't want them to think ill of Mary Ann.'

'We can't be certain it is her in the bagnio at the moment. But you re right, if she's there the less Bow Street people who know about it, the better.'

'Does that include Mr Fielding?'

'I'm not certain yet.'

'We're here,' called the boy, and stopped short.

John and Nicholas stood transfixed, staring into the window, struck to the heart with horror.

They had dressed Mary Ann like a doll, her face painted, her hair bouncing round her head in a mass of ringlets. But to ruin the effect she had wept, in fact was sobbing even as they watched her, smudging her maquillage and covering her face with streaks.

'I'm going in,' said Nicholas, and would have run into the building had not John stayed his arm.

'Don't be so hasty. You'll ruin everything. We must carry the plan through whatever happens.'

'But she's suffering.'

'Not for much longer. Now, be calm.' John raised his voice. 'Run back and tell Mr Harris I like her,' he said to the boy. 'Here's a coin for your trouble.'

'Thank you, Sir.'

'Now, in we go,' he said.

The bagnio, probably because it was so specialised, catering for those whose needs could only be satisfied by the very young, almost had the air of a nursery about it. Every corner was carpeted, there was no noise or uproar; indeed, a feeling of luxury and pleasure pervaded the atmosphere. To add to the general quiet, there seemed absolutely no one in sight as they came through the front door, though lurking in shadowy corners John could make out the shapes of several hulking men, the bully-backs employed by brothels to throw out unruly clients. However, all charm and smiles, seated behind a large desk in the spacious hall, was Mrs Tredille herself, a vivacious redhead, no more than forty years old.

She got to her feet and curtseyed as John and Nicholas approached. 'Good evening, gentlemen. How may I help you?'

'We have been sent here by Jack Harris,' the Apothecary answered. 'He told us about the girl in the window, and to be frank with you I am more than interested. So interested, indeed, that I would like to hire her, my friend to follow immediately afterwards.'

Mrs Tredille dimpled a smile. 'I must warn you, Sir, that she is completely new. We've had no time to train her. She'll probably put up a bit of a fight.'

'As I told Harris, I might find that quite stimulating.'

'Then, gentlemen, if you would like to have a Turkish bath and some champagne, we'll take the girl upstairs for you.'

'We won't bother with the bath but the champagne will be in order.'

'Excellent.' Mrs Tredille rang a little bell. 'By the way, Sir, payment is always in advance. Twenty guineas. Each.'

'I am treating my young friend,' the Apothecary answered smoothly, and felt for his pocket book, praying that he had enough money on him.

Fortunately he had had the foresight to borrow from the shop, a bad habit but useful on this occasion, avoiding any possible hitch in his role as a rich young pervert, able to squander money to satisfy his degraded whims. And John was still acting out this part, a look of lecherous delight on his face, his tongue flicking over his lips, as he finally climbed the opulent staircase and was shown along a softly carpeted corridor.

Mrs Tredille, who had lit his way with a candelabra, curtseyed once more outside a door. 'We have dressed her prettily for you, Sir, but she's had no training in manners. Still I hope you will be satisfied,' and she turned the door knob. 'Mary Ann,' she called, 'here's your first gentleman. Now just you behave yourself or you'll fetch up with a beating.'

Silently, the Apothecary stepped inside and looked around him. The room was decorated in deep red, the hangings of the great bed the same opulent colour as the walls, the sheets and pillows, by contrast, virgin white. In the midst of this sensuous elegance, sitting up and hugging her knees, sat the Blind Beak's niece, her eyes enormous in a chalk-pale face, her small stature dwarfed by her surroundings, her shapely young body naked but for a lace shift.

'If you come near me I shall kill you,' she whispered defiantly, though her lower lip trembled at the hopelessness of her situation.

'No need for that,' the Apothecary answered, and stepped out of the shadows. 'I'm here to take you home, you horrible child, despite the fact that you've led me one of the most impossible dances of my life.'

Mary Ann hesitated, looking at him with all the special beauty of a girl on the very brink of maturity. 'Oh don't be cross with me, Mr Rawlings,' she said pitifully, and broke down into a sad and sobbing little bundle of humanity that begged to be taken care of.

Chapter Seventeen

'And how, my dear boy,' said Sir Gabriel, his voice rising in a crescendo of incredulity, 'did you ever get the wretched child out of such a sink of iniquity?'

John waved a hand to show that he was chewing a vast amount of toast and marmalade.

'With immense difficulty,' he answered after a convulsive swallow. 'Nick and I had made a last-minute plan, speaking in whispers over the champagne. He was to announce that he was going for a stroll while he waited for me — as the money had already been paid we knew there would be no objection to that — then search round the entire area for the Runners and return with them. We had hoped not to involve anyone else but could not see an alternative. In the event, though, Nick couldn't find them and came across Sukie, the female peacher. It so transpires that she has several little bastards and consequently no time for the likes of Mrs Tredille. In a short space of time she rallied several of her larger friends, to say nothing of Little Will, and they all came charging into the bagnio like the hounds of hell, waving cudgels and God alone knows what else. Hearing the racket, I bolted down the stairs with Mary Ann and threw a few fists to get us out into the street.

''Zeeth! And what of Nick?'

'He fought like a demon and loved every minute of it. I do believe that in his mind he saw himselfas a knight of yore rescuing his beloved from the clutches of evil.'

'And the beloved herself? How did she behave?'

'With remarkable coolness once she had got over her fit of weeping. The little imp actually played cards with me while we waited to be rescued.'

'I am afraid,' said Sir Gabriel severely, 'that I suffer an overwhelming urge to land a well-aimed smack on that particular party's arse.'

'She can be immensely irritating,' John answered with a grin.

'And what yarn did you pitch to the Magistrate – or did you tell him the truth?'

'I decided on the truth. It seemed to me that he of all people should know about Mrs Tredille's establishment.'

'Particularly in view of the refuge he has opened for orphaned girls.'

'Quite. Anyway, I returned scantily clad Mary Ann to the arms of her family.'

'And?'

'Her aunt cried and cuddled her. Mr Fielding gave her six of the best and cuddled her. And Nick, in a moment of total frenzy, asked for her hand in marriage, and cuddled her.'

'God's truth!' exclaimed Sir Gabriel, gulping his coffee. 'What then?'

'The Beak, may his patience be blessed, paid my poor apprentice the honour of listening to him with great seriousness, then suggested that all such proposals should be shelved until Mary Ann reaches the age of eighteen.'

'And do you think the little minx has learned a lesson from all this?'

John, mouth full again, nodded. 'Yes. She was very frightened indeed. I shall never forget her face as I walked into that room. It is criminal that children should be exploited in such a way.'

'Which leads me naturally to my next question. When do you return to Bath?'

'Today, dear Father. Joe Jago is taking on the task of seeing Toby and trying to find out what he knows about the mysterious coachman. And I intend to track down that same young coachman and learn the truth. I also want to follow a thought of my own.'

'Which is?'

'That the disappearances of Meredith Dysart and Lucy Allbury are in some way connected. It is not as far-fetched as it sounds. The Dysarts' Somerset home is only twenty miles from Bath.'

'Umm,' said Sir Gabriel, considering. 'You may well be right.' He smiled mischievously. 'Of course, there is one other thing that you will be anxious to discover as well.'

'Which is?'

'Just how much Miss Coralie Clive has missed you while you have been apart.'

'That,' John answered, 'is the thing I want to find out most of all.'

He travelled overnight as he had done before, ensuring he slept by taking a mild draught, and awoke next morning aching in most of his limbs but refreshed. Booking himself a room at The Bear, John enquired whether a Miss Clive was staying and was told no. However, a detailed description yielded the information that a Marchesa di Spinotti was in residence and resembled the lady he had depicted.

'Of course,' the Apothecary answered, and murmured something about the Marchesa using an alias when travelling abroad. 'And is the lady here now?' he asked.

'No. Madam has gone to the baths. You may well catch up with her in the Pump Room, Sir. I think it is her habit to go there.'

'Thank you,' said John, and went to his room to unpack and repair his dishevelled appearance before presenting himself to his beautiful mistress.

Afterwards he was glad that he had done so, for the Pump Room was more like a Welsh fair than ever that day. The musicians were in fine loud form, blowing for all they were worth, while the chatter and aspect of the crowd resembled an aviary swarming with birds of brilliant hue. John, gazing around, saw Coralie at once. Surrounded by a swarm of gallants, she held court in their midst, her dark hair glistening as she turned her head to listen to first one, then another. Very straight-faced, the Apothecary approached.

'Madam la Marchesa,' he said in thrilling tones, and bowed to the ground.

Coralie wheeled round, and it was only her acting training which saved her from giving the game away. 'Er...' she said, as if she couldn't quite remember who he was.

John bowed again. 'Rawlings, Marchesa. John Rawlings. We met at the assembly given by Serafina de Vignolles when you were last in London.'

'Of course,' Coralie cooed, tapping him lightly on the cheek with her folded fan. 'How could I forget? You are an actor, are you not?'

'An apothecary, Ma'am.'

She pealed with laughter, in which all the gallants joined. 'There you are. I knew it began with an "a".'

Her Italian accent was a triumph, trilling up and down as if she were singing. John, shaking his head very slightly at the sheer audacity of his mistress, fell in love with her all over again. None the less, he decided to give her a run for her money.

'I attended your husband just before I left town,' he said casually.

He saw the amusement spark in the depths of Coralie's eyes. 'Beloved Marco. How is he?'

'I have been trying to persuade him to join you here, Marchesa. He really would benefit from taking the waters.'

She sighed. 'But he is so busy with his diplomatic duties, alas.'

'But he might surprise us yet and arrive unexpectedly.'

'I hope not,' said a shrill little voice. 'We want the Marchesa all to ourselves.'

It was young Sidmouth joining the party, stomping up on high red heels, his small mouth petulant at the thought of an elderly husband appearing without warning and spoiling his flirtation. He eyed John briefly, then recognised him.

'Mr Rawlings,' he screeched, jumping into the air in his excitement. 'We've missed you here. Orlando was quite put about after you left. He'll be delighted to hear that you've returned.'

'How is he?' asked the Apothecary, drawing the silly creature to one side.

Robin Sidmouth pulled a face. 'Rather poorly. His health ain't all it should be.'

'He does tend to overdo things.'

'By that do you mean his drinking or his fornications?'

'I know nothing about the latter. They are entirely Orlando's affair.'

'You wouldn't say that if you were an irate mama.'

'A condition in which I am very unlikely ever to find myself.'

'Oh la, la,' said Robin, giggling.

Coralie approached them. 'Gentlemen, we have decided to go and eat Sally Lunn's buns and undo all the good of taking the waters. Do you care to join us?'

John bowed. 'It would be a pleasure to spend some time in your company, Madam.' He offered his arm. 'May I escort you? I would like to talk further about your husband's health.'

'That would be most enlightening,' said Coralie, and curtseyed formally.

It was enormous fun, strolling along as if they hardly knew one another, discussing the ailments of poor old Marco and all the time sending each other hidden messages with their eyes. Eventually the gaggle of gallants, about half a dozen in total and all very much the stamp of young Sidmouth, emasculated nothings who swore pretty oaths and painted their faces, drew ahead of them and they were able to speak freely.

'You are lovelier than ever,' said John. 'I've missed you so much.'

Coralie gave a graceful shrug. 'It's only been a few days.'

'If I say that every minute seemed like an hour I suppose you'll laugh.'

'Yes, I think I well might.'

'Then I won't say it, 'John responded. He bent his head closer to hers. 'How have you got on with your investigations?'

She lowered her voice. 'I have met Orlando a couple of times. I think he is quite taken with me but so far I have received no invitation to dine, which is very annoying indeed.'

'So you've had no chance to talk to Jack the coachman?'

'None. But, strangely, I've seen him. Sir Vivian Sweeting came into town the other day and Orlando presented him to me. I noticed a young man sitting on the coachman's box as Sir Vivian stepped out of the carriage. A handsome fellow, about twenty-one years old.'

'That's him. By the way, how is Orlando? Young Sidmouth said he was ill.'

Coralie shook her head. 'He might well be. He wasn't at the ball last night.'

John fingered his chin thoughtfully. 'I wonder if I dare risk calling.'

'Why shouldn't you? You are an apothecary, after all.'

'Yes, but his uncle knows that I am interested in Hannah Rankin. I was forced to hide in a most uncomfortable cupboard last time I was there in order to avoid him.'

The actress frowned, considering. 'But supposing I were to go, expressing concern for my new-found friend. Sir Vivian can hardly ask me to leave.'

'No, in all politeness, he can't.'

'Then we shall cross the river this very afternoon. You can accompany me and wait in an ale-house while I call laden with fruits and flowers.' Her eyes glowed. 'Then supposing I beg for a carriage home. Do you think Sir Vivian might lend me Jack?'

'There is another, more senior, coachman beside him, you know.'

'Which one I get is a chance I shall have to take.'

There was no point in arguing with her, one glance at Coralie's face told John that. She was like a player with a grand new part dangled before her, determined to obtain and succeed in it.

'There's an ale-house on the banks of the Avon, The Ship. If you get into trouble of any kind you are to leave the house and find me there,' he said firmly.

For answer, Coralie, after glancing round to see that they were not observed, gave him a kiss on the lips which left the Apothecary in no doubt that her feelings for him really were of the most affectionate kind.

They crossed the river at noon, complete with a pair of chairmen whom John had hired in Bath to take Coralie from the ferry up the hill to Welham House. The men had then been instructed to depart, deliberately leaving her without transport for the return trip, a ruse which both of them hoped might enable Coralie to have a private conversation with Jack. This stratagem arranged, and having seen his mistress safely on her way, the Apothecary retired to The Ship.

Whether fortune would favour Coralie that day remained to be seen, but it most certainly favoured John. As he went up to the bar, a figure in the corner waved its arm and a voice called out, 'Lady Allbury's nephew, isn't it?'

For a moment the Apothecary's mind went blank, then he remembered the old ferryman and the yarn he had spun him. Turning, he saw that the gaffer was sitting in exactly the same spot as when John had last seen him, almost as if he hadn't moved. Blessing his luck, the Apothecary went to join him, determined to extract some more information, but before he could speak the old man started to babble excitedly.

'I've got that name for you, the one you wanted. I seed him in the street, by God's cods, and I went and asked him.'

John was completely bemused. 'What name? Who are you talking about?'

'Last time we met, Sir. You asked me the name of the man who finds things out. The one who tried to locate poor Lucy Allbury.'

'Yes, of course,' the Apothecary answered, now remembering clearly. 'Well, what is his name?'

'Dick Chandler, Sir. A tidy enough man in his way. He lives just outside the city at Widcombe.'

'How can I find him?'

'Very easily. He informed me he's given up discovering things — too old for it, he said — and has become an attendant at the King's Bath instead. I told him about you and he said he'd like to talk to you. You won't be able to miss him, Sir. He stands over six foot and has hair like an old badger, all black and white stripes. Very unusual it is.'

'It sounds so.' John reached in his pocket and produced a guinea. 'Thank you for all your help. Let me refill your glass.'

'I won't say no, Sir.' The ferryman held out an enormous tankard. 'Glad to have been of service.'

The Apothecary joined the old fellow in a quaff of ale, then stood up. 'I think I'll walk along the riverbank, if you'll excuse me. Another fill?'

The ferryman nodded. 'Never said no to that in my life.'

John obliged, then, well satisfied with this latest turn of events, stepped outside.

August was nearly over and it was a high, bright, glorious day with just a hint of autumn in it. Across the Avon to the west, Bath glimmered in the afternoon sunshine, while the river water, picking up the radiance, had little golden rivulets swirling over its blue expanse. Fisher boats were out everywhere, their sails rigged to catch the breeze, and John caught a glimpse of a larger craft, white sheets billowing purposefully, going downriver in the direction of Bristol. Beneath the surface of the waterway, fish swam in lazy dark shoals, defying the anglers who stood on the banks, ever hopeful. Overhead flew river birds, wheeling and crying to the sun, and in the shallows a heron perched sedately on one leg. It was a peaceful scene and John could have watched it, totally absorbed, for another good hour. But thoughts of Coralie were creeping in and he found himself wondering if she were safe. Almost reluctantly, he turned his back on the Avon and started to climb the hill towards Welham House.

But the Apothecary was not destined to reach the top. Halfway there, with the gates and the lodge just coming into view, he suddenly heard the sound of horses' hooves approaching at speed. Staring upward, John saw a coach and four come charging out of the drive and start heading downhill towards him at a frightening rate. Instantly jumping aside, it was only as they drew level that John saw that the horses were not attached and were pulling away from the vehicle, running free, swerving to one side in a frenzied quartet, while the coach rolled on at an ever increasing pace, driven by its own momentum. Helplessly, he stared as the conveyance careered past him and on towards the bottom of the hill. It could never stop, of that the Apothecary felt certain, and he started to run after it as the carriage hurled itself towards the river.

In the distance he could see its uncontrolled velocity slow a fraction as it reached the flatter terrain at the bottom of the hill. But the reduction in pace was not enough. Crashing towards the riverbank, the coach thundered into the Avon, the driver shooting off his box like a rag doll, his very limpness indicating to John that he had already hit his head and lost consciousness before entering the water. Running like a hare, the Apothecary sped towards the scene of the accident.

A couple of fishermen were already there before him, one swimming round frantically, the other standing with a rope ready to throw to the coachman. Without hesitation, John flung off his coat, hat and shoes and dived in, keeping his eyes open, looking for the unconscious man, wondering whether he might be trapped as he hadn't yet come to the surface.

Jack was at the bottom, right enough. In a grim parody of the way in which Hannah Rankin had been found, the coachman lay on the riverbed, one of the carriage wheels on his chest, weighing him down so that even if he regained consciousness he would drown. Frenziedly, John tore at the obstruction but it was too heavy for him. Not wasting a moment, he shot to the surface, dashing the water from his eyes as he reached the top.

'He's down here,' he called to the other swimmer. 'There's a wheel on his chest. Can you help me?'

The fisherman nodded, and the two men dived together to where Jack lay trapped. Heaving in unison, they shifted the obstructing wheel and the fisherman, bigger and brawnier than John, placed his hands under the coachman's inert arms and drew him to the surface. His companion had waded in thigh deep, ready to give assistance, and it was he who grabbed

Jack and pulled him on to the bank. Scrambling out of the water, John rushed to apply every technique he knew to save those who had almost lost their lives through drowning, only hoping he was in time for this poor young man.

To tip Jack up and empty the water from his lungs, something that the Apothecary would have done to a child, was an impossible feat with an adult. Instead, John turned the coachman on his face, pulled his mouth open, and pumped furiously on his lungs from the back to force the fluid out. After a few minutes of silence, during which the Apothecary feared the worst, Jack finally spluttered and the water poured from his mouth.

'You've saved him,' said the fisherman who had brought the coachman to the surface.

'Yes,' John answered, investigating the cut on Jack's head and thinking it needed a stitch. He looked over his shoulder. 'Did you see what happened?'

'The coach shot over the embankment into the river. Only missed our boat by a few feet. There was no sign of the horses.'

'I'm not surprised. They broke loose from the trace.'

'Completely? That's unusual.'

'Almost impossible,' the Apothecary answered grimly. He stood up. 'Look, this poor fellow comes from Welham House. Perhaps you could help him get back...' He stopped short. 'No, on second thoughts, I think he might be better off in The Ship until I return for him. Could you carry him there?'

'Yes, quite easily. But what are you going to do? He's been injured and might need attention.'

'I won't be long,' said John, 'but I must go in search of those horses. There's something I want to look at.'

Halfway up the hill he found them, grazing in a field, still joined together by their harness, which had not been damaged at all during the frenetic flight. Making encouraging noises, the Apothecary approached the second pair, the two who would actually have stood directly in front of the coach, the trace, the bar attached to the vehicle to which the back pair of horses was secured, between them. They were quite docile, only looking up in mild interest as he picked up their tack and examined it.

It was just as he thought. The long strap, attached at one end to the horse's collar, at the other to the strut running across beneath the driver's box, had been almost cut through with a knife, the remaining thread torn jaggedly by the terrific strain it had been put under when the creatures started to pull. This had been done on both sides, so there was no question of the tear being accidental. Further, the buckle of the shaft tug, the small piece of leather that secured the horse to the central trace, had simply been left undone, again on both animals, a fact that might easily be overlooked by a coachman in a hurry.

So a person unknown had deliberately set out to destroy the harness with the clear intention of causing an accident. But why? Was it, John wondered, because Jack knew too much and had been on the point of telling someone the entire story?

Chapter Eighteen

Things began to happen rather fast. Wondering if Coralie could possibly be in danger, yet horribly aware that an injured man required his help, John finally compromised by running to The Ship and paying a fisherman's lad to go to Welham House with a note. This he wrote in great haste in the ale-house, signing it Serafina, and asking Coralie to return to Bath at once as her presence was urgently required. Then he took a barely coherent Jack back on the ferry and straight round to a physician who stitched the wound on the coachman's head with two sutures made of gut. This done, the Apothecary booked Jack in at The Bear and put him to bed with a strong dose of laudanum to sleep off the effects of his terrible experience.

It was by now six o'clock and John had not yet dined. Indeed, he was ravenously hungry after all the exercise he had taken. Yet his worries about Coralie would not permit him to leave The Bear, knowing that she would come back there as soon as she was able. Therefore he was not best pleased when young Sidmouth, Orlando's crony, came strutting in and called his name.

'My dear Mr Rawlings, there you are. I have been sent to fetch you.'

'Fetch me? Where?'

'To Lyndsey's. Orlando and Violetta have gone there for a late dinner and asked me to convey you to them.'

The Apothecary felt a surge of irritability. 'And who is Violetta, pray?'

Sidmouth's little mouth formed a small O of surprise. 'Why, the Marchesa of course. I thought you knew her.'

'Not well enough to be on Christian name terms,' John answered, feeling anger set in with a vengeance.

'Oh, I see. Well, my dear, are you ready?'

There was no way out of the situation. The only thing was to go to Lyndsey's with as good a grace as possible. Yet the thought of Orlando rising from his sickbed in order to accompany Coralie back into town filled John with that most uncomfortable of emotions — jealousy.

Even though the dining hour was passed, Lyndsey's was packed with ladies drinking tea and bright young sparks imbibing stronger stuff. Orlando sat at his usual table, looking at death's very portal, his face so pale that the Apothecary thought he had no need of enamel to whiten his complexion. Wondering to what extent the beau was involved in the near-fatal coach accident, and whether that might be the cause of the young man's ravaged appearance, John sat down. Coralie, in her role as elderly diplomat's wife, did little more than exchange a few pleasantries with him, a fact that depressed him even further. Determined to get something out of the evening, John decided his only course of action was to find out as much as he could about what had taken place at Welham House that day.

'I thought you were ill, my friend,' he said, addressing Orlando. 'I had not expected to see you up and about quite so soon.'

The beau shifted uncomfortably in his chair. 'It was either that or the prospect of staying at home in the clutches of my beloved uncle. So when the beautiful Marchesa called to see and cheer me, she inspired me to brave the rigours of Bath once more.' He took a deep mouthful of wine. 'But I haven't said how pleased I am to see you, my dear. I could hardly believe my good fortune when Robin told me you had returned to us.'

John felt guilty. There could be no doubt that Orlando genuinely meant what he said.

'I had an excuse to return and having enjoyed such congenial company on my last visit I came as quickly as I could.'

'Excellent,' answered the beau. 'One meets so few fellow spirits in this dreary life that I believe anyone of merit should be cultivated.'

The Apothecary couldn't help it. 'I wouldn't have thought of myself as quite the sort of person you would like. A bit too down-to-earth, perhaps.'

Orlando shook his head, and John got the impression that even his neck hurt. 'I admire that in you. It is part of your charm that a little bit of you is a dull fellow. We can't all be birds of paradise.'

It was said with such insouciance that John could not but chuckle. Beside him he felt Coralie quiver as she tried not to laugh out loud. Feeling in a better mood, the Apothecary turned to her.

'So, Marchesa, did you meet Sir Vivian Sweeting today?'

His mistress looked him in the eye, trying to tell him something. Unfortunately John was not quite certain what it was.

'Oh yes,' she answered blithely. 'He was very delightful to me. Sadly, though, Orlando's uncle had to go to Bristol and so could not ask me to dine.'

'But he wants you to come later in the week,' the beau put in. 'I think he was very taken with you, Madam.'

'Such compliments,' said Coralie, and fluttered her fan.

John leant forward. 'Who drove him to Bristol, pray?'

Orlando looked thoroughly startled. 'His coachman. Why?'

'Do you mean Jack?'

'No. Jack's the second coachman. Ruggins drove him. Why are you asking these questions?'

Deciding that he would learn nothing by secrecy, John said, 'Because this afternoon Jack was involved in a very serious accident which I happened to see for myself. I had crossed the river to do some walking and to look for herbs when I saw a runaway coach heading down the hill outside your gates. The horses had broken free and galloped off in a panic. The coach plunged into the Avon, throwing Jack in as well.'

Orlando's eyes bulged in his head and he looked as if he were about to have a fit. 'Oh my God! Oh God's mercy! Is he...?'

'No, he's alive. I ran to give what help I could but two fishermen had got to the scene before me. Between us, we got him up and brought him back from the dead.'

'But how...?'

John risked all. 'Listen! Later on I found the horses in a field. They were still wearing their harness. I examined it carefully. The two leading straps had been almost cut through, cut to the point where the first bit of strain would make them snap. Further, just to make certain that the horses would slip from the trace, the shaft tug buckle had been left undone. Whoever took the coach out that day would have had very little chance of survival once it gathered speed.'

It was not possible for Orlando to look worse, so harrowed were his features. He tried to speak but no words came out.

'I see you are shocked, my friend. And I am not surprised at it. Whatever the differences in your station, you must have regarded Jack as a childhood companion.'

The beau got to his feet, swaying. 'He was my greatest confidant,' he gasped, then he staggered from the room, everyone staring at him, audible remarks being made about drunkenness and lack of manners.

John looked from Coralie to young Sidmouth, 'Should I go after him?'

'I think you'd better,' Coralie interjected, while Robin stuttered something about Orlando preferring to be alone.

But the Apothecary's instincts to tend the sick made up his mind for him. As discreetly as he could, he left the table and followed Orlando out into the twilight. The beau had crossed the road and was splashing his face with water from a small fountain, his shoulders heaving, though he wasn't audibly sobbing.

Banging his feet so that Orlando would hear him and not take fright, John approached. 'My friend, don't distress yourself. Jack is alive and will make a complete recovery, I assure you of that.'

The other turned. 'Yet somebody attacked him, somebody set a trap for him, that is what is so terrible.'

'Who did it? Do you know?'

'Not for sure, no.'

'But you have an inkling?'

'Certainly.'

John laid his hand on the beau's arm and saw him wince with pain. 'What is the matter with you, Orlando? What has made you ill?' he asked quietly.

The same terrible expression that the Apothecary had seen before appeared in Orlando's eyes. 'My sins,' he said, with a parody of a laugh.

John looked at him closely. 'Somebody's beaten you, haven't they? You can hardly move.'

The beau wept. 'Oh God, John. It is almost too much to bear.'

'Let me have a look. Let me dress your wounds.'

Orlando drew away. 'Nobody shall see. My shame shall not be shown to the world.'

'I am hardly that. I am an apothecary, not some gawking busybody. I am used to such things.'

'Not like this, you're not.'

'Who did it? Sir Vivian?'

'Of course. Who else?'

'Is the man mad? Or just plain malicious?'

'Both,' said Orlando, repeating that same terrible smile. 'He is the Devil come to earth and put in human form.'

'The children. The children he brought up? What is the truth about them?'

The beau shuddered, deep to his bone. 'The truth is that none of us remained children for very long. Does that answer your question?'

'Only too clearly,' said the Apothecary, then he put out his hand to support Orlando as he sunk to his knees, suddenly faint.

It had not been an easy evening. Every plea to the beau to allow John to examine him had met with an adamant refusal. In the end, the best that the combined forces of the Apothecary, Coralie and young Sidmouth could achieve was to persuade Orlando to book himself into The Katherine Wheel in the High Street and extract a half-hearted promise from him that if he were no better in the morning he would allow someone qualified to examine him. And with that they all had to be satisfied. Hungrier than ever, as he still had not eaten a thing, John saw the wretched young man into a chair and then went back to Lyndsey's to dine.

Young Sidmouth, thankfully, had by now gone to join other friends, so that Coralie and John were alone for the first time.

'Well?' he said.

'There's evil in that house,' she replied fearfully.

'Did Sir Vivian say anything?'

'Yes. In fact it was extremely unpleasant. He looked at me with those dark pebble eyes of his and remarked that I reminded him very much of a certain actress he had seen at the Theatre Royal.'

'A Miss Coralie Clive?'

'No less.'

'What did you do?'

'Bluffed my way through. Became more Italian than the Italians. But all the time I had this terrible feeling that he was smirking at me, laughing at my performance, that he did not believe a word I was saying.'

'What of Orlando? Did he convey anything to you at all?'

'He was lying in a darkened room but made an attempt to rally when he saw me. It seems that he had fallen foul of his uncle for spending too many nights away from home and that Sir Vivian had taken the horsewhip to him by way of punishment.'

'No one whips a man of twenty-odd.'

Coralie's lovely face grew dark. 'There is something awful happening there, I feel certain of it. What with the beating, then the attempt on the coachman's life. Those young men aren't safe.'

'Well, they are both in Bath and quite secure, at least for tonight. And now, my sweetheart, I must eat.'

And the Apothecary fell to with relish as the waiter began to pile before him the enormous helpings of food that he had so eagerly ordered.

Later, when he was replete, John and Coralie walked back through the darkened streets of Bath to Cheap Street where The Bear was situated. Once there, they whispered their secret plans, then went their separate ways. Looking in on Jack's room, John saw that the coachman still slept peacefully, no sign of the day's dramatic events showing on the young man's handsome countenance. Having thus checked that his patient was completely at ease, the Apothecary stole along the corridor to Coralie's chamber and there knocked quietly.

'Come in,' she called.

She was sitting on the bed wearing her white nightrail with the red ribbon trimming and looked so delicious that he could have kissed her from head to foot.

'Oh, sweetheart,' he said, and snuggled down beside her.

'I have missed you,' the actress responded, turning to him. There was no reply. 'My dear?' she said. But the Apothecary was already sound asleep.

Chapter Nineteen

It was a slow awakening. After the violent escapades of the previous day, the Apothecary slept deeply, though not peacefully. Orlando's pitiable state, the fact that he had suffered a beating at Sir Vivian's hands, must have impinged deeply on his consciousness, for all night long he dreamt of children in peril; of Petronelle, small and lost and sad, roaming the streets of London with no one to care for her; of Jack the coachman, knowing nothing of his parents, brought to Welham House, his only memory a garden.

'A garden, a garden,' John repeated in his sleep, and then very gradually, almost as if layers of oblivion were being peeled away, he woke up, wondering what it was that he ought to know, what piece of information ought to be crystallising in his mind, giving him the answer to a vital question.

Beside him, Coralie Clive moved, and the Apothecary turned to look at her. She was like a rose, he thought; her lissom body the stem, the cloud of dark hair tumbling over the pillow the petals. With a tilt of his heart, he realised, yet again, that he had finally achieved his ambition, that at long last she shared his bed and his life, at least as far as she would allow herself to do so at this stage of her career.

'One day,' John whispered, and Coralie smiled and stirred but did not wake. Kissing her very gently, the Apothecary got out of bed, his thoughts turning to Jack, wondering how that particular young man was faring after his narrow escape from the hands of a murderer. Very conscious that he must see to him, John stole down the corridor to his own room, where be washed and shaved and put on fresh clothes before going to his patient.

It was six o'clock in the morning, and the dose of laudanum that John had administered the night before should easily have cleared Jack's system by now, leaving him refreshed and ready for the day. Quietly confident that he would find the coachman much better, the Apothecary knocked on the door. There was no reply so he knocked again, this time a little louder. Slightly alarmed that there was still no response, John turned the handle and went inside.

The room was empty, the bed-linen neatly folded back, the pile of clothes that the landlord of The Ship had lent Jack, his own being too wet to travel in, gone from the chair on which they had been neatly laid. The nightshirt that John had loaned the coachman lay in their place. Of Jack himself there was no sign whatsoever. With frightening thoughts of kidnap running through his mind, the Apothecary rushed downstairs.

A maid was struggling about in the hall, armed with jugs of hot water to take to the various rooms as the guests awoke. She looked up warily as John approached.

'Was I late with your ewer, Sir? It's been a bit of a rush this morning. I hope I haven't put you out.'

He cut through the pleasantries. 'It's about the young man who slept in number six last night. He'd had stitches in his head and went to bed early. Do you recall him?'

'Yes, Sir.'

'Well, he's not in his room. Have you any idea where be can be?'

'Yes. He's gone to London, Sir.'

John stared at her. 'Gone to London?'

'Aye. He came down at five and caught the stagecoach leaving just after. He said to tell you he felt much better and to thank you for everything. He also said he'd see you again.'

'Did he have enough money to settle his account?'

'Aye. The gentleman who called on him late last night gave him some, or so the young man remarked to me.'

'God's love,' said John irritably, 'what gentlemen was this?'

'I don't know, Sir. I was catching a wink. All I can tell you is that the young man with the mauve eyes told me that a friend visited during the night and lent him some money, otherwise he would have been in trouble.'

'But you didn't see the visitor?'

'No, Tim did.'

'And where's Tim?'

'Asleep, Sir.'

It was hopeless. Disturbed and definitely disgruntled, John stepped out into the street to gather his thoughts. During the night, then, someone had called on Jack, someone who knew where he was, and had given him enough money to pay his bill and to travel to London. But who was that someone? The only person that the Apothecary could possibly think of was Orlando, and the more he thought about it the more sense that answer made. If the motive for the whole thing were for Jack to escape from a murderous Sir Vivian Sweeting, then the pieces of the puzzle certainly fitted. But why London? Why so far away? There were other places in which to hide nearer at hand, surely. Could the reason for going to town be entirely different? If the mysterious coachman who called on Hannah Rankin was indeed Jack of Welham House, then might not something connected with the murder be the cause for Jack's sudden disappearance to the metropolis?

The Apothecary had been walking while all these thoughts rushed through his mind, so that now, gazing around him consciously for the first time, he found that he was only a hundred yards or so away from the King's Bath. Looking at his handsome watch, a present from Sir Gabriel for his twenty-first birthday, he discovered that it was not yet seven o'clock. Acting on a whim, John went inside the Bath, hired drawers, a waistcoat and turban, and prepared to enter the Dragon's Lake.

It seemed more vapour-filled and desolate than ever this morning, the whispers of the few dippers present echoing off the walls like the voices of the dead. With his usual sense of apprehension, John descended the steps into the steam, his feet seeking the hot waters that he knew lay in wait for him, and lowered himself with care into the cauldron.

Out of the mist a voice spoke, right by his ear. 'Mr Rawlings?'

John's turbaned head shot round, but he could see nothing. 'Yes?'

'What are you trying to do, raking up memories that should be allowed to die?'

'I don't know what you mean.'

'You little bastard,' whispered the voice, 'you know perfectly well.' And with that a pair of brawny arms seized John round the waist and dragged him below the scalding surface.

It was a ghastly sensation, just as if he were being drowned in a vat of boiling oil. Wriggling like an eel, the Apothecary threw frenzied punches with as much strength as he could muster, but his assailant was standing behind him and nothing was hitting home. Gasping for breath, John kicked out backwards as hard as he could and felt his foot come into contact with soft flesh. He was abruptly released and, spluttering and hawking, managed to get his head above the surface and take some deep breaths. Whirling round, he peered through the steam and saw a tall man, bent double and clutching his privy parts, groaning as he did so.

'Serves you right,' stated John, his voice echoing back off the dripping walls. He eyed his opponent more closely, and the unusual head of hair, striped like a badger's, confirmed what he had begun to suspect. 'So you're Dick Chandler, who went in search of Lucy Allbury,' he said. 'What a fool you are, man.'

The other looked up aggressively but did not have the wind to answer.

'I thought that you, of all people, would have had the sense to check your facts before you attacked someone at your place of employment,' the Apothecary went on. 'Why, I could have you dismissed, you blundering idiot.'

'Don't call me names, you bloody liar,' gasped the other. 'You are no more Lady Allbury's nephew than I am. Her true nephew died at sea.'

'Yes, I must confess I falsified that detail in order to extract as much information as I could from the old ferryman.'

A distant voice called out, 'Could you make less noise, if you please. Some of us are trying to bathe in peace.'

John moderated his tone. 'We can't talk here,' he hissed. 'Go about your work and when I have finished bathing I shall seek you out.'

Chandler looked cynical. 'I'll believe that when I see it.'

'And see it you will. Now, give me a quarter of an hour, then I'll go to a changing cubicle. Bring my clothes to me so that we can discuss the situation in private.'

Dick sneered, but at least had the good grace to head towards the steps, where he disappeared into clouds of vapour. Wondering what further misfortunes could possibly befall him, John groaned and submerged his aching muscles in the suddenly comforting warm water.

Fifteen minutes later, having traversed the bath twice for good measure, the Apothecary headed for the changing cubicles, to be instantly greeted by a hovering Chandler.

'Your clothes, Sir,'

'Thank you. Could you bring me a towel, please.'

'Certainly, Sir.'

This formality dispensed with, John went into the cubicle and Chandler followed a moment or two later. The Apothecary lowered his voice to a whisper.

'My name is John Rawlings and I am in Bath on behalf of Mr John Fielding, who is London's Principal Magistrate and who presides over the court and Public Office at Bow Street. He is investigating the death by foul play of a woman called Hannah Rankin, who at one time worked for Sir Vivian Sweeting of Welham House. When she applied for work in London, Hannah gave as one of her references Lady Allbury of Bath. When I came here to find Lady Allbury I discovered that she had killed herself after the disappearance of her youngest child, Lucy. The ferryman told me that you investigated that disappearance at the time. Tell me, Mr Chandler, do you believe that Hannah Rankin was involved in the affair?'

Chandler's somewhat pointed face, a feature that made him appear even more badger-like, had undergone a transformation from mistrustful to interested as the Apothecary had spoken. Now, though, it looked sorrowful.

'I don't know, Sir. All I can tell you is that the girl must have been snatched by someone she knew, and Hannah was Sir Vivian's trusted servant. I combed the gardens of Prior Park and nowhere could I see any sign of a struggle: kicked-up earth, broken branches, that kind of thing. She must have been called to while she was playing hide-and-seek, then gone with a person that she considered a friend. Perhaps a bribe of some kind, a promise of a treat or sweetmeats, was used. Who can say?'

'But why was she abducted, in your view? For what purpose?'

Chandler sighed deeply. 'To act as some perverted beast's little lover, that is my opinion. I believe that she was taken to London and either sold on the open market or to someone who had ordered her in advance.'

'Did you find any evidence of this?'

'In a way. I travelled the route myself and asked at every inn and posthouse if a girl answering Lucy's description had passed that way, either by stagecoach, post chaise, or private carriage. Several remembered such a child travelling in the company of a dark-haired woman.'

'Hannah!' John breathed.

'Possibly, Sir.'

'What did you do?'

'I went to London — Lady Allbury was paying all my expenses — and there I searched the brothels and bagnios. There was no sign of her, Sir. She had vanished into a private residence, of that much I am certain. I spent a month combing that hell-hole of a city and in the end I had to come away empty-handed. Whoever had taken Lucy had concealed her well from prying eyes.' Chandler coughed a little, then said, 'I'm sorry I attacked you, Mr Rawlings. I thought the worst when the ferryman told me that Lady Allbury's nephew had returned from abroad.'

'That's perfectly understandable. I regret kicking you in the cods.'

Chandler gave a rough laugh. 'Not for the first time in my life, I might add.'

They shook hands.

'Now, is there anything further you can tell me?' John asked. 'I know it may not seem relevant but I am convinced that Lucy's disappearance is linked with a similar incident involving a boy in Paris, unlikely though that may appear.'

Chandler scratched his chin. 'I can't think of a thing, Sir. Lady Allbury had no connections in France.'

'Did you know Sir Vivian Sweeting at all? Or Hannah?'

'I had heard of her, though I never actually met the woman. Sir Vivian is a different matter, however. He is a member of Bath's beau monde. I remember that way back he was bringing up a great many of his deceased relatives' children.' Dick stopped and stared at the Apothecary. 'You don't think he trafficked...?'

'Yes, I do, I'm afraid. The presence of Hannah Rankin in his household, to say nothing of a remark made by one of those children, now grown up, convinces me that Sir Vivian is — or was — a child molester.'

'Then the man must be stopped.'

'As I said, perhaps that has already happened. There is no sign of children in Welham House now. And Hannah left years ago. Perhaps something frightened the man and he ceased his evil trade. But, Mr Chandler, if we are to solve this whole mystery, please rack your brain for any detail that might assist me further.'

'My mind is a blank. What can I say? Lucy was born in 1741, a little bastard alas. She vanished seven years later. Nothing was ever heard of her again.'

'Very well, I'll have to be content with that. Now, I'd best get dressed. I'm beginning to feel cold.'

'Would you like another towel, Sir?'

'No, I'll put my clothes on quickly. By the way, I'm staying at The Bear, just in case you should think of anything more.'

'Very good, Sir.'

It had been an interesting conversation, John thought as he hurriedly put on his garments. Indeed, most enlightening had been the facts about Lucy's journey to London in the company of a woman who surely must have been Hannah Rankin. Yet how much further had his talk with Chandler got him? Other than for that piece of information, not a great deal forward. Still, the conviction that because of their similarity Lucy and Meredith's disappearances were somehow connected continued to haunt John as he finally tied his stock and set forth, hatless, in the direction of the Pump Room where, hopefully, he might discover Coralie or even the suffering Orlando.

It was early, however, and the usual jollities were not yet under way. Taking a glass of the horrible stuff, the Apothecary, feeling tremendously virtuous, paced the almost empty room, listening to the band strike up and watching as various aged invalids hobbled forward to consume their daily dose of health-giving water.

'My spleen has never been better,' commented one old fellow.

'Nonsense,' replied the other. 'I believe it is all in the imagination. I cannot credit that a glass of disgusting liquid like this could be of any benefit at all.'

'Well, the Romans thought so. They came here and bathed and no doubt drank the water, and they were an advanced civilisation.'

'Rome fell, didn't it,' responded his companion, chuckling.

'You are very cynical, Thomas. I personally find it fascinating to know that another culture sported here before us. Which reminds me, have you seen the head of Minerva?'

'No, I haven't. Where is it?'

'It's on display at the baths themselves.'

John froze, a black hole in his mind where there should have been a memory. Who had spoken to him about the head of Minerva, and recently at that? Who had told him it was lucky to touch it? Without waiting for the answers to come, the Apothecary turned on his heel and literally ran back to the King's Bath. As luck would have it, Dick Chandler, a bundle of towels over his arm, was standing in the doorway.

'The head of Minerva,' gasped John. 'Where is it?'

'There,' Chandler answered, and pointed upwards.

John followed his finger and looked to where the gilded bronze head of a statue stood in a small niche in the wall. Underneath was a handwritten notice.

'Head of a Roman statue,' it read, 'found by a workman in Stall Street, 1727. Believed to be the goddess Minerva.'

The Apothecary thumped his forehead with his fist. 'Who was it?' he said aloud. And as Dick stared at him, obviously thinking he had gone completely mad, it came to him. Once again, John saw those terrible tortured eyes and heard the mad girl's dying voice. She said she would take me to see Minerva's head. It was lucky to touch it.

'Petronelle,' he said aloud.

A ghastly expression crossed Chandler's face. 'Did you say Petronelle, Sir?'

'Yes, I did. Why? You didn't know her, did you?'

'In a way I did, for it was Lucy's second name. Lucy Petronelle Allbury was the girl I went looking for all those years ago.'

John turned on him a ravaged face. 'Then, my friend, it grieves me to tell you that your search for her is finally over.'

Chapter Twenty

It had been no use. Instead of seeking company, John had deliberately avoided it. When he should have made strenuous efforts to find Orlando and ask him exactly what was happening, instead the Apothecary walked through Bath alone, ignoring the passing parade and concentrating solely on his thoughts.

The revelation that poor tragic Petronelle and the missing child of ten years earlier were the same person had come as a great shock, yet in a way it had not been unexpected. Petronelle's fear of Hannah Rankin, Forbes, the warder's, belief that the poor lunatic had met the woman before, both served to confirm John's certainty that a child abduction ring had at one time flourished in Welham House and that Lucy Allbury had been snatched by that very circle. And now, aware that the Dysarts had lived only twenty miles from Bath, his conviction that Meredith's disappearance must somehow be linked grew even stronger. The boy had been over two years old when he had left the country to live in Paris, not too young to have attracted the attention of an English kidnapping gang. Despite flaws in the argument, John's conviction remained. Reaching into his pocket, he drew out the address given him by Ambrosine Dysart. 'Westerfield Place, Westerfield Abbas, Somerset,' she had written. Filled with an absolute certainty as to what he should do next, the Apothecary walked back to The Bear to enquire about transport.

It had not been an easy journey. Study of a map had revealed that the only towns of any size reasonably close to Westerfield Abbas were Wells and Glastonbury, and enquiries at The Bear had resulted in John catching the stagecoach to Glastonbury. From there, the Apothecary was advised to hire a man with a trap to take him the rest of the way.

It was some while since John had travelled by stage, preferring the faster post chaise or flying coach, therefore he was much amused to find himself boarding the Bath Magnet, an antiquated, lumbering affair that went as far as Taunton and back. The design of it was not of the latest, to say the least, yet it could accommodate an unbelievable fifteen passengers. The coachman's box hung forward, secured to the main bodywork by a series of leather straps. Dangling their feet into the space thus provided were three travellers, two men and a woman, all sitting on the roof, while beside the driver was squeezed one more. Similarly, at the back perched two other people alongside the guard, while in the basket behind squatted a couple of passengers, sitting on their luggage and a pile of parcels. With a heave, John went in with them, and he, together with the six travellers within, made up the full complement. Dreading to think what would happen if the conveyance shed a wheel in mid-career, the Apothecary gritted his teeth as, with a blast of the coachman's horn, the four-horse team strove to pull the loaded vehicle over the cobbles and away.

Getting his bearings, John saw that two other young men shared the basket with him.

'James Jinks,' said one, bowing his head and holding out his hand. 'Thomas Hasker,' added the other, doing likewise.

The Apothecary returned the compliment. 'John Rawlings, at your service, gentlemen.'

'Travelling far?' asked Jinks.

'To Westerfield Abbas. I'm getting off at Glastonbury and hope to hire a trap.'

'Then allow me to offer you a ride, Sir. My conveyance will be waiting for me and as I am travelling in that direction I can drop you where you wish.'

'How very kind. I'm actually going to Westerfield Place.'

Jinks and Hasker, who were clearly acquainted, looked at one another.

'The Dysart house, eh?'

Instantly sensing something of interest, John said, 'Yes. Why?'

Jinks grinned. 'I come from close by, a small place called Meare. My papa used to play cards with Lord Anthony. Knew the family quite well before they left for France.'

'Then you would have been acquainted with their daughter?' John asked casually.

'Not really. I was just a child at the time. But my elder brother was much smitten with her. She was known as the Beauty of the County, you know.'

'Wasn't she involved in some sort of scandal?' the Apothecary said, his face ingenuous.

'Ran off with a footman and pregnant into the bargain. Just about as scandalous as you can get,' Jinks answered cheerfully.

Hasker looked at him reprovingly. 'Steady, James. Mr Rawlings is probably a friend of the family.'

John instantly became bland. 'No, no, not at all. I am merely going to the house to deliver something. I hardly know the Dysarts, though I must confess something I heard about them recently intrigued me.'

'Oh? What was that?'

'Did a child of theirs vanish in Paris, or have I got it all wrong?'

Jinks shook his head. 'No, you're right. It was Lord Anthony's grandson. The progeny of the Beauty and her runaway husband who, sadly, were both killed in a coaching accident.'

As he said the words, the stagecoach bumped over a large stone in the road and the three occupants of the basket flew aloft, laughing despite the seriousness of the topic.

'Anyway,' Jinks continued, ramming his hat back on his head, 'they left behind a baby, aged about two years or so. After they died the child was brought to Westerfield by Gregg the steward...'

He and Hasker exchanged another look and Hasker shook his head slightly.

'...who looked after him until Lord Anthony and Lady Dysart arrived from France to fetch him. Anthony was the British Ambassador, you know. Anyway, they took the boy back with them, then one day he vanished from their garden in Paris, never to be seen again.'

'What a terrible tale.'

'Terrible and rum, don't you think?'

'Very rum,' John answered, watching Hasker while he and Jinks conversed, wondering why he had indicated 'no' when Gregg's name came into the conversation. He decided to find out.

'I've been told to make my delivery to Lord Anthony's steward. Would that be the same man you mentioned?'

Jinks, who was clearly the greater gossip of the two, answered, 'Oh yes, old Gregg is still there. I reckon he'll keep the post until the day he dies.'

'That's unusual, isn't it? I thought old servants were pensioned off.'

Jinks opened his mouth but Hasker spoke up firmly. 'Gregg is more of a friend to the Dysarts, Mr Rawlings. He was a child working round the place when Lord Anthony was a boy. Though they will relieve him of duties in the years to come, he will always retain the honour of being steward.'

He spoke with an air of finality, giving John the impression that there was a lot more to the story which would not come out until Jinks was left on his own. Quite deliberately, the Apothecary changed the subject.

'Do you live in Meare also, Mr Hasker?'

'No, I reside in Wells, just outside the town to be precise. However, James and I have known each other since schooldays, and whenever we have the time we go into Bath for the balls and theatre.'

'How delightful! I envy you that. I think it a charming spot. I only have one friend living there, though, Orlando Sweeting. You don't know him, by any chance?'

Jinks and Hasker shook their heads. 'Can't say we do.'

'He's the nephew of Sir Vivian Sweeting.'

Still they looked blank, and John felt a vague sense of disappointment. He had somehow hoped that a connection, however tenuous, between Sir Vivian and the Dysarts could be established.

The conversation, conducted between bursts of laughter and fierce drawings in of breath as the track became ever more perilous, now changed to general topics. Those sitting on the roof beside the guard joined in, and the Apothecary had to come to terms with the fact that Jinks would say no more until after his friend had left the coach. Indeed, pleasant though young Hasker was, it was quite a relief when The Magnet rumbled into the courtyard of The Swan with Two Necks in Wells and he got off.

His place was taken by an enormously fat, belligerent woman, determined to get a seat within the coach itself. Furious that nobody would give up their place for her, she finally flopped into the basket like an angry flounder and glared at John and James as if it were all their fault.

'No manners,' she said loudly, crushing baggage and parcels as she heaved her weight from one side to the other.

'Perhaps you'll acquire some soon,' the Apothecary answered, just loud enough for his companion to hear.

'Eh?' the woman asked suspiciously.

'I said, "Perhaps you'll expire at noon", to my friend.'

She glared all the more. 'Why should you say a thing like that?'

'Because he's a very bad traveller, Ma'am. Prone to sickness and all sorts of terrible things. He's been known to go into a faint and be taken for dead. That's why I said it.'

The woman, as best she could, moved to the far side of the basket. 'If you feel vomitous you're to lean over the side, young man. D'ye hear?'

Jinks made a terrible retching sound and rolled his eyes.

'It might be too late,' said John sorrowfully.

'Oh Gawd!' she responded, and turned her back.

Hardly able to control themselves, the Apothecary and his new companion indulged in an entirely silly conversation until the short haul to Glastonbury was complete and the passengers got off to dine. Tempted to have a meal, John saw that this would be out of the question. A smart coach, complete with coachman and postillion, awaited James Jinks, who, John guessed, must be an extremely well-breeched young man, despite the fact that he liked travelling on the common stage.

'Sorry that we haven't got time to eat, but I'll drop you off at the Place,' Jinks said as they climbed aboard his equipage. 'I'm sure old Gregg will look after you.'

'Do you know the man well?'

'Only from seeing him round the house when I used to visit. As I said, my elder brother was mad for Alice, and I used to be taken along when he went to pay his respects. But then, of course, Gregg's role in the establishment became somewhat different after the scandal.'

'What do you mean?'

Jinks stared at him. 'You don't know?'

'No, I'm afraid I don't. As I said, I am the merest acquaintance of the Dysarts.'

James adopted a gossipy look. 'Then you wouldn't be aware that Gregg was the father of the fornicating footman, the one who ran off with the Beauty of the County.'

'Do you mean...?'

'Yes, I do. He and Lord Anthony were both grandfathers to the same child. Meredith Gregg, the boy who vanished.'

'Then the steward didn't lose his position despite his sinning son?'

'He came close to it, I believe, but he and his master went back a long way. In fact I've heard tell that Gregg saved Lord Anthony's life when they were both boys and the Duke's son went skating on thin ice, quite literally.'

'By the Duke's son you mean Lord Anthony, I presume?'

'Yes. He's the late Duke of Bristol's middle boy, brother to the present Duke.'

'So old ties saved Gregg from dismissal?'

'That, together with Lord Anthony's natural sense of fairness. After all, a father can't be held responsible for his son's follies, can he, now?'

Thinking of wise Sir Gabriel and his recent advice to John regarding Coralie, the Apothecary could only smile and say no.

'Strange affair, ain't it, though,' James Jinks offered.

'I think,' John replied thoughtfully, 'it's going to get a great deal stranger before all the answers come out.'

To approach Westerfield Place from the village of Westerfield Abbas was a breathtaking experience indeed. The village itself was in truth little more than a spread of houses, though it did have a church at its centre, and even an ale-house, called The Star. But leaving it and heading out on the road towards Meare, travellers soon became aware of a great wall, running for miles alongside the track.

'The estate?' asked John.

'The estate indeed,' Jinks confirmed. 'It's huge, as you've probably gathered. The Dysarts are the biggest landowners in the county, though my papa ain't too far off 'em.'

'I'm pleased to hear it,' the Apothecary responded, then widened his eyes at the sight of the great gates, a lodge house built on either side of them, that gave access to all the splendour that was the Dysart acreage.

'To see Mr Gregg,' John called to the lodge-keeper, and the gates were swung open to allow Jinks's coach to pass through.

As they trotted down the elm-lined drive, the house, a magnificently proportioned edifice that had obviously been rebuilt at the time of James I, could be seen in the distance. John had discovered from his conversation with Jinks in the stagecoach's basket that King John had had a hunting lodge on the site, and there had been people residing at Westerfield for five hundred years. Something of this showed in the very antiquity of the house's surroundings. For here was land well trodden, well hunted upon, well used and loved by the many generations who had dwelled and continued their heritage on the venerable spot.

The house had a sheen to it, a patina created by scores of people living out their lives there, rejoicing or sorrowing within its solid, comforting walls. Yet at the same time there was an air of sadness about the place, as if being empty were an anathema to it. Saddened yet excited by what he was seeing, John descended from Jinks's coach and rang the bell. It echoed through empty rooms and desolate corridors, and his heart bled for Westerfield Place that it had no heir to fill it once more with laughing children.

James Jinks's cheerful face appeared in the carriage window, accompanied by a waving arm.

'Is anybody in? Will you be all right?'

But already great locks were turning and a fresh-faced footman was appearing in the doorway.

'Yes, Sir?'

'I have come to see Mr Gregg. My name is John Rawlings and I do not have an appointment, but Lady Dysart has written to him asking that he should expect me.'

'Very good, Sir. Would you step within? I shall find out if Mr Gregg is available.'

'He's at home?'

'He's round and about the estate, Sir,' the servant answered warily.

John turned to Jinks. 'Gregg is here. I think all should be well. Thank you for your help.'

'A pleasure. If you get into difficulties come to Meare Manor. Don't forget.'

'I won't,' said John, and waved his new friend a thankful farewell, thinking that travelling companions of his ilk were worth their weight in gold.

'If you would follow me, Sir,' said the footman, leading the way into an overpowering hall, so large and so full of treasures that the Apothecary quite literally stopped in his tracks and stared round, gazing at everything open-mouthed.

The servant allowed himself a small snigger. 'The hall of Westerfield Place is one of the most glorious in England, so they say. Would you care to sit in one of the window embrasures that you may continue to observe it, Sir? Or do you wish me to conduct you to an anteroom?'

'I'll stay here,' John answered, unashamedly impressed and not caring who knew it.

'Very good, Sir.'

'If you could take Mr Gregg my card and remind him that I am here with the blessing of Lady Dysart.'

'Indeed, Sir.'

The man went, leaving John to study the immense splendour in which he found himself, and at which he must have stared for at least five minutes before a voice spoke at his elbow.

'Mr Rawlings, I believe we met in London.'

Not having heard the steward approach, John leapt to his feet, his heart pounding.

'Ah, Gregg,' he said rather breathlessly. 'I'm sorry to foist myself upon you like this, but Lady Dysart told me to call when I was in the area.'

'Of course, Sir. How may I help you?'

It was a strange experience, knowing that this man was Meredith's other grandfather, aware that his blood had flowed in the missing child just as much as had that of the Dukes of Bristol. John decided to be perfectly honest.

'Gregg, I have come here because I believe there may be a link between the disappearance of Lord Anthony's grandson in Paris and the kidnapping of a child from Bath a few years later. The two cases are so similar in the way the children vanished that I cannot get it out of my mind that they are connected. Where can we go that we may talk privately?'

'Have you eaten, Sir?'

'No, I haven't.'

'Then may I suggest that you follow me to my quarters where we may dine and discuss the situation.'

He was even more bear-like than John remembered; a powerful being who breathed calm and reassurance and strength. Small wonder that Lord Anthony had kept the man in his service despite the transgressions of Gregg's son.

In a somewhat daunted silence, John mounted a staircase of vast proportions and, having traversed a long and silent corridor, entered a suite of rooms that were friendly and lived-in. A sputtering fire burned in the main parlour and a maidservant hovered anxiously, ensuring that all was well.

'Are you ready to be served dinner, Mr Gregg?'

'There will be two of us tonight, Millie. So we'll wait a quarter of an hour or so.'

'Very good, Sir. I'll make the necessary arrangements.'

John held out his hands to the blaze, feeling that the first fingers of autumn were in the early evening air,

'Gregg, I'm afraid that I am going to rake over old ground. I hope that this will not distress you.'

'What do you hope to achieve by it, Sir?'

The Apothecary looked solemn. 'Nothing, really. Nothing I can do or say will ever bring Meredith back.'

'Then why...?'

'To satisfy my own curiosity. To reassure myself that the cases of Lucy Allbury and Meredith Dysart are not related at all and that the similarities are nothing more than mere coincidence.'

A slow, sad sigh came from Gregg's hulking frame. 'Meredith Gregg, Sir, for that's who the poor child was. For all his father brought shame to the family, Lord Anthony's grandson still bore my son's name.'

'So it is true. I had heard a rumour that you were Meredith's other grandfather but wondered whether it was just gossip.'

'No, it's a fact. My son Richard seduced Alice.' Gregg poured John a glass of claret, and the Apothecary could see that the older man's hand was shaking. 'But it wasn't like a seduction, Sir. They were brought up together, just as I was with Lord Anthony. Look, let me show you something.'

He stood up, beckoning John to follow him, and by the light of candles, for the evening was beginning to draw in, they retraced their steps to the towering staircase, then made their way down another corridor. Throwing open a door, Gregg led the way into a large and beautiful salon, whose long windows overlooked the dusk-drenched park.

'Here,' he said, and, lighting a silver candelabra, held it up to a painting.

As was the fashion, it showed Lord Anthony and Ambrosine with their only surviving child, Alice, together with several of their servants. The picture had been painted in the grounds and Westerfield Place appeared in the background, large and impressive yet delicate as a fairy castle. Lord Anthony and Lady Dysart were seated, while Alice stood by her mother. Grouped round them were several of their servants, including a turbaned black slave. Unusually, at their feet sat four boys, aged roughly between ten and fourteen years old. The portrait was signed James Thornhill, whose name John recognised as that of William Hogarth's father-in-law, and was dated 1722.

'Look at Alice,' said Gregg, his voice suspiciously hoarse.

John followed the line of the steward's finger, peering closely, and could easily see how as a young woman the child would have earned the nickname of Beauty of the County, for she was an exquisite little thing, with Ambrosine's gorgeous lilac eyes and a great mop of tumbling fair ringlets.

'There's Richard,' said Gregg, not without a note of pride, and John looked to the smallest boy, probably about ten or eleven years old, dressed simply as a kitchen lad, but for all that an extremely handsome child. 'And that's me,' Gregg continued, pointing to the figure of a man of thirty or so, standing behind his master and easily recognisable as a younger version of the steward.

'Remarkable,' said John, and taking the candle tree from the other man's hand, he held it close.

For no reason his eye was drawn to the line of boys, and he wondered what it was about one of them that was attracting his attention. For there was something about that particular lad's face that was faintly familiar. Yet try as he might, the Apothecary could not put a name to it, and he shook his head, dismissing the impression as an optical illusion caused by the light.

Gregg interrupted his train of thought. 'They were always friends, Richard and Alice. Then they became lovers. It seemed the most natural thing in the world to them. But they had flown in the face of social convention and they had to pay the penalty.'

'What happened?'

'When they discovered that she was pregnant, they eloped and were secretly married. But Lord Anthony would not recognise the match and they were forced to go and live in the direst poverty in a cottage that I would have described as a hovel. When Meredith was born, Lady Dysart relented and made Alice an allowance, but up till then she had had to take employment as washerwoman to a big house, while Richard became a footman.'

Almost absently, John asked, 'Where did they live?'

'Across the river from Bath in a place called Bathwick.'

A million clarion calls sounded in the Apothecary's brain. 'And what was the name of the man who employed them? Gregg, it is vital that you answer me correctly.'

The older man frowned deeply. 'I really can't recall, Sir. We are talking about something that happened many years ago.'

'Then where did Richard and Alice work? What was the name of the place?'

'Ah, that I do remember. It was Welham House, Sir. For some reason that has always stuck in my mind.'

'Welham House,' repeated John, and sat down rapidly because of the sudden excitement that bubbled through him like champagne.

Chapter Twenty-One

It was a strange experience, spending the night in the vast echoing emptiness of Westerfield Place. Shown into a bedroom in the completely deserted East Wing, John, not prone to fancies, found himself unable to sleep, certain that deep in that huge deserted house a dead girl sobbed for her missing baby. Once, when he had drifted off into an uneasy slumber, he woke suddenly, convinced that someone was whispering outside his bedroom door. But lighting a candle and going to investigate he found no one there, though he could have sworn that the figure of a woman was just drifting out of sight as he stepped into the corridor.

Over breakfast, Gregg had stared at the Apothecary's somewhat haggard appearance. 'Did she bother you?'

'Who?'

'Alice. She's supposed to haunt the place, though I've never seen her. She whispers in the passageways and weeps on the stairs, or so it's said.'

John blenched. 'I certainly did hear something.'

Gregg looked grim. 'Some old gypsy woman who came to the kitchens to sell brooms said Alice would never rest until her son came back to Westerfield.'

'But he might well be dead after all this time.'

The steward looked at him narrowly. 'You don't altogether believe that, do you? I think you reckon as I do. If the boy was taken for slavery or prostitution he might yet find his way home.'

Having had much the same thought, John found himself unable to disagree.

Perhaps because he looked so tired, perhaps because Gregg felt like a change of scene, perhaps because of a combination of both, the steward, as soon as the meal was over, offered to drive John back to Bath. Indeed, he took the reins himself, swinging up on to the box, a stalwart, comforting figure, calling to John over his shoulder, 'Shouldn't take long, Mr Rawlings. I can get up a better speed than the stage.'

'How many miles is it?'

'About twenty-four, Sir. I'll have you there in a couple of hours at most.'

Glad to be saved the rigours of the stagecoach, John promptly closed his eyes and fell asleep. When he opened them again he was on the outskirts of the city, and a glimpse through the window revealed Gregg, stoic as ever, driving his team of four with the ease born of long practice. Hoping that

Coralie was not going to be furious with him for disappearing overnight, John disembarked at The Bear, persuaded the steward that he should take a well-earned break before attempting the return journey, then went into the inn to buy him some ale.

Going into the parlour, John saw that Orlando, of all the unlikely people, was asleep in one of the more comfortable chairs. He looked ghastly; white and ill, a wreck of humanity. Not knowing quite what to do, John murmured to Gregg, 'I know that young man but don't particularly want to have a conversation with him at this moment. Will you walk to The Crown and Sceptre with me? It's only just up the road.'

The steward looked over in the beau's direction. 'Poor soul. He looks fit to drop. What's the matter with him?'

John shook his head, not wanting to reveal the connection with Welham House. 'He tends to live to the full, I fear. And this does not please his uncle, who chastises him if he stays away from home.'

'Then I pray for him, Sir, I really do, for there can be very little happiness in his life if he burns it all out on folly.'

'I wish he could somehow be rescued,' answered John, not specifying exactly what he meant.

They walked in thoughtful silence to the neighbouring inn, where they spent a pleasant hour or so before Gregg, announcing himself refreshed and his horses undoubtedly well watered by the hostlers at The Bear, took his leave.

'I shall be returning to London shortly, Sir. I'll tell Lord Anthony and Lady Dysart that you called at Westerfield.'

'Please do. And can you also say that I shall visit them in Mayfair as soon as I am able?'

'I certainly will.' The steward bowed then shook John's hand warmly. 'I hope that what I told you was of some help.'

'It answered all the questions I had,' the Apothecary replied. Then waving Gregg off, he walked back into The Bear, full of a fierce determination to prise Orlando from the clutches of Sir Vivian.

The beau was just waking up, stretching in his chair and yawning widely, his enamel, which looked as if it must have been on all night, cracking here and there as he did so. Beneath the concealing mask, John glimpsed, as he had on another occasion, strong features and what could well be a handsome countenance. Desperately sorry for the poor creature, the Apothecary spoke earnestly.

'Orlando, you are not to return home. You must leave Welham House for good. I truly believe that your uncle, if that is what he really is, traffics in children – or at least has done so in the past. I beg you, for your own salvation, quit Bath and start a new life away from his corrupting influence.'

As had happened before, somebody else looked at him out of Orlando's eyes. 'With what, my dear friend?' drawled the beau, hiding that other being. 'I have no means, I have no training. I could not make a living. I would be dead within a few months.'

It was out before John could stop the words. 'You'll be dead in a few months if you don't go.'

The sad being behind the great fop's veil nodded agreement. 'Oh yes, assuredly I will.'

'Then get a grip on yourself, man. Sign as an older apprentice, find work in a counting house, do something that would suit you, but get away from that corrupt creature who dominates your life.'

Orlando got to his feet, and one tragic tear stole out of his eye and ran down his cheek, smudging the kohl line drawn beneath his lashes. 'You don't understand, John, do you? Sir Vivian has cost me my soul, and without that there cannot be any life at all.'

'For God's sake, Orlando,' the Apothecary shouted, physically shaking him, 'what do you mean by that? You speak of your sins but never say what they are.'

'If I did you would turn your back on me for good, and you are the only friend I've got who has an ounce of worthiness within him.'

John's arms dropped to his sides in a gesture of helplessness. 'What more can I say? Do you want me to go on my knees and beg you to start your life again?'

Orlando put his hands on John's shoulders in a movement that was so loving yet so hopeless the Apothecary felt he might weep. 'Don't demean yourself on my account, my dear. Return to town and forget you ever met me.' He turned to leave.

'Wait!' said John. 'Tell me one thing. Why did you send Jack to London, for it was you, wasn't it?' Orlando nodded. 'What did he go there for?'

'He went to settle an old score.'

'But Hannah Rankin is dead.'

'Have you never heard of a nest of vipers?'

And with that Orlando did leave, hurrying out of the door and up the street, before John could ask him another thing.

It had taken a fine display of penitence to placate Coralie. In fact only by catching her imagination with his recounting of the story of his haunted night at Westerfield Place had he managed to get the actress's attention away from her desire to be angry with him.

Green as a cat's, Coralie's lovely eyes had narrowed as she had looked at him.

'I am not the sort of woman, Sir, to be fobbed off with scribbled notes and sudden disappearances. And if that is the way you intend to act in the future you can consider our connection at an end.'

It would be better by far, John thought, to humble myself completely now. Acutely aware of how much she meant to him and how devastated he would be if she were to end their association, he said, 'Forgive me. It was entirely my fault I was forced to leave in a hurry, but it would have been a great deal more sensible to have missed the stagecoach and to have told you what was happening.'

'Yes, it would.'

'But I had just discovered the truth about Petronelle and was not thinking clearly. I had a fondness born of pity for her. Not love, you understand, for all of that I keep for you.'

He was winning; Coralie was starting to smile. She changed the subject, a very, good sign. 'Tell me – do you really think Westerfield Place is haunted by the ghost of Alice?'

'Gregg seemed to believe it, and he is the very last person on earth to suffer from a colourful imagination; built like a bear and solid as a rock.'

'How exciting. The ghost I mean, not Gregg. I would love to spend a night there.'

'Talking of that,' said John, 'do you think you could bear to spend a night in a post chaise?'

'If all else fails. Why?'

'There's one leaving for London in half an hour and it is now essential that I see Mr Fielding. The fact that Lord Anthony's daughter and son-in-law worked for Sir Vivian Sweeting is conclusive evidence in my view. He obviously saw Meredith and took a fancy to the child.'

'But before he could get his hands on him the boy was removed to Paris?'

'Something on those lines, yes.'

'Surely Sir Vivian would have lost interest at that point. Snatching a child from another country would have presented too many difficulties.'

'Not when that child was the Ambassador's grandson and easy to find.'

Coralie looked uncertain. 'It sounds a somewhat tenuous argument to me, John.'

'Not at all,' he responded roundly, absolutely certain that not only had he found the link between Meredith and Lucy but that everything pointed to Sir Vivian Sweeting and Hannah Rankin as the people behind the child abduction ring.

'Not enough evidence,' said the Blind Beak, adjusting the black bandage that hid his eyes and sighing somewhat wearily.

'What?' exclaimed the Apothecary wrathfully.

'My dear Mr Rawlings, be calm, I pray you. I entirely agree with you that that wretched man in Bath is probably one of the most evil creatures ever to walk the earth, but the few strands of evidence that we have against him would be torn to shreds by a clever advocate.'

'But...'

'Listen to me, my friend. A girl dies in St Luke's Hospital; she is called Petronelle. The child that was abducted in Bath, who would now be the same age as the dead woman, is called Lucy Petronelle. That is the only link between them. There is nothing else.'

'But I know they are one and the same. I feel it in my gut.'

'I agree with you,' Mr Fielding answered calmly. 'I feel it too. But there is no evidence to connect them with Sir Vivian Sweeting and Hannah Rankin...'

'Petronelle feared her.'

'That proves nothing.'

Joe Jago, who had been sitting in the corner, listening silently, spoke up. 'Mr Fielding is right, Sir. We'd be laughed out of court. So far there is nothing but coincidence.'

'But Joe, you think I'm right, don't you?'

'I do, Mr Rawlings, I truly do. But we cannot bring a man to justice on such paltry findings.'

'Then there's the matter of the boy,' the Magistrate continued. 'He may indeed have been seen by Sir Vivian as a child, yet he disappears from Paris. Even worse. No connection at all could be proved. I'm afraid, my dear friend, that the case is as full of holes as a watering can.'

'Then what are we to do?'

'Either obtain irrefutable fact — or get a confession out of someone.'

'But who?'

'Sir Vivian himself.'

John gave a contemptuous laugh.

'Or the dirty old Frenchman,' put in Joe. 'My money is on him, Sir. Just how long had he known Hannah Rankin, that is the question. If he and she had worked together stealing kinchen, then we might be able to take a step forward.'

John fingered his chin and nodded, and the Blind Beak gave a rumbling laugh. 'It's a good thought, Jago. Well worth following up.'

'Which reminds me.' John turned to look at the clerk, who winked a light blue eye. 'Did you get any further with Toby Wills?'

'Yes and no. He told me no more, yet his very silence revealed something.'

'What?'

'That he fears he knows the identity of the weirdly masked figure that wheeled in Hannah Rankin. Or possibly...'

'Yes?'

'That he let that person into the grounds himself.'

''Zounds!' said John. 'Is it conceivable?'

'I think it could be. His anonymous friend had told him evil stories about Hannah; his sad, mad son was fond of Petronelle. I think that might have been enough to make somebody of Toby's temperament cooperate in bringing about her death.'

'Dear God,' said John, 'how convoluted this terrible story is!'

The Blind Beak cleared his throat. 'Mr Rawlings, may I suggest that you call on the Marquis and try, by whatever means you consider necessary, to obtain information from him. Crack his facade, if you can. I believe there is much in what Jago says. In fact that terrible old man may hold the key to all of this.'

John's spirits soared from despair to exhilaration. 'I'll go now, straight away.'

'No, Sir. Go home and get some rest. It is perfectly obvious that you travelled overnight for you are somewhat red of eye. Tackle the Marquis an hour or so before he goes to dine. In that way you might catch him in and also take him by surprise.'

'I'll do as you say.'

'Very good. And, Mr Rawlings...'

'Yes?'

'You are right, of course. Sir Vivian is the culprit as far as those children are concerned. Now all we have to do is find out which of the poor souls killed that wicked wretch Hannah Rankin.'

September sunshine became that most elegant of buildings, the French Hospital. As it shone off its well-proportioned walls, casting pretty shadows on its delightful gardens, the Apothecary was struck again, as he ascended the gracious sweep of its steps, by how well planned and attractive a place had been created to house those poor emigrants who had fled from France because of their religious beliefs.

The same elegant, unfriendly maid answered the door.

John swept off his hat. 'I have come to see the Marquis de Saint Ombre.'

'Do you have an appointment?'

'Oh yes,' John lied with ease. 'He is expecting me to dine with him.'

'Then come in. You know where his apartment is.'

'Of course,' the Apothecary responded, wondering whether he could remember the way.

She stared after him as he turned left, hoping he was correct, gazing at the identical entrances that led off the corridor at regular intervals and praying he could recall which was the Frenchman's. Proceeding hesitantly, John eventually came to a door that looked as if it might well be the one he sought. He gave a tentative knock.

'Entrez,' said a voice.

He went in to find an extremely pretty young woman reclining in a hip bath. Covered with confusion, the Apothecary bowed his way out again, whereas she smiled cheerfully and assured him in delightfully broken English that there was really no need for him to leave at all.

Back in the corridor, John took stock, wondering what to do next. Beautiful though the French Hospital was, it was for all that an institution, and there was nothing individual about the apartments or their entrances. Wondering how many doors he was going to have to bang on before he located the Marquis, the Apothecary suddenly caught sight of one that stood slightly open. Through it he could just see the outline of a brocaded wing chair very similar to, if not the same as, the one he had sat on when he had originally called on the Frenchman. Thinking that this must surely be the right place, John knocked. There was no answer, though the door swung inward a little beneath his touch. He knocked again and it opened a fraction more.

The Marquis was asleep in the capacious fauteuil which stood opposite the wing chair, his back to the door, his white-stockinged legs and buckled shoes sticking out in front of him.

'Monsieur,' John called from the entrance.

There was no reply.

'Monsieur le Marquis,' he repeated, more loudly.

Still there was no answer. Not quite sure whether he should go in or not, the Apothecary took a step into the room. The Frenchman did not stir.

The silence became intense, only the ticking of a little clock on the mantelpiece disturbing the calm. Suddenly alarmed, John walked round the chair so that he could see the Marquis face to face.

A small neat hole with extensive black powder burns covered the area of the old man's temple, and on the other side of his head was a matching hole where the pistol's ball had made its exit. The Marquis's old-fashioned, curling white wig was scarlet with blood, its redness in hideous contrast with the bleached enamel paint that still adorned his face. Lifting the wig carefully, his handkerchief covering his fingers, the Apothecary looked down at the Frenchman's head and his stomach heaved at what he saw, so violently that he hurriedly dropped the headpiece again and saw it settle grotesquely askew.

Then his attention was caught by something else. Lying on the floor by the Marquis's feet was the obscene picture of the child and the fairies. It had been slashed to ribbons with a knife. so that the subject-matter would have been unrecognisable unless one had known what it was before. Whatever perverted acts the Frenchman had committed in his lifetime had obviously been paid for in full.

Chapter Twenty-Two

Without seeing a soul, and thankfully avoiding the austere maid, John left the French Hospital only too aware that he should go straight to Bow Street and inform Mr Fielding of the latest turn of events. Yet the sight of what was left of the old Frenchman's head beneath that garish scarlet wig had made him feel physically sick. Trained apothecary or no, John Rawlings felt in need of a large tot of brandy, and knowing that The Shepherd and Shepherdess inn was just a matter of a quarter of a mile away at the top of Ratcliff Row, he turned in that direction without another thought. Two glasses later, and somewhat restored, he felt able to marshal his ideas.

Hannah Rankin's murderer had clearly struck again, for the Apothecary had no hesitation in thinking that the two killings must be linked. Yet who had had the opportunity to commit both crimes?

The most likely person, of course, was Jack. Mother Hamp had seen a coachman outside her door and that very same coachman, or presumably so, had disappeared to London only recently. But what of Orlando, who by his own admission had given Jack the money to travel to town? Had he left The Bear and gone straight to some form of public transport? If so, he would have arrived in London well before John and Coralie. Then, of course, there was Sir Vivian Sweeting himself. Could the old Frenchman have known too much about the past, forcing Sir Vivian to silence him for ever?

Yet, the Apothecary considered, the Dysarts were also very much on the scene. Had they discovered more about the kidnapping of their grandson than they were prepared to admit? If John had been able to unearth as much as he had, why couldn't they have done the same? And what of their faithful servant, Gregg? Or Toby? Was he shielding someone, or was that just a fabrication? Could he have killed Hannah and the Marquis in order to settle an old score regarding Petronelle?

It was a considerable enigma, and the more John thought about it the worse he felt. Yet through all the confusion one idea kept coming back to him. Surely Mother Hamp could, if pressed, be more specific about the coachman she had seen. If he were to question her once more perhaps she could come up with a better description of the man. Full of brandy and determination, and yet again delaying the visit to Bow Street, the Apothecary left the hostelry and made his way down Ratcliff Row to the house where Hannah Rankin had once lived.

As luck would have it, the old besom Hamp was standing outside, chewing the fat with an equally slatternly neighbour. John put on his best face and she gave him a toothless grin in return.

'Coming to see me, my lovely boy?'

'I thought you might be good enough to accompany me to The Old Fountain, Ma'am.'

'Well, I'll be at clicket!' exclaimed the neighbour. 'Your luck's high, Mill. That's the second time this week.'

Mother Hamp made an obscene gesture. 'It's my good looks, that's what it is.' She turned to John, puffing stinking breath into his nostrils. 'Ain't it, lovely boy? That's what gets the young coves asking.'

She was drunk again but not objectionable.

John bowed low. 'It is indeed, Ma'am. Now, shall we go?'

He offered his arm, which she hung on to heavily. 'I likes going out with the handsome culls, I really does.' And she gave a frighteningly coquettish toss of her head accompanied by a gummy leer.

'Then let it be my pleasure to escort you,' the Apothecary answered, thinking he deserved a medal for bravery.

As it was very close to the dining hour, several customers had gone into the ale-house for a pre-dinner tot. This suited John's purpose, well aware as he was that it was easier to extract information against background noise than it was when people spoke in whispers. Having plied the old woman with a large measure of gin, he got straight to the point.

'Mother Hamp, it's about the coachman that you glimpsed one night, the coachman who frightened Hannah so much.'

Instead of turning on him her usual brainless expression, the old woman looked at him out of cunning eyes.

'What about him?'

Something had changed, John knew it. He took a wild guess. 'You've seen him again, haven't you?'

She cackled soundlessly. 'What if I have?'

'When was this?'

The cunning look grew cannier. 'What's it worth?'

'A guinea.'

'Make it two.'

She held out her hand. John dropped a coin into it. 'One now. The other when you've finished.'

Mother Hamp swigged down her gin and offered him the empty glass, which the Apothecary refilled for her, watching her carefully while he stood at the counter. She appeared mighty pleased with herself and from her gleeful expression he deduced that she truly had a good story to tell.

'So?' he said as he handed her the drink.

'He – the coachman – called on me the other night. He'd been to the lunatic asylum first and they had given him my address. He brought me here, the little swell, just for a chat.'

'What did he want?'

'He asked about the Marquis, Hannah's light-of-love. I told him where he could find him. He was very pleased.'

'When did this happen?'

'The night before last.'

So it had to be Jack. 'What did he look like?'

'Pretty. Dark hair and handsome face. Beautiful eyes.'

'What colour were they?'

'Violet.'

'As I thought,' said John with a note of triumph.

Mother Hamp's face contorted into a ghastly grin. 'There's something else besides.'

'What?'

'Another gin and I'll tell you.'

Much as it irritated him, the Apothecary did as she asked. 'Well?'

'He was different.'

John leant forward, more alert than he had felt all day. 'Can you explain that?'

Mother Hamp rocked with laughter. 'That's got you interested, hasn't it?'

Fighting off a strong desire to throttle her, John said, 'Are you telling me that this coachman — the young handsome one — was not the same as the one who scared Hannah?'

'Of course I am. You'll have to do a lot more thinking, my friend. There's two of 'em about the place and you're going to have to find them both.'

It was midnight when they brought the Marquis de Saint Ombre to the city mortuary, taken from the French Hospital by Mr Fielding's famous Flying Runners. Covered with a cloth, the body was carried into the darkened building, then the door was closed heavily behind him as John and Joe stepped into the street and breathed fresh air.

'Well, well,' said Jago, who had seen to all the arrangements, Mr Fielding for once being indisposed and having taken to his bed.

'I suppose it must have been Jack who killed him,' stated John with a sigh.

'Yes, I think it must. But until that is proved, Sir, we can make no assumptions. I mean, weighty though the evidence is against him, it could still be that a madman came in off the streets and killed the Marquis at random.'

'Quite so,' answered the Apothecary, and the two men stared at one another, straight-faced.

'I'd be getting to your bed, Sir. You look quite done in,' said the clerk.

'Thank you, Joe, I'll heed your advice.'

And so saying, they bowed to one another politely and went off to their individual homes, knowing that the next day the Beak Runners would have to start their investigations into the mysterious death of the man who had once been Hannah Rankin's lover.

* * *

'So there *are* two coachmen,' said Samuel Swann incredulously.

'Yes. Jack is one, for sure. The physical description tallies and Mother Hamp found out what he did for a living by the simple means of asking him.'

'Then who is the other?'

'If we knew that I think we would be near to solving the whole wretched mystery.'

'Whom do you suspect?'

'No one and everyone. Our only hope is to break Toby down and make him reveal the name of his mysterious friend. But Joe Jago got no further with him than I did. He refuses to say another word.'

'Then how...?'

'Unfortunately I am duty bound to return to Bath and try to find Jack. I've got to face him and ask him about the Marquis's death.'

'He killed him, didn't he?'

'Almost certainly.'

Samuel looked thoughtful. 'Perhaps you shouldn't look for him too hard, John.'

'Perhaps I might find him and he could change my mind for me,' the Apothecary answered.

The two friends were sharing a hackney coach heading towards Mayfair and the home of Lord Anthony and Ambrosine Dysart, where an evening of supper and cards was to be held. Samuel, delighted to have received an invitation, was dressed very finely in a suit of dark blue velvet which became him and hid the fact that he could easily become plump if he did not exercise. John, knowing that he was to see Coralie that night, was wearing green embroidered with silver, a romantic compliment to his mistress's eyes:

Lady Dysart had set things out very well, a fact they discovered on arrival. The entire house had been brilliantly lit with dozens of candles, the light spilling out into the street beyond, while inside, the dining room and the great saloon, these two rooms leading into one another, had been set for supper. Card tables were arranged in the Red Room, so called because of its flocked wallpaper, and there was already a good mingle of guests, laughing and talking and generally adding to the light-hearted atmosphere. Ambrosine, her unusual eyes glinting in the brilliance, was receiving her visitors personally and made much of welcoming John and Samuel. But after the usual pleasantries her expression changed and she drew the Apothecary to one side.

'I suppose there is no news?'

He knew at once what she meant. 'Madam, I have not found Meredith, if that is what you are asking. When I promised to look I offered little hope on that score. However, for what it is worth I believe I have found a connection between his disappearance and that of Lucy Allbury.'

'The girl from Bath?'

'The same. I consider the link to be a man called Sir Vivian Sweeting who lives across the Avon in Welham House.'

The fascinating eyes, staring so appealingly into the Apothecary's, flickered, there could be no doubt about it. From somewhere, somehow, Ambrosine Dysart recognised the name.

'You know him?' John continued, never taking his gaze from hers.

Ambrosine's look dropped to the floor. 'The name is familiar. You must remember that before the scandal we went in and out of Bath a good deal. It is possible that we might have met him.'

'And after the scandal,' John continued remorselessly, 'your daughter and son-in-law went to work for Sir Vivian. Surely you were aware of that?'

'I...er...'

'Gregg, your steward, knew. It was he who told me.'

Another voice entered the conversation. 'All that happened a long time ago, Mr Rawlings. However, I do recall Sir Vivian in that context. But what could he possibly have to do with Meredith?'

John looked round to see that Lord Anthony had joined them. He bowed politely. 'My Lord, it is my belief, though admittedly there is no sure evidence to prove it, that Sir Vivian, in league with a creature of his called Hannah Rankin, was running a child abduction ring. It is my further belief, though again one I cannot establish, that he may have noticed Meredith as a little boy and snatched him from Paris, perhaps through the agency of a Frenchman calling himself the Marquis de Saint Ombre.'

Both their faces had stretched themselves into masks, utterly expressionless, revealing nothing. Then, simultaneously, they gave John a half-smile, a fact that would have been amusing had it not been so bizarre.

'What an unpleasant story,' Ambrosine said, and shivered.

'As you say, it cannot be proved,' Lord Anthony added. 'And personally I think your theory somewhat far-fetched.'

The Apothecary bowed his head. 'I accept that, my Lord. As Mr Fielding said, the case against Sir Vivian is as full of holes as a watering can.'

'Mr Fielding?' asked Lord Anthony, his eyebrows raised.

'Yes,' answered John. 'I work for him from time to time, you know.'

So saying, he bowed very low and excused himself making his way to where Samuel and Coralie stood talking and laughing and generally being two of his greatest friends in the world. Longing to tell them what he had just seen, John put an arm round the shoulders of each and drew them close.

'There's much that I would discuss,' he said in an undertone, and planted a swift kiss on Coralie's lips, shielded from the gaze of the other guests by Samuel's broad frame.

'What is it?' asked the Goldsmith, agog with the excitement of the latest developments.

'The Dysarts know more about this business than they care to admit. They are putting on an act.

'But why?'

'That I don't know.' John leant close to Coralie's ear. 'Did Samuel tell you that the terrible old Frenchman has been shot?'

'Yes, he did.'

'Coralie, I will have to go back to Bath because of it.'

'I can't come with you. Bartholomew Fair is over and the theatres have reopened. I appear in Twe!fth Night the day after tomorrow.'

'I shall miss your company, yet I have a strange feeling that this visit is not going to be nearly as pleasant as the last, and you wouldn't be happy.'

'Things are coming to a head,' said Samuel portentously.

'I agree with you, yet there is still a lot to uncover. At the moment we do not have corroboration of a single thing.'

There was a deferential cough at John's elbow, and he looked up to see Gregg, very solid and smart in his evening clothes.

'How are you keeping, Sir?'

'Very well indeed, though extremely surprised to see you here. It was not so long ago that I bade you farewell as you set off for Westerfield Abbas.'

'Only to pack up the house, Sir,' Gregg answered urbanely. 'Then I left forthwith for London.'

John felt Coralie nudge him with her foot, while Samuel made a strange flapping motion with his arm.

'Then it seems we all departed for town together,' said the Apothecary jovially.

'So it does, Sir. So indeed it does,' responded Gregg, then he bowed and walked away, leaving the three friends to stare questioningly at one another.

It had been John's intention to catch a post chaise early the following morning, but in that he was forestalled by a most unexpected event. Sir Gabriel Kent, who was never ill, went down with a feverish cold. He had attended the Dysarts' party on the previous evening but quite unexpectedly had left early, pleading a headache. Yet all this had been done discreetly, and his son, enjoying himself with the younger people, had not realised his father had gone until it was too late to accompany him. However, by the time the Apothecary had got back Sir Gabriel had been in bed, and it had not been until the next day that John had realised quite how unwell the older man was. He had sent for Dr Drake at once, at the same time prescribing a decoction of the green leaves and roots of colt's foot for his father's cough. The lowering of the fever he had left to the physician.

Having stayed with Sir Gabriel all day, indeed until he was satisfied that there was no danger, John consequently left the house that evening, only to find the only available travelling space to be had was aboard the overnight post chaise to Bath, which did not stop except to change horses and allow its passengers time to relieve themselves. Cursing his luck, but at least grateful that he had obtained a seat within, John got on board at eight o'clock, prepared for a terrible night but knowing that he would reach his destination at ten o'clock the following morning.

An elderly couple were already inside, sitting on the seat facing the driver, a rug tucked cosily about their knees.

'Good evening,' John said, removing his hat and bowing as best he could in the confined space.

'Good evening,' said the woman, while the man responded, 'Thought we were going to have the whole conveyance to ourselves.'

Despite the obvious rebuke, the Apothecary smiled pleasantly. 'Not a popular ride this one.'

'Very good if you are in a hurry,' the woman said, trying to be civil.

'Quite so,' John replied, sitting down.

Ten minutes later there was the usual shout of the hostlers and the stamp of the team, which, together with the coachman's whip, meant they were off. Then, at the very last minute, the door was flung open and another passenger leapt in, hurling himself on to the seat beside John as the coach began to pull away.

'Just in time, eh?' said the Apothecary, and turned to look at the newcomer. Then his mouth fell open and he drew in breath.

It was Jack.

Chapter Twenty-Three

The shock was so great that the Apothecary sat for a moment, gulping, before he searched in his coat pocket and, drawing out a hip flask, had a good-sized nip of brandy. Then the sight of Jack's equally stricken face had him wiping the mouthpiece with his sleeve and passing the beaker over, smiling cynically at the sheer outrageousness of the situation.

'Well,' John said, when the coachman had taken several large swigs, 'it seems that you are unable to elude me altogether, hard though you might try.'

Jack laughed, clearly seeing the ridiculous side of the situation. 'God love you, Sir. I owe you a great deal. It was only necessity that made me bolt. I'll say more of it later.'

And he winked a brilliant eye, then rolled it slightly in the direction of the aged couple. Understanding, John winked back and they sat in a remarkably companionable silence until the rhythm of the coach had its desired effect and the two old people fell asleep, their heads rolling inwards towards each other and their snores blending in a strange sort of harmony.

'Now,' said the Apothecary, a determined expression on his face, 'I want you to tell me the truth, and the whole truth at that. I have to know all that went on at Sir Vivian Sweeting's home in the days of Hannah Rankin if I am going to get anywhere in solving the puzzle of her death. Am I right in thinking that all the children, including yourself, were abducted from other homes and brought to Welham House against their will?'

Jack put his hand out for the hip flask and took another deep draught. 'Oh yes, you are quite right. There were dozens of us, mostly sold on to brothels or into private slavery for people with perverted minds. And don't think they were all male buyers either. Dreadful old women purchased boys for their delight; some bought girls too. It was the most terrible trade the world has ever known — and still is to this day.'

'And what of you children that Sir Vivian kept? What was your function?'

'He retained those to whom he took a fancy, plying us with drink and teaching the little girls the arts of love — he had a defloration mania, of course.'

'And the boys?'

'They were sodomised. Often he would dress us all up as little Arabs and call us his harem, abusing us one after the other, girls and boys alike. You will never know the degradation we children endured. In the end I fought back, biting and kicking him so savagely that I thought he was going to kill me. But he decided to let me work in the horse dung instead. And eventually I think he almost forgot about me. That is until he tried to kill me a few days ago.'

'Was that because I had appeared on the scene, asking questions?'

'It was. He thought I was going to tell everything, either to you or the Marchesa.'

'And were you?'

'Yes indeed, regardless of the consequences to myself.'

'What do you mean by that?'

'I personally don't care what happens, but I would never betray the person who killed Hannah Rankin; they did a service to mankind. But I knew that the time had come to end all the secrecy and expose Sir Vivian for what he is.'

'Do you know who murdered Hannah?'

'Yes, I believe I do.'

'Are you going to tell me who you think it is?'

'No I'm not.'

And this was said with such an air of finality that John knew he would get no further down that track and that he must change the topic.

'There was a girl called Lucy Petronelle Allbury who was kidnapped from Prior Park while you were at Welham House. Do you know anything about that?'

The coachman nodded wearily. 'She had been seen by one of Sir Vivian's friends, a depraved old nobleman who adored fair-haired young girls. Hannah Rankin actually did the snatching, then the child was taken to London. But as soon as he had despoiled her, the nobleman lost interest, and she was turned out on to the streets like an unwanted animal, forced to fend for herself. I know this because I heard Sir Vivian discussing the girl with Orlando.'

'And what of him? And what of you? Where did you come from originally?'

Jack smiled a sad, sweet smile. 'Both of us were brought from across the water, I think probably from France. After we were abducted Orlando and myself, along with several others, were held in a house near a port. Then the man in charge of us brought us here by ship. Hannah met us at the quayside and took us to Welham House. It had all been prearranged.'

'Are you then French?' John asked, his spine icy, remembering how Jack had told him of a garden and the Apothecary had dreamt about it but been unable to make the link until this moment.

'Perhaps. I told you, I believe my name was once spelt with a "c" and a "q".'

Jack reached for the flask again, and John saw that his hand was shaking violently. 'It was at that time, when Orlando and I were together in that terrible house near the port, that we swore to be brothers. We had no one but each other. We also swore that one day, when we were older, we would kill Sir Vivian Sweeting and all those involved in our degradation and downfall.'

'And have you?'

Jack's violet eyes flashed. 'That would be telling you, now, wouldn't it?'

'Very well. Just two more questions. Why did Sir Vivian stop trading in children? For he obviously must have done. Hannah left years ago and there are no longer any around the place.'

Jack gave a frightening and humourless laugh. 'If I say, you will never believe me.'

'Try.'

"He fell in love with Orlando. He taught him everything he knew about abuse and humiliation, then he found he adored the boy. So when Orlando, to save others like us, asked Sir Vivian to end his vile trade of abduction, the disgusting creature agreed. But at a price.'

'What price?'

'That Orlando became the grand seducer. That he initiated to lust all young and innocent and defenceless creatures that crossed his path, then told Sir Vivian every detail.'

Man of the world though the Apothecary considered himself, he felt his stomach heave.

'This is hideous,' be said.

'Thank God I escaped and was banished to the stables. At least I felt clean in the horse shite.'

'I presume it was the Marquis de Saint Ombre who brought you to this country.'

'I didn't know it at the time but Orlando found out from Sir Vivian and told me who the man was.'

'Did you kill him? Is that why you got up from your sick bed and, aided and abetted by Orlando, headed for town? In order to commit a murder? Is that what made your perilous flight so necessary?'

'Mr Rawlings,' said Jack, leaning forward and putting his hand on John's arm, 'there is no defence for shooting a man in cold blood. Do you really think I would betray myself thus?'

'You just have by telling me how the Marquis was killed, a fact that I did not mention. So it had to be either you or Orlando who did the deed, swearing to it as blood brothers might. I cannot think that Sir Vivian would shoot one of his former henchmen.'

'Why not? You have no proof who it was,' Jack answered. 'And you most certainly are not going to get anything further out of me.'

And folding his arms across his chest, the coachman closed his eyes firmly, signifying that conversation and questions were at an end.

John stared out of the coach window into the darkness, allowing the fearfulness of the story to sink into his brain. To say that he was appalled by it was not fully stating the case. It was the most terrible tale of human corruption that he had ever heard in his life. Being honest with himself, he no longer had the wish to find the murderer — or murderers — of Hannah Rankin and the old Marquis. Only natural curiosity and the feeling that having once started a task he must finish it now inspired him. Sipping from his hip flask, John gazed bleakly into the blackness of the night.

Eventually, though, the jolting of the carriage and the amount he had had to drink combined to send him into a doze, deep sleep being impossible in such uncomfortable conditions. But almost as soon as he closed his eyes, John had a strange vision. Surprisingly, not of the horror story he had just heard but rather of the Dysart family portrait which Gregg had shown him at Westerfield Place. In his mind's eye, the Apothecary looked again at the four servant boys sitting on the ground, and something stirred in his subconscious, something that he should have seen earlier but which was at last becoming clear to him.

Terrible though the journey had been, the coach was punctual and swept into the courtyard of The Plume of Feathers in Southgate Street at exactly ten o'clock. Jack and John immediately disembarked, leaving the old couple to descend at their leisure.

'Where to now?' John asked his travelling companion.

'To Welham House.'

'Is that safe?'

Jack pulled a long face. 'Probably not, but I will not abandon Orlando to his fate. I've always been there to dress his wounds and dry his eyes. We are brothers, remember.'

'Then for the love of God try to get him out of there. He told me he has nowhere to go and no trade to ply, but surely, between you, you could make a living. For pity's sake take him away from that house of corruption.'

'I know Orlando of old. Once he has made up his mind nothing will sway him. He has been in the thrall of Sir Vivian too long for him to change now.'

John shook his head. 'Then what can I say except farewell.'

Jack made a polite bow. 'Farewell, Mr Rawlings. I doubt that we shall meet again.'

'Now that,' said the Apothecary, returning the salute, 'is where you are very much mistaken.'

Later that day, tired out with travelling but for all that content, John stood before the Dysart family portrait and knew some of the answers to some of the questions, though admittedly there were still several things to discover before the last pieces of the puzzle slotted into place.

He had hired a man with a carriage and, within half an hour of his arrival in Bath, the Apothecary had left again, hastening towards Westerfield Abbas and the great house just outside the village. Gaining entry had been easy enough. The same footman who had answered the door on the previous occasion had, as luck would have it, been on duty again. Making an excuse that he was running an errand for Mr Gregg, John had found himself once more in that empty, haunted house. Dwarfed by the vast staircase, he had made his way to the room where the portrait hung, and now he studied it again.

There were the Dysarts: Anthony, Ambrosine and Alice, the two females with their beautiful eyes, the man with his handsome, strong features. There was Gregg, young and vigorous, a proud father. There was his son, the future parent of Meredith, one of the cross-legged boys seated upon the ground. And there was that other face, instantly recognisable now that John had finally made the connection.

'Well, well,' he said, and shook his head in amazement.

'Will you be staying for dinner, Sir?' asked the footman, coming into the room and standing behind him.

The Apothecary smiled. 'No, though I thank you for the invitation. I must return to Bath. There is much to be done there.'

'Have you seen all you wanted to see?'

'Yes,' answered John, then added, almost to himself, 'I have indeed seen enough to leave no further room for doubt.'

Chapter Twenty-Four

Despite the fact that he was dropping with fatigue, the Apothecary found it impossible to sleep when he lay down on his bed in The Plume of Feathers. It was five o'clock in the afternoon, and since arriving in Bath he had journeyed to Westerfield Place and back, and this, after a night when he had merely catnapped, now made him feel utterly exhausted. Yet every time he closed his eyes he saw Orlando's ravaged face jumbled up with that of Jack; the two tragic small boys who had adopted one another as brothers and who had stayed together throughout all the years of humiliation and despair. A sense of unease filled the Apothecary, and he had the odd sensation that he was wont to describe to others as the pricking of his thumbs. Deep within himself he had the inescapable feeling that something, somewhere was desperately wrong.

Eventually he could stand it no longer. He rose from his bed, poured a ewer of cold water into a basin, and dipped his head into it. Then, changing into fresh clothes of the practical travelling variety, the Apothecary slipped a pistol into a deep inner pocket and left the inn, heading in the direction of the Avon ferry. While he crossed the water, he tried to rationalise his behaviour, but was unable to do so. He was acting on pure instinct, and was probably just about to walk into a hornet's nest of trouble as a result. However, not quite all good sense had abandoned him, and he decided that a discreet method of entry into Welham House would be far preferable to going to the front door only to find himself refused admittance.

At the time of his uncomfortable confinement in a cupboard he had made his escape through an open window, situated conveniently close to the ground. Now he wondered if he might be lucky and manage to do likewise, this time going in. Yet there were still the main gates to contend with, and as John drew close he wondered what he ought to say. However, a tug at the bell of the gatekeeper's lodge solved his problem, for the man recognised him as the person for whom Orlando had sent a carriage.

'Calling on the young master, Sir?'

'Yes,' John answered smoothly, 'I have been asked to dine.'

This was a mistake, for the gatekeeper looked surprised. 'Have you, Sir? Sir Vivian usually leaves a list with me of those who have been invited.'

'Perhaps he forgot on this occasion.'

'Not like him at all.' And the man shook his head, simultaneously clicking his tongue.

The only course of action appeared to be a bold one. 'Do you wish me to leave, in that case? I can explain to Master Orlando by letter why I failed to keep our appointment.'

The gatekeeper became flustered. 'No, Sir, that wouldn't do at all.' He opened the wicket in the wall. 'Please go through.'

Yet there was something a little grudging in his manner, and John felt the man's eyes boring into his back as he set off down the long, straight drive. In fact the Apothecary had got almost as far as the front door before he dared veer off into the shadow of the trees.

It was about six o'clock, not yet dusk but for all that an overcast evening. Keeping his head low and removing his hat, John cautiously dodged from sheltering tree to sheltering bush, keeping his gaze on the house all the time, hoping to find some means of entry. Eventually, after skirting round most of the building and almost giving up hope, he saw a sash window which had been opened just a fraction, enough to enable him to push it up further and get inside.

Stepping out had been easy; climbing in was rather a different matter. Eventually, John was forced to scramble up a drainpipe and cling on to it with his knees while he shoved the window higher, a hazardous process to say the least. Then he was obliged to heave himself up by resting his forearms on the sill, hoping to heaven meanwhile that there was nobody sitting quietly on the other side waiting for him to appear. Finally, though, with a mighty hoist, the Apothecary manoeuvred one leg on to the sill and from that position was able to wriggle through into the room beyond. Looking around cautiously, he saw that he was alone.

Entering in this strange manner and into this unknown room, he found the house suddenly transformed into a maze, a dusky, candlelit rabbit-warren full of shadows and empty corridors. With his heart pounding, the Apothecary crept along, cautiously looking for some sign of the mansion's occupants. Then, hearing the sound of footsteps, he slunk back into the darkness of a doorway, only to see a footman carrying food up a back staircase. So that was it. In company with many a grand family, Sir Vivian had his dining room on the first floor in order to command a view over the grounds. As stealthily as he could, John followed the footman up the servants' staircase, which was wooden and creaking and lethally spiralled.

Reaching the first-floor landing, he stopped, attempting to get his bearings. The corridor stretched in either direction, doors leading off it at regular intervals. To his right and in the far remoteness, the Apothecary could glimpse the imposing central staircase, fluting up giddily to the floors above. Beyond it, and only just visible in the vastness of the house, a great deal of light shone from beneath one particular door. He could also hear the distant drone of voices coming from the same direction. Aware that he had located the dining room, the Apothecary crept forward. But as he did so, the footman he had seen earlier appeared again, this time with an empty tray. Once more, John shrank into a doorway and saw the man walk past him, close enough to' touch.

Sir Vivian Sweeting's voice rang out. 'You are all dismissed. My nephew and I wish to converse privately.'

There was a general stamp of feet, then four servants came through the door. 'We all know what that means,' said one to the others. There was a muffled snigger and they passed on their way.

Wildly nervous, John crept forward. 'I'm telling you, my dear, that your bad behaviour has to stop,' said Sir Vivian.

In the darkness, the Apothecary shivered, for somehow the older man's tone was not sinister enough; indeed it was almost caressing, as if this were the prelude to sex and the arousing beatings that he regularly inflicted on the object of his affections.

From the candlelit room, Orlando's voice could be heard. 'Precisely what do you mean, Sir?'

'Do you dare to question me?'

There was no doubt about it; this was an oft-enacted ritual.

Orlando spoke again. 'Yes, by God, I do.'

Sir Vivian Sweeting chuckled, low and deep. 'Then, young man, you deserve a lesson. And a lesson you shall have. Step outside with me to the sanctum sanctorum. Nobody will disturb us there.'

Listening in the dusk-filled passageway, John felt himself grow tense, ready to rush in and defend Orlando by whatever means were necessary. Then the beau whispered a reply, his voice so low that the Apothecary had to strain to hear it.

'I'll see you in hell first, you bastard. God give me strength, but you've struck me for the very last time.'

There was a sharp intake of breath, quite audible. This was not part of the rite so often and so vilely enacted.

'What do you mean?' asked Sir Vivian, his voice suddenly harsh.

'I mean that you have done enough evil in this world, and now I fully intend to send you to the next.'

'Christ's mercy!' screamed the older man, clearly frightened.

A chair scraped back and somebody stood up. 'Say your prayers,' said Orlando, his voice strong and true. 'Ask your ruler Satan to help you, you wretched devil, because nobody else will.'

John's hand was on the knob and he pushed the door just the merest fraction, not wanting to startle Orlando or give Sir Vivian the chance to rush the younger man. The sight he saw then was one that he would never forget, coming to him as it did through a small crack of light.

The huge dining table, at least eight feet in length, had been formally laid at both head and foot. so that the two diners had no option but to converse down the extent of it. There were candles everywhere, filling the room with glittering light which sparkled on fine china, gleaming cutlery and crystalline glass. Beyond the table, and occupying almost the whole of one wall, were floor-length French doors leading on to a stone balcony overlooking the gracious parkland, misty in the gloaming. The heavy drapes that covered them had not yet been pulled and remained ruched back in tasselled cords. At the foot of the table, Orlando, dressed from head to toe in scarlet satin, stood, a pistol in his hand pointing straight at Sir Vivian's head. With eyes dull and opaque, hard as pebbles, the older man stared back at him, his tongue, like that of a serpent, occasionally flicking over his lips. Not daring to move, John remained motionless, watching.

'You filthy corrupting sodomite,' said Orlando, still in that same firm voice. 'You do not merit the quick and painless death that I am about to deliver you. Oh no, you deserve the agony and persecution that you have inflicted on your victims all these years. By rights I should drag you off to your torture chamber and pay you back in your own kind. But I can no longer wait. My blood is up.'

And there was a click as the beau cocked his pistol. John stood, frozen in time, and observed soundlessly as Orlando took aim, fired, then watched, quite unable to move, as Sir Vivian's wig split open and the top of his head came off and hit the wall behind, before he crumpled like a straw man and fell to the floor, Slowly, in an almost leisurely fashion, the beau strolled to where the body lay, emptied the rest of the pistol's balls into it, then kicked the corpse repeatedly before he sauntered on to the balcony to take the evening air.

At last John was released from his catalepsy. Throwing the door fully open, he rushed into the room, glancing at the body, fleeting images of the scores of innocent children who had passed through Sir Vivian's hands and emerged as corrupt and vile as he, filling his mind.

'Orlando,' he shouted, his tone shrill. 'I saw what happened.'

The enamelled face, heavy with beauty spots, turned towards him. 'John, my dear fellow, what a habit you have of arriving at quite the strangest moments. So what are you going to do about it? Report me to the constable?'

A ghastly parody of the Apothecary's crooked smile twisted his features, and when John spoke his voice sounded so strange that he hardly recognised it, even though the words he said were conversational enough.

'By an odd coincidence I met Jack on the stagecoach. He's come here looking for you. I think he must be downstairs somewhere.'

The beau laughed and ruffled John's hair with languid fingers. 'Then I'd better go and join him, my dear.' And so saying he leant one hand on the elegant stone balustrade with which the balcony was made safe, and jumped up on to it.

A cry came from the dimness below. 'Orlando, in God's name what are you doing?'

'What I should have done many years ago,' the beau answered, staring down into the shadows of the garden to where Jack stood, before turning his head to look at the Apothecary.

John saw again the terrible expression of despair which he had glimpsed on Orlando's face on two other occasions, and realised instantly what the beau intended. 'Don't, Orlando,' he shouted. 'Nothing's worth that.'

'Oh my friend,' came the tragic reply, 'you simply don't know. He taught me his sins and worse. It became my lot to corrupt and deprave young creatures when he no longer chose to do so. I cannot stand for another instant the horror of what I have become.' A dreadful laugh rang out.

'Look no further for your murderer, my dear. I killed Hannah Rankin and the Marquis, and I glory in the fact that I did so. Dear God, spare a prayer for poor Orlando.'

Then he raised his arms as if he could fly and stepped off the balustrade into the night.

Just for one second John did not move, rooted to the spot by what he had witnessed. Then he rushed from the room, hurling himself down the staircase and through that rabbit warren of a house to where a door led into the garden.

Jack was already kneeling beside Orlando's body, cradling him in his arms, the tears running silently down his cheeks.

'He's dead, he's dead,' he kept repeating.

'Let me see,' answered John, and leant over Orlando to listen for his heartbeat. There was nothing, yet still the Apothecary tore at the beau's coat and shirt so that he could put his ear to Orlando's chest. But the heart was silent, and John could see by the first faint rays of the moon that the poor creature had crashed on to his head, smashing his skull to an oozing pulp.

'He died instantly,' he said to Jack.

'But he's gone, my poor brother, the only friend I ever had.'

'He killed Sir Vivian before he took his own life.'

'You're wrong there,' Jack answered bitterly, 'Sir Vivian killed him years ago, as he did us all.'

'Rest in peace,' said John, and went to draw the shirt back over the whitening skin. And then his eye was caught by something, and the Apothecary gasped at what he saw. On the left of Orlando's chest, as distinct and clear as a patch of blood, was a red birthmark, a port wine stain.

He looked at Jack, who still knelt beside the body, weeping.

'Has Orlando always had this?'

'Yes, since the day I first met him.'

'God's mercy,' said the Apothecary.

For he knew then that in his arms, quite dead, lay the last mortal remains of Meredith Dysart.

Chapter Twenty-Five

'So it's finished,' said Mr Fielding, sitting very straight in his high-backed chair, the black bandage that concealed his blind eyes turned in John's direction, his expression intense.

'Yes, Sir. Before he killed himself, Orlando confessed to both murders.'

'I see.' The Magistrate steepled his fingers. 'Yet what puzzles me is the fact that there are so many inconsistencies, so many pieces that do not fit. One small example: how did Orlando find out where Hannah Rankin went after she left Sir Vivian's employ? He had to know where she was in order to go there and murder her, if you see what I mean.'

'Presumably Jack knew her whereabouts. He saw her for some years after she left Welham House, usually dragging some wretched child about.'

'And the Marquis? How did Orlando know where to locate him?'

'Oh, that was simple. Mother Hamp told Jack — for that is definitely who it was who called on her — all about him.'

'Mm. Well, it's a neat ending, I must say.'

'But you are not convinced?'

'Yes and no. I said to you we needed either proof or a confession. Now we have one. Yet there are too many questions left unanswered, Mr Rawlings. I mean, which was Toby's anonymous friend — Orlando or Jack? And how did they know him in the first place? And how exactly did they track Hannah down? For I am not convinced that Jack knew her whereabouts all along. And why was Jack in London when the Marquis was shot, when it was Orlando who confessed to shooting him?'

Joe Jago spoke up from his corner. 'That final confession poses more problems than it solves, if you ask me, Sir.'

'Indeed,' answered the Apothecary, and wished that he were not in the same room as the finest brain in London, together with the cunning fox Jago.

For ever since Orlando's tragic funeral, attended by Jack and himself, young Sidmouth and the servants of the house, but none of the beau monde, there had been a scene in John's pictorial memory that refused to go away. In this scene he was in the Bath Assembly Rooms with Orlando and he had just told him of the death of Hannah Rankin. As clearly as if the poor thing were present, John saw the beau's features transform into a mask of loathing, followed swiftly by a further change to pure triumph as he learned that she was dead. Was this the reaction of a murderer, he wondered? Could anyone who knew she was gone have acted quite so convincingly? Yet John shied away from investigating further, believing with all his heart that sleeping dogs should now be left to lie.

Mr Fielding was speaking again. 'We tread a fine line here, Joe. The case is concluded, Mr Rawlings has brought us the admission of guilt that we needed, yet there are loopholes of which all three of us are aware. Still, I believe we would be quite justified in closing the book on Hannah Rankin.'

'I agree with you there, Sir.'

'Do you think I can safely enter the fact that she was murdered by a young man known as Orlando Sweeting, as was the Marquis de Saint Ombre, together with that vile kidnapper, Sir Vivian Sweeting?'

'Absolutely, Sir,' said the clerk, and quite deliberately gave John a light-eyed wink which spoke volumes.

From his high-backed chair Mr Fielding said, 'I wonder,' and then there was silence.

'So what's afoot?' asked Samuel, rubbing his hands together excitedly.

'Everything and nothing. As you know, the case is closed. Mr Fielding is writing his report and that will be that. And yet...'

'Yes?'

'Samuel, I don't think Orlando killed anyone except Sir Vivian. When I informed him that Hannah was dead his face was exultant. It was his instantaneous response. I would stake my very life on the fact that I was the first person to tell him and he reacted naturally.'

'Dear God. Then why did he confess?'

'In order to protect those who really did the deeds. He took their guilt on himself so that they could walk free of fear.'

'Was it Jack then?'

'In the case of the Marquis, I'm sure it was. But somebody else murdered Hannah Rankin.'

'Who? Do you know?'

'Yes, I think so.' And John uttered a name. Samuel listened, wide-eyed.

'What do you intend to do about it?'

'I'm not quite sure yet. So first of all you and I are going to the Peerless Pool to relax, then to The Old Fountain for a drink.'

'And then?'

'I am going to Coralie's house. I shall take the necessary action tomorrow regarding the murderer, that is if I do anything at all.'

Samuel looked at John most acutely. 'There's something else, isn't there? Something you want to tell me but are afraid to say.'

'Yes.'

'Is it about Orlando?'

'Yes. You are very observant.'

'What is it?'

'The poor thing was the missing Meredith Dysart, or Gregg, however one likes to think of him. I have found Lord Anthony's grandson, yet how can I tell them? It will break Ambrosine's heart.'

'Are you absolutely sure it was him?'

'Absolutely. He had the birthmark exactly where Lady Dysart said it was.'

'But couldn't it just as easily have been Jack? You said both boys were brought from France.'

'Jack certainly thought they were, and Orlando's birthmark proved it.'

'Well, then,' said Samuel.

'Well, then, what?'

'Just well, then,' answered the Goldsmith, and smiled expansively.

It was September and beautifully fine and warm, but for all that the swimming pool was not as full as it had been that other time; that day when Hannah Rankin's body had been found lying on the bed of the Fish Pond and John had started on the trail that had led him to such sordid truths. In fact today the waters were reasonably empty, and both the Apothecary and Samuel were able to enjoy a long, leisurely swim. Afterwards they plunged into the cold bath, a withering experience, and then, feeling virtuous, went to have food and wine and sit in the sunshine. As chance would have it, and very much as John had hoped, Toby Wills served them.

'Well, well,' said the Apothecary. 'How are you, my friend? It seems a long while since we met.'

The waiter turned on him an uncommunicative look, his features set, his face expressionless. Irritated, John decided to give the man the shock of his life.

'I suppose you have heard that the killer of Hannah Rankin has been discovered and the investigation is now closed?'

The waiter's hands shook violently as he attempted to pour claret into a glass. 'Really, Sir?'

'Oh, yes. The murderer confessed before he killed himself.'

Toby's face was the colour of ash, and he could hardly mouth the next words. 'So who was it, Sir?'

'Nobody you would have known,' John replied airily. 'Hannah once worked in Bath and it was a person connected with that phase of her life, a young man called Orlando Sweeting. He had been badly used by her as a child and he decided to take revenge.'

There it was; relief, joy, exuberance even.

The Apothecary narrowed his eyes. 'You came from round that way, didn't you, Toby?'

'I was born in Somerset, Sir, but I did not hail from Bath.'

'No, I never thought you did,' John said, as the final question was answered.

Chapter Twenty-Six

At eight o'clock the following morning, John walked briskly from the house of the Clive sisters in Cecil Street, then made his way via The Strand, St Martins Lane and Castle Street towards Leicester Fields and home. There he changed into sombre black, suitable for the task that lay before him, and collected Jack, who had been staying at number two Nassau Street ever since Orlando's funeral. The Apothecary then spent some while in choosing which of his many suits he should lend the coachman, and finally decided on violet satin, a shade that strongly enhanced the colour of Jack's unusual eyes.

'But what is all this finery for?' the young man asked.

'Just so that you look your best,' the Apothecary answered enigmatically, then they set off together in Sir Gabriel's coach, especially borrowed for the occasion.

The driver took them through Piccadilly to Berkeley Square, behind which lay the new development of Mayfair. And there they stopped outside the home of Lord Anthony and Lady Dysart.

'Jack, can you amuse yourself for an hour?' John asked, presenting his card to the footman who answered the door.

'You don't want me to come in with you?'

'Not at the moment. Return at noon, by which time my business will be concluded.'

'Very well.' And the young man went off, a handsome figure in his borrowed clothing, looking very slightly bemused by the secrecy of everything that was taking place.

Inside the house, a normal day progressed; servants about their duties, the master in his library, reading the newspaper, the mistress out shopping with her maid.

'Lord Anthony will receive you now, Sir,' said the footman, who had shown John into an anteroom. 'Would you follow me?' And they went from the reception hall to the book-lined room where the Apothecary had sat with his host and first met that stolid figure, Gregg the steward: in the company of, though he had not know it at the time, the two grandfathers of that saddest of young men, the beau known as Orlando Sweeting.

Lord Anthony looked up from his copy of The Spectator and gestured to John to take a seat.

'My dear Mr Rawlings, do sit down. Would you care for a glass of sherry?'

'Very much indeed,' the Apothecary answered with feeling, and took the glass offered to him on a silver tray by the footman.

'Now how may I help you?'

John waited until the servant had left the room, then he leant forward in his chair. 'Lord Anthony, it is hard to know where to begin. On the face of it you know nothing of the death of a woman called Hannah Rankin who worked at St Luke's Hospital for Poor Lunatics, and who was found in the Fish Pond close to the Peerless Pool, severely beaten then thrown in alive to drown.'

The nobleman folded his paper meticulously and put it down on the table beside him.

'No, you are quite right. I had not heard of such an incident until this moment.'

'Yet you knew of Sir Vivian Sweeting. Knew that when your daughter Alice was struggling to make ends meet after marrying Gregg's son Richard, against your wishes, she took in washing from Welham House, Sir Vivian's home.'

'Yes, I knew that.'

'Well, Hannah Rankin also worked there at that time. Did your paid informants not tell you that?'

'I repeat, I had never heard of Hannah Rankin until just now.'

'Did you not also discover, years later, that Sir Vivian masterminded a child abduction ring and that his creature in this hellish trade was the very same Hannah?'

Lord Anthony looked down his long, patrician nose. 'I don't know what you're talking about, young man. Believe me, if you were anyone other than Gabriel's son, I should ask you to leave forthwith.'

'Please, Sir, give me a hearing. A man has already admitted to killing Hannah, then bitterly paid the penalty by taking his own life. There is nothing to fear from the law. It is only my desire to learn the truth that makes me say what I do.'

His host did not reply, which the Apothecary took as a sign that he should continue. He hurried on.

'I do not know how you made the connection between Hannah and Meredith, but make it I believe you eventually did. Gregg was in this country when the boy vanished, and he may have hit on something before he joined you in Paris, something which did not make sense till many years later. Alternatively, one of your informants in France could have pointed you in the right direction. Whatever transpired, it clearly took you a very long time to catch up with her. But then Toby Wills, the waiter at the Peerless Pool, suddenly provided you with the information you needed, I think.'

Lord Anthony drew in his breath but said nothing.

'He worked for you as a boy. In fact he's one of the children in your family portrait. I didn't recognise him at first, but once I had done, everything slotted into place. It is my belief that as a childhood friend of Richard's, he always kept in touch with Gregg, whom he probably looked on as a father figure. He knew the anguish you all went through, knew the names of the people you were looking for. Then one day, by chance, a strange woman appeared in The Old Fountain and Toby asked who she was. Probably no one could have been more surprised than he to learn that her name was Hannah Rankin and that she worked close by at St Luke's Hospital. An easy step from there to find out where she lived, then to write to his old associate Gregg and tell him that the search was over. Then Gregg called on her, no doubt to check that it was the same woman. He drove your coach with the coat of arms on the door, and she grew so afraid that she packed her bags and was ready to leave had not you, Lord Anthony, stopped her doing so.'

'You are accusing me of this woman's murder?'

John hesitated. 'I believe the final link in the chain was when the truth was learned about her association with the Marquis de Saint Ombre, whom you had met in Paris. I think then you felt you had enough proof to proceed.'

'Are you saying I killed her?' Lord Anthony repeated.

'No, it was probably your steward who did so, but I believe you and Toby cooperated. I think Gregg waylaid her crossing the fields to Ratcliff Row on the way home from St Luke's. Then I imagine he took her to a remote spot and beat her to a pulp, then put on the disguise he had brought with him and waited while Toby brought the wheelbarrow from the Pleasure Gardens and left the gate open for him.'

'You're right,' said a voice from the doorway. 'That is exactly how I did it, Just as I intended to finish them all.'

'No,' interjected Lord Anthony, his tone commanding. 'Don't listen to him. It was I who killed her. I was the one who threw her in. I was the one who put the death sentence on her. Just as she once put it on my grandson, Meredith.'

'I have heard enough,' John declared decisively, "and I have also heard nothing. Gentlemen, be advised that I do not want you to tell me such a story again. A gallant young man, a young man whom destiny brought low but who achieved splendour in his final moments, confessed to the murders before he put an end to his own short life. That is good enough for me.' He cleared his throat, then said cautiously, 'You know that Meredith is dead?'

'My grandson died while he was the Marquis's prisoner in France. The odious creature held several children in a house in Calais. Some perished from his mistreatment. Meredith was one of them. I was shown his grave. I never spoke of it to Ambrosine for she lived in hope, and I could not bring myself to shatter that.'

John shook his head. 'No, my Lord, you are wrong. Despite what you think, two of the boys did survive and were brought to England. It is my belief that Meredith did not die in France.'

He spoke carefully, neither saying too much nor too little.

Lord Anthony drew himself up. 'If only that were true.'

'My Lord, I took the liberty of bringing with me the sole survivor of those two boys whom the Marquis held captive. He thinks he once was given the French name Jacques, he can remember a garden and being brought to this country across the sea. He is a very remarkable young person and I would like you to meet him.'

'Is he…is it…?'Lord Anthony asked hoarsely.

But before John could say another word there were sounds of confusion from the hall. Ambrosine's voice was raised loud and clear.

'Oh, Simmons, be careful. You always try to carry too much and end up dropping the parcels.'

John heard Jack's voice. 'Allow me to help pick them up, my Lady.'

'Oh, good gracious, and who might you be?'

'I am here to see Mr John Rawlings, Ma'am. I have arranged to meet him at noon.'

'What very unusual eyes you have,' John heard Lady Dysart say, and there was a strange note in her voice. 'Simmons, whose eyes do this young man's remind you of?'

'Why, yours, my Lady. And Miss Alice's, of course.'

The door flew open and Ambrosine appeared, her face a picture of wonder.

'Oh, Anthony, Anthony,' she called out. 'Mr Rawlings gave me his word and he has kept it. He's come back to us! Oh, my darling, Meredith is here at last!'

Chapter Twenty-Seven

'So there's a thing,' said Sir Gabriel, carefully pouring four glasses of champagne despite the rocking and bumping of the hired coach taking them to the grand ball at Westerfield Place, at which Jack the former coachman was being presented to the entire county as the missing grandson of Lord Anthony and Lady Dysart.

'A wonderful story,' said Coralie, green eyes abrim. 'How touching. La, it would make a good play.'

Samuel gave an extremely jolly wink. 'The Dysarts have found their grandson, Jack has found a family home. All's well that ends well, say I.'

'Shakespeare said it before you,' Coralie answered, smiling.

Sir Gabriel, who looked stunning in a mélange of black and silver fit to dazzle the gaze of mortal man, raised his brows. 'Bear with me. The boy who died was really their grandson, wasn't he?'

'Yes, if the birthmark was anything to go by. But then Dr Drake was the first to assure Ambrosine that such marks are not uncommon and also can fade with the passing of the years.'

'But the Dysarts claimed to recognise Jack by the colour of his eyes, is that correct?'

'Absolutely.'

'And how do you account for that?'

'Happy coincidence, I imagine,' said John, and, draining his. glass, held it out for a refill. Sir Gabriel looked thoughtful. 'It is certainly a truism that people see what they want to see and believe likewise.'

'As many a wife has done when she has gone into marriage,' said Coralie, and was somewhat put out when all three men grinned at her instead of taking up the cudgels.

'D'ye know,' said John's father, raising an elegant brow, 'Anthony wrote me that even the ghost of Westerfield Place, poor little Alice, has departed.'

'She wept for her missing child and now, I suppose, she feels he has returned,' Samuel answered.

'And in a way, he has,' said Coralie.

John was silent, and in the darkness raised his glass in an unspoken toast to Orlando, who had given up his terrible young life so that others might be free to live without fear. And who, with his ultimate sacrifice, had at long last become the person he was truly destined to be.

Historical Note

John Rawlings, Apothecary, was born circa 1731, though his actual parentage is somewhat shrouded in mystery. However, by 1754 he had emerged from obscurity when on 22 August he applied to be made Free of the Worshipful Society of Apothecaries. He became a Yeoman of the Society in March, 1755 – the reasons for the delay are interesting but not to be told here – giving his address as number two Nassau Street. Well over a hundred years later, this was the address of H.D. Rawlings Ltd, Soda Water Manufacturers, proving conclusively that John Rawlings was probably the first apothecary to manufacture carbonated waters in this country. His ebullient personality has haunted me for years and now, at last, I am bringing him out of the shadows and into the spotlight.

LaVergne, TN USA
13 December 2010
208543LV00001B/133/A